The
Brewery
Murders

ALSO BY J. R. ELLIS

The Body in the Dales
The Quartet Murders
The Murder at Redmire Hall
The Royal Baths Murder
The Nidderdale Murders
The Whitby Murders
Murder at St Anne's
The Railway Murders

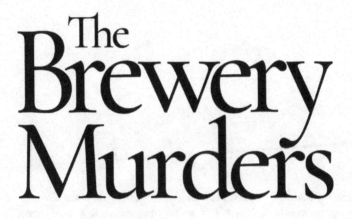

The Brewery Murders

A YORKSHIRE
MURDER MYSTERY

J.R. ELLIS

THOMAS & MERCER

Text copyright © 2023 by J. R. Ellis
All rights reserved.

Published by Thomas & Mercer, Seattle

www.apub.com

Amazon, the Amazon logo, and Thomas & Mercer are trademarks of Amazon.com, Inc., or its affiliates.

ISBN-13: 9781542031394
eISBN: 9781542031387

Cover design by @blacksheep-uk.com
Cover images: © Peter F. R. Forster & Lina Mo / Shutterstock;
© Brian Scantlebury / Getty Images

Printed in the United States of America

The
Brewery
Murders

Prologue

Brewing beer in Yorkshire has a long history going back to the time of the medieval monasteries. The oldest commercial brewery was established in the eighteenth century. Yorkshire people are fiercely proud of their beers, especially the traditional cask bitter: amber hued with a full-bodied flavour and a rich, creamy head.

April 1995

'And it gives me great pleasure to declare that the winner, yet again, is Wensley Glory Bitter, brewed in Markham by David Foster,' announced the chairman of the Yorkshire Ale Society. There was a round of applause and some cheers. David Foster of Yoredale Ram Ales in the town of Markham, Lower Wensleydale, Yorkshire, mounted the rostrum wearing a flat cap and a faded tweed sports jacket, creased checked shirt and brown tie. He had a red face and untidy hair. He smiled and nodded to acknowledge the applause.

The annual gathering of the Yorkshire Ale Society was taking place in a hotel in Harrogate and concluding with the prestigious title of Beer of the Year, awarded to the best brew in the county. The large room was full of representatives from the Campaign for Real Ale, brewery owners, publicans and members of local chambers of commerce. The contest had been closely fought and the judging protracted and difficult, but Wensley Glory had won for the third time. The judges loved the depth of flavour and the distinctive texture. It was a beer that managed to combine earthiness and sweetness. There was an edge of hoppy bitterness and a uniquely subtle malty flavour.

Wensley Glory was shrouded in mystery. No one, even at the brewery in Markham, knew exactly how it was brewed. Foster had developed the recipe with his father Brian years before and now kept it a close secret from everybody.

A man of few words, Foster thanked the president of the Yorkshire Ale Society and said what an honour it was to be awarded this prize again. He then called a number of Yoredale employees on to the stage, including his head brewer Wilfred Scholes, for a group photograph. After that he left the stage holding his trophy to further applause. He did not make any kind of protracted speech and refused to say anything about the ale for which he was famous. But he was very happy because he knew that this award would promote sales of Wensley Glory and his other beers like no other publicity could.

A number of his rival brewers surrounded him, clapping him on the back and offering their congratulations.

'Well done again, David,' said one. 'It's a cracking beer, that Glory. I don't suppose on this special occasion you'll agree to tell us anything about it?' He grinned mischievously.

'Nay, I can't do that, Walter. Once I start saying stuff there'll be all kinds of folk trying to copy it. It's going to stay up here.' Foster tapped the side of his head. Despite the joking, bantering and even a measure of pleading, Foster would say nothing about Wensley Glory except to encourage people to drink it. This they did in large quantities, and the celebrations went on far into the night.

Foster's resolution did not fail. He never spoke about the recipe for Wensley Glory, even to members of his family. He personally supervised the brewing of this special beer and everyone else was excluded at certain crucial stages of the process. The only person who was rumoured to know anything was Wilfred Scholes, but he never said anything about the beer either.

There was some speculation concerning who Foster would eventually hand on the recipe to, but when he died suddenly from a heart attack at the comparatively early age of seventy, no written version of the recipe was discovered among his papers, nor in any safes or bank vaults. It looked as if Wensley Glory Bitter had, sadly, had its days of glory and would never be drunk again.

One

Timothy Taylor's was established in Keighley in 1858 and still brews beer in the town, drawing water from an artesian well at its Knowle Spring site. Taylor's most famous beer is Landlord, a pale ale which has been Champion Beer of Britain four times at the Great British Beer Festival. It is a well-loved beer all over Yorkshire and beyond.

It was a warm and sunny Saturday in April and the rural town of Markham was looking very attractive. Tubs and troughs of yellow and white daffodils decorated the large market square, which was bustling with people. The sun shone strongly through the trees that surrounded the edge of the square. The branches were still leafless, although here and there was a vibrant suggestion of the new green ready to burst into life. In the distance the fells of Upper Wensleydale, criss-crossed with dry stone walls, rose up majestically.

The Spring Beer Festival was in full swing. Two large marquees had been erected in the centre of the square. The atmosphere was lively and cheerful, not to say raucous in places, no doubt encouraged by the copious amounts of alcohol being consumed and the small folk bands dotted around the square to which people were singing along and dancing.

Many families and groups of friends were making a day of it, bringing chairs and rugs to sit on. The areas outside the marquees were dotted with groups eating picnics along with drinking beer from plastic cups.

The festival was a mecca for real ale enthusiasts and brewery owners throughout the north of England, and a significant number of tourists were also wandering around enjoying the cornucopia of drinks and snack foods on offer. The cafes and pubs around the square were doing a roaring trade and the marquees were packed with busy stalls run by different breweries. Each paraded their imaginatively named products – from Squirrel Tail Bitter to Cow's Udder Stout and Muddy Stile Mild. Bottles and cans were presented in colourful displays and samples were being drawn from traditional oak casks.

The reason for holding this event in a small town like Markham was that there were two well-known breweries in the town who both had set up shop at the festival. In one marquee, Yoredale Ram Ales had a pop-up bar and tables crammed with presentation boxes of canned and bottled beer and books about the brewery's history. Above the bar was a large model of a fierce-looking dark ram which dominated the marquee. The stand was run mostly by men.

In contrast, the Ewe's Ales stand in the other marquee was busy with women serving samples of beer from a similar bar. Above them was a fluffy white model of a ewe nurturing her lambs, which were gathered beneath her. The distance between the stands symbolised the frostiness in the relationship between the two companies.

A handsome bearded man in his late thirties, dressed shabbily in corduroy trousers and a worn jacket, stood at a slight distance from the Yoredale Ram stand, leaning against one of the marquee pole supports. He brushed his fingers through his longish black hair, stroked his full beard, and looked on with a half-smile on his face. He was watching a tall, energetic man of about the same age who was greeting members of the public and talking very animatedly: Richard Foster, the owner of Yoredale Ram Ales. As Foster talked, he noticed the bearded man looking towards him and the smile left his face. Excusing himself, he came over.

'What are you doing here, Scholes? I'm very busy today, as you can see.'

'You didn't reply to my message, Richard. I've got something that I know you'll be interested in.'

'Mr Foster to you, never mind this familiarity. I don't remember getting a message. What are you talking about?'

Scholes lounged against the pole with his hands in his pockets and ignored Foster's outrage. 'I've got what you've all been looking for, Richard.'

Foster regarded him with great suspicion. 'What do you mean? Do you think I'd ever trust you again after what happened and how you've behaved in this town?'

Scholes ignored him. 'I've got the recipe: Wensley Glory Bitter. I can prove it if you don't believe me.'

Foster's eyes widened at this extraordinary claim. 'What?'

'It's true and it could be yours . . . for a sum of money, of course.'

Foster laughed scornfully. 'Don't be ridiculous. How on earth could you have found my father's recipe? It's been missing since he died. We don't even know for certain that he ever wrote it down. And you're asking me for money based on some preposterous claim? How dare you?!'

Scholes remained calm. He shifted his feet and smiled as he continued to lean against the pole. 'How I came by it is my business, Richard, but just consider what you could do with that recipe: revive the legendary Wensley Glory Bitter. It would be a sensation. Think of the money you could make – and you'd get well ahead of your sister's outfit, wouldn't you?'

Foster was nearly speechless with anger. 'Get out of here, you lying—'

'Careful, Richard. This is a public space. It doesn't belong to the Yoredale Ram Brewery, though I know you like to think you own the whole town.' Scholes straightened and nonchalantly brushed dust off his jacket. 'Anyway, it's up to you. If you're interested let me know, otherwise I'm sure there will be plenty of other people who will jump at the chance. Here's my number.' He gave Foster a card. 'You might find me in the Wensley Arms; I'm still a regular when I'm in Markham. Bye for now.'

He waved a hand sarcastically at Foster, walked away from the stand and left the marquee. Foster gazed after him and tried to collect his thoughts. He didn't believe for a moment that Brendan Scholes had somehow obtained his father's recipe for Wensley Glory; the man was untrustworthy.

But there was, annoyingly, just the slightest of doubts: what if he had been telling the truth? Surely it was not possible, but . . . Foster frowned as he continued to look at the receding figure of Scholes.

～

Scholes was making his way to the other marquee when he nearly bumped into a large, burly man who appeared from the side of a tent. This man's eyes widened when he saw who it was.

'Scholes? What the hell! I said if I ever saw you again, I'd . . .' He was red in the face with anger.

Scholes looked at the man in surprise and then said, 'Steady, don't give yourself a heart attack. I've come back to torment you all, but hopefully not for long before I leave you in peace.'

The other man's brow furrowed. 'What the hell are you talking about, you bloody rogue? Get out of this town before I kick you out. You were told never to come back.'

'What's the matter with you?' said Scholes, keeping his distance.

'What's the matter . . . ? How dare you? Get out of my sight!' The man glared at Scholes, who laughed and walked smartly away. The other marquee, containing the Ewe's Ales stall, was also busy. He couldn't see the person he wanted to speak to, so he went up to a young woman pulling samples of beer at the bar.

'Is Emily around?' he asked.

The woman did a double take, seeming surprised to see him. 'She'll be back in a minute, but she won't want to speak to you.'

Scholes smiled. 'Oh, I think she'll be interested in what I have to say. I'll just wait here.' He sat down on a folding chair near the bar.

Before long, a woman slightly younger than Scholes strode into the marquee. She was tall with short blonde hair and was wearing the same outfit as the other women on the Ewe's Ales stand: green dungarees with an image of a fluffy white sheep embroidered on the front. She already looked very angry, and her mood was not improved by the unexpected sight of Brendan Scholes.

'What are you doing here? You'd better be careful who sees you.'

'I have some important information for you.'

'Hmm.' Emily Foster shook her head. 'Have you really?'

Scholes again decided that coming straight to the point would be the most effective strategy. He stood up. 'I've got your father's recipe for Wensley Glory. Of course, we would need to agree a sum if I was to hand it over to you. I've already told your brother and he's thinking about it.'

Emily was brought up sharp. Her brow furrowed. 'What? Stop playing ridiculous games. What are you after?'

'Money, Emily. Money. I'm being quite open about it. The recipe will go to the highest bidder. I would prefer you or Richard to buy it – that would keep the tradition in the family, wouldn't it? But if I'm not satisfied with your offers, I shall go elsewhere.'

Emily looked at him with incredulity. 'My father's recipe? How on earth could you have got hold of that?'

Scholes laughed. 'That's exactly what your brother said, but I'm giving nothing away.'

'If you do have it, it's my father's property, which you've stolen.'

Scholes laughed again. 'You'll have a hard time proving that. How do you know he didn't give a copy to someone?'

'Why would he do that and not give one to me or Richard?'

Scholes shrugged. 'Who knows? And he's not around to ask, is he?'

Emily dismissed him with a wave of her arm. 'Just get lost. I haven't time for this nonsense.'

Scholes smiled in a smug manner. 'OK, I'll be around if you change your mind. This is my number.' He handed her another of his cards.

Emily hesitated for a moment then put it in the pocket of her dungarees and turned away.

'Hello, Brendan.' Another member of the Ewe's staff spoke to Scholes – the first friendly voice he'd heard that day. 'I haven't seen you for a while. How are you?'

Scholes turned to her, looking a bit confused. 'Oh, hi,' he said. 'Sorry, I can't stop. I'm not popular round here.' And he walked out of the marquee.

The woman looked puzzled as she turned to join a group of Ewe's people, who were being addressed by an angry Emily.

'Have you seen what's strung up outside?' Emily was saying. 'I've bloody well had enough of this now. I'm going over to have a word with that lot.' She strode out of the marquee, followed by two of the women who reached the entrance and looked across to where a banner had been strung between two trees. In large letters it contained the slogan: 'Ewe's Beer: Made by Girls for Girls.'

There was a cartoon drawing of a ewe, cross-eyed, cross-legged, and obviously drunk.

'Oh God! That's awful,' said one of the Ewe's employees, whose name was Abigail.

'Can you two pull it down?' asked Emily, and she continued across to the other marquee and straight to the Yoredale Ram stand. Her brother was talking to a member of his staff and didn't see her approach.

'Richard! I don't think it's funny. What the bloody hell do you think you're playing at?' Her voice was raised.

Foster turned round abruptly. 'Calm down. What're you talking about?'

'Don't pretend you don't know. You've seen it. It's out there in full public view.'

'What is?'

Emily noticed a couple of young men on her brother's staff were listening and sniggering as they exchanged glances. 'Perhaps it was two of your juvenile staff who enjoy schoolboy pranks,' she said as she glanced at them with contempt, 'but I still hold you responsible.'

'I don't know what you're talking about.'

Emily pointed to where the banner was and stabbed aggressively with her finger. 'There's a nasty comment on that about our beer. It's a blatant act of sabotage.'

Foster turned to the two men who were trying to stifle giggles. 'Oh, you didn't? You idiots!' he said. 'I'm sorry, they were talking about putting up something as a joke. What does it say?'

'"Ewe's Beer is Made by Girls for Girls",' said one of them and they both collapsed laughing.

Foster turned to his sister. 'Look, I'm sorry but . . .' Emily was incensed to see that her brother was trying to prevent himself from laughing, too. 'I'll get them to take it down.'

11

'Don't bother, two of my staff have already removed it.' She glared at Foster. 'You don't get it, do you? You think it's all a bit of fun. This is exactly the kind of thing that drove me away. Men will never take the idea of women running a brewery seriously.' She turned round and walked out.

'Oh dear,' said Foster and looked at the pranksters. 'You shouldn't have done that!' They started laughing again, but stopped a moment later when Emily walked back in.

'By the way, have you seen Scholes?'

'Yes. Has he been peddling the same tale to you about Dad's recipe?'

'Yes.'

'Well, it's crap, isn't it? There's no way he could have a copy.'

Emily looked at him for a moment. 'No, I'm sure you're right,' she said and left the marquee again.

~

As the beer festival continued, an expensive Audi was being driven towards nearby Ripon. Tim Groves, a senior forensic pathologist based in Harrogate, had been called out to where a body had been found in a drainage tunnel at an old sewage works near the city. The body had been discovered, as so often happens, by a local dog walker. Detective Constable Jeffries from the Ripon station was supervising the police operation.

The body was now extracted from the tunnel. It had been wrapped in an old carpet, which the scenes of crime officers had removed.

Groves was tall, and had to kneel by the side of the body in his protective clothing to conduct his preliminary examination. The body was that of a man and was not in a pleasant state. The smell of putrefaction was strong, and Groves had to wear a mask. The body had been stripped of clothing. There was a lot of blood around the head, and the face was badly disfigured.

'Obviously badly decomposed,' Groves said to Jeffries. 'He's been dead for some time. Up to a couple of weeks, but not months or years. Large wound to the back of the head which was probably the cause of death. Facial features are unclear for identification purposes.'

'Yes,' said Jeffries. 'I saw that. Unless we find anything on the body, we'll have to see what we can do with fingerprints and dental records, and hope it's someone local.'

'Any missing persons reported?' Groves liked to dabble a bit in the detective side of things, although it was not his area.

'No, only a teenage girl, so not much help in this case. The murderer obviously went to some lengths to try to hide the body, but they were unlucky. I suspect those heavy rains we had a couple of days ago moved the body nearer to the entrance. And then we had a dog that was a keen sniffer. It went right in the tunnel, apparently – wouldn't come out and the owner had to crawl in to get it; that's how they found the body.'

'I'll know more when I get it into the lab,' Groves said. 'And I'll inform you as soon as I can. Best of luck in finding the culprit.'

'Thanks.'

DC Jeffries drove back to Ripon HQ in a thoughtful mood. Meeting Tim Groves again had reminded him of when he had worked with DCI Oldroyd on a dramatic case at nearby Redmire Hall. Groves had been the forensic pathologist on that case, too. What exciting times those had been!

Ever since then, Jeffries had badly wanted to be involved with another baffling mystery being investigated by DCI Oldroyd, who had become a hero to him. Too much police work felt rather mundane and routine. It was always different with the chief inspector who had become famous in the area for solving difficult cases.

Brendan Scholes made his way from the beer festival to the Wensley Arms, just off the square, where he could drink in greater comfort. Normally he would talk to the local regulars, but today he remained aloof, sitting in a tiny snug bar with his pint of bitter and thinking about his encounters with the Fosters. The rest of the pub was full. The attractions of the beer festival had brought in plenty of visitors.

He was feeling rather pleased with how things had gone when his phone rang.

'Hello? Yes, this is Brendan Scholes— Your daughter? Who are you? . . . Right, well, don't worry, I won't be seeing her again— She's what? How do you know it was me? . . . Steady on! No need to start being nasty— Look, I'm sorry, but it's over! . . . Yes, I'm leaving the area soon and I won't be back . . . Don't call me again or I'll tell the police you were threatening me! Goodbye.' He ended the call and frowned; it hadn't exactly been the discussion he'd expected, but he thought he'd handled it well. Nothing was going to interrupt his pursuit of the grand prize which he believed was in his grasp. He was sure that someone would be unable to resist the chance to brew Wensley Glory again.

After a while, he left the pub, got on his motorbike and rode the nine miles to Ripon where he owned a small, terraced house. This had formerly belonged to his father who had recently died. He was confident that he would be contacted again soon, but he passed a quiet Sunday, and it wasn't until the middle of Monday evening that his phone rang while he was watching television.

'Yes, hello,' he said, smiling to himself with anticipation. 'Who's speaking? Oh, yes – you're interested, are you? . . . I understand. At the brewery, yes, that's fine. There'll be no one there at this time . . . Forty minutes – see you there . . . OK, at the side entrance, yes.' He ended the call, left the house, got on his motorbike and rode back to Markham. As he locked up his bike in a lane off the now empty market square and near the brewery, he was seen by a person who then followed him at a discreet distance.

~

The failing light was casting long shadows as Scholes arrived at the brewery. He passed the big metal main gates and headed down an alley to a side entrance reached by climbing up a flight of stairs. He saw that the door was open, and a light was on. He went inside and along a short corridor with doors into various offices.

'Hello?' he called.

'Over here,' replied a rather muffled voice in the distance. At the end of the corridor was a door out into the works section. Scholes opened it. There was very little light, but he was vaguely aware of the large, round, steel fermentation tanks below him. There was a strong yeasty smell.

Scholes stood by a metal railing looking around for the person he was supposed to be meeting. He was unaware of the shadowy form closing in behind him. The figure struck him hard on the back of the head, and he slumped to the floor.

His assailant hauled up the unconscious body, searched all the pockets and removed a mobile phone and other items before tipping the body over the railing into a tank. It fell in with a huge splash. The killer quickly left the building as Scholes' body floated, face down in the yeasty liquid.

~

'Well, if you have to go, sir, it's a good way, isn't it? Drowned in a vat of beer?'

'Yes, Andy, very funny. I suppose you could even say he got too much of a good thing, although, as that beer was not properly fermented, it wouldn't have tasted very good.'

Detective Chief Inspector Jim Oldroyd and his assistant Detective Sergeant Andy Carter were looking at the body of Brendan Scholes, which had been lifted out of the tank and laid on the ground. The yellow yeast had been scraped off to reveal sodden hair and clothes. There was a matted clump of dark-red blood and hair on the back of his head. The skull was depressed.

'Also,' Oldroyd said, 'by the look of that head wound he was probably dead before he was thrown into the tank. We'll know more when Tim Groves gets here, but we shouldn't really joke about such things. Although I suppose it helps us to cope with sights like this.'

'Yes, sir.'

It was Tuesday morning. The body had been discovered by the first workman to arrive at the brewery, who had immediately called the police. DC Jeffries had attended from Ripon station before requesting assistance from Harrogate HQ. He couldn't believe his luck when DCI Oldroyd arrived. His wish had been granted.

Oldroyd turned to Jeffries, who was standing just behind him and Andy.

'So . . . who found the body, Jeffries?'

Jeffries consulted his notes. 'Philip Welbeck. He's a foreman here; arrives first thing every day to open up. He was here at eight o'clock; noticed yeast and water on the floor by this tank and took a look inside. He called us, and we got the body out. I've called forensics and I expect Mr Groves will be here soon.'

'Good work. And do we know who the victim is?' said Oldroyd, staring at the lifeless body.

'A couple of the staff here have identified him as Brendan Scholes – a local chap. He used to work here at the brewery a few years ago; they said he left under a cloud but claimed not to know any details. Apparently, he lives in Ripon now, but had recently been seen around Markham. They also thought he was a bit of a wrong 'un generally, but didn't say why.'

'Right. Well, we'll see if they're more forthcoming when I speak to them. It sounds as if we might have some motives to work with.' He looked up as another man entered the room. 'Ah! Here's Tim.'

Groves and Oldroyd had worked together for many years and enjoyed some good-humoured, if often rather gruesome, banter.

'Good morning, Jim. Sergeant. Constable.' Groves acknowledged everyone, and then knelt down by the body. 'Was he drowned in a tank of beer like the Duke of Clarence in a butt of Malmsey wine?' he observed breezily, before looking at Oldroyd. 'Which Shakespeare play was that, Jim?'

'Richard the Third,' replied Oldroyd, who had studied English at Oxford before entering the police force. 'And not exactly. I think you'll see this victim wasn't drowned.'

'Ah, no indeed,' said Groves as his long, gloved hands felt around the head wound. 'He would certainly have been unconscious and on his way out when he entered the tank. Especially with a head wound like this. Inflicted by our old friend, the blunt instrument.' He paused as his sensitive fingers continued to examine the wound. 'Hmm, there is something unusual about this head wound. It's not been inflicted by a standard type of hammer . . . if it was even a hammer at all. I would say the instrument had a narrow edge and it looks as if there was a thin groove cut into the surface.'

'What do you think it could have been?'

'I'm not sure. I've not seen anything quite like this before. I'll have to do some more work back at the lab.'

'How long has he been dead?'

'About twelve hours, consistent with being murdered last night and placed here. Most likely killed hereabouts, wouldn't you think?

It would have been a big job to have dragged him here and got him into this container. Bodies are heavy, as I've said to you before.'

'We found bloodstains on those railings, and also on the floor beside them, sir,' said Jeffries, pointing up to where Scholes had been standing when he was attacked. 'I think he was up there, probably lured here by the killer, who then surprised him, smashed him over the head, tipped him over the railing, and into this vat. That's why there was such a big splash.'

'You're probably right,' observed Oldroyd and Jeffries beamed at the praise. 'Anything of interest on the body?'

'No phone, sir. I fancy that would have been removed by the killer because of incriminating phone calls. There's a wallet with the usual collection of bank cards plus a little cash. There's a side entrance to the building, sir. You climb up some steps which take you to that level.' He pointed to the railing. 'There's a corridor where the offices are and a door out on to that platform. I expect it was designed like that to allow the boss to look down over the workers and check they were all doing their jobs. It's an old building; dates back to the nineteenth century when the brewery was started.'

Oldroyd looked up to the railings. 'Yes, he must have arranged to meet his killer here. Why else would he have been in the building at that time of night? And why would there also happen to have been a random killer around?'

'We've found a motorbike locked up in a lane nearby, sir,' said Jeffries. 'It could have belonged to the victim who rode here from Ripon to meet his killer.'

'Excellent.'

'So, what might be the motive, sir?' Andy asked. 'Jealousy? Blackmail?'

'Too early to say. We've got plenty of work to do,' said Oldroyd, rubbing his hands together and relishing the prospect of a fresh mystery. 'We'll start with the man who found him and then we must talk to whoever owns this place.'

'That's Richard Foster, sir. He arrived a little while ago. Very agitated, as you can imagine. I told him to wait in his office for you to arrive.'

'OK, we'll start with him, then. Jeffries, I'd like you to find out all you can about the victim: family, work, relationships, enemies – you know the kind of stuff.'

'Right, sir. The office is up there in the corridor.' Jeffries pointed again to the door on to the platform. 'Go up the metal stairs, through the door and it's the first office on the right, sir. I'll send Philip Welbeck to wait outside. Then my team will carry on taking statements, sir.'

'Thank you, Jeffries.'

'Well, Jim, I'll be off,' said Groves. 'I think it's all pretty straightforward from my point of view. I hope finding the perpetrator is a bit more demanding or you'll get bored. You like the unusual cases, don't you?'

Oldroyd laughed. 'I'm sure there'll be a challenge somewhere, Tim.'

Groves nodded to everyone. 'Didn't think I'd be seeing you again so soon,' he said to Jeffries.

'How's that?' asked Oldroyd.

'The body of a murder victim was discovered not far from here on Saturday,' said Jeffries. 'Mr Groves attended the scene with me and other officers from Ripon station.'

'I see. That's quite a coincidence, isn't it?' remarked Oldroyd. 'Two bodies within four days. Any connection, do you think?'

'Well . . . murder, obviously. The victims were both male, and of similar age. But then young men are the most common victims of violent attacks like this. The body in the drainage tunnel had been strangled.'

19

'There's nothing so far to link them, sir,' added Jeffries.

'Have you found out who the first victim was yet?' asked Oldroyd.

'No, sir,' replied Jeffries. 'The body was badly decomposed; we've done a fingerprint check which revealed nothing. The next step is to look at dental records when Mr Groves gives us the information.' He smiled rather cheekily at Groves.

'Don't worry, you'll have it soon. Anyway, I'm off. Plenty of work to do back at the lab.' Groves picked up his case and walked off, followed by the detectives.

~

'That lad Jeffries is coming on well,' observed Oldroyd as he and Andy climbed the metal staircase to the level of the platform. 'He's absolutely on the ball. When you get promoted to inspector, I've got my eye on him to replace you. If we can prise him away from Ripon station.'

Andy laughed. 'Well, sir, who knows when that will be? I'm happy where I am at the moment.' Andy had joined West Yorkshire Police at Harrogate a few years earlier, moving up from London to take a position as detective sergeant. He was now quite settled in Yorkshire with his partner Stephanie Johnson, the other DS who was regularly a part of Oldroyd's team. They lived in a converted warehouse flat in the centre of Leeds, overlooking the River Aire.

'Yes, but you mustn't become too comfortable. You and Steph have the potential to rise in the force. And we don't want your talents wasted.'

'It's very nice of you to say that, sir,' replied Andy politely. Inside he was bursting with pride that his revered boss had such a high opinion of him and of Steph. Wait till he told her! At the same time, he reflected on his boss's remarks about getting too comfortable. Maybe there was some truth in it, but somehow he found the idea of moving on quite unsettling.

They went through the door, into the corridor, and arrived at the office. Inside they were greeted by a harassed-looking Foster. He was behind a solid old wooden desk and the detectives sat on chairs at the other side. There was also a formally dressed man wearing spectacles who was just leaving. Foster introduced this man as his finance director, Peter Morgan.

'I understand this has been a shock for you,' began Oldroyd.

'Yes. It's terrible,' said Foster. 'And very bad publicity. Suddenly your product is contaminated. When it comes out that he was found in a tank of beer, people feel they might be drinking stuff that's had a body in it. Ridiculous, of course, but these subconscious things matter; they're bread and butter concerns in the field of marketing.'

Oldroyd frowned. It seemed rather callous to make such a point when someone had been murdered. 'Did you know the victim?' he asked.

Foster nodded. 'Of course, everyone around here knew Brendan Scholes. It won't surprise anyone that he's ended up like this. He was the town villain, if I can put it that way. Him and that brother of his.'

'He had a brother?'

'Yes. Frederick. He was much quieter than Brendan, but he was also in trouble quite regularly. He was in my year at school here in Markham but not in my class. My sister was in the same class as Brendan; we both went to the local primary school before Dad sent us to a private high school in Ripon.'

'Tell me more about Brendan.'

Foster took a deep breath before he replied. 'His father, Wilf, worked for my father for years in the brewery, eventually becoming head brewer. He was excellent at his job, and Dad would never get

21

rid of him no matter what happened with Brendan. He even got Brendan a job.

'The problem was that Wilf's wife Marjorie died when the boys were still young. Wilf found it hard to cope and his sons went off the rails. Brendan was an awkward character and constantly disrupted the class at school. He was expelled for a time.

'He grew into a good-looking and charming young man. That was when the problems with women started: two-timing local girls, having affairs with married women, stealing jewellery to give to them . . . stuff like that. At the same time, he was working on Dad's office accounts when money started to go missing. He ran a little sports car and was fond of nice clothes, and we all wondered how he financed it on the wages he earned. Dad was forced to sack him in the end, when the evidence against him was clear. By then he was in debt all over the place and he ran off. It wasn't long before Dad retired. I think he regretted employing Scholes. It was a favour to Wilf, who must have felt terrible about how his son behaved.'

Foster paused, thinking about the past. After a moment, he looked directly at the detectives. 'Before you ask, I did see Scholes recently after a long time. He was here last Saturday when the beer festival was on. He came into the tent where we had our stall and spun me some fantastic yarn about having a copy of my father's recipe for Wensley Glory.'

'I've heard of that,' said Oldroyd. 'It was the famous beer your dad brewed to a secret recipe. The recipe was lost after his death, wasn't it? I remember something in the *Yorkshire Post* about it.'

'That's right. Brendan wanted money from me, of course, but I told him where to go.'

'You didn't believe him?' Oldroyd looked at Foster with his penetrating grey eyes.

Foster laughed. 'No, I didn't. I don't think that recipe will ever turn up. As I told him, we don't even know whether or not Dad wrote it down. He wasn't good with writing. And if he did, the last person I would trust on such a matter would be Scholes.'

'Do you know where Scholes went after he saw you?' asked Andy. 'We need to track all his final movements.'

'Apparently he went over to my sister with the same story and got the same reception.'

'Your sister?'

Foster sighed. 'Emily Foster. She runs Ewe's Ales. That's the other brewery in the town. It's a long story, but we don't get on.'

'Yes, I've heard about the two breweries. But maybe we'll get the details another time,' said Oldroyd. 'So . . . you didn't see Scholes again after the beer festival?'

'No.'

'And where were you last night?'

Foster was taken aback. 'Does this mean I'm a suspect, Chief Inspector? That's ridiculous.'

'Not at all, I'm afraid,' was Oldroyd's unyielding and blunt reply. 'Scholes may well have had a copy of the recipe, and it's not beyond the realms of possibility that you bumped him off to get it. Or your sister did. We'll see what she has to say for herself. So where were you?'

Foster looked flustered. 'I . . . I was with some friends at the house of one of them near here.'

'We'll need some names if this is your alibi, sir,' said Andy.

'Yes, yes, of course. I'll make a list and send it on to you. I haven't got all their numbers on my phone.'

'OK. As far as you were aware, did Scholes have any particular enemies who would have been capable of being violent towards him?'

Foster shrugged. 'How long have you got? He wasn't exactly popular. I don't like saying this, but there's a bloke called Norman Smith; he's a joiner. He has a workshop behind a garage on Sheep Street. He's done a few jobs for us. Scholes had an affair with his wife. Norman's a bit hot-headed. I heard he threatened to do all sorts to Scholes if he didn't move away from here.'

'So, did Scholes leave the area? You said earlier that you hadn't seen him for a while.'

'Yes. His father had lived in a cottage belonging to the brewery while he was working but when he retired, he bought a terraced house in Ripon. I heard that Scholes was living there with him.'

'Is his father still alive?'

'No. He died about two months ago.'

'The victim and the murderer were able to access this building, without breaking in. Do many people have keys?' asked Andy.

'I can give you a list of the keyholders, but there's always the possibility that people acquire sets in various ways. We've never really gone for very high security; there's nothing much to steal. Everything's pretty massive; people couldn't move the huge tanks and coppers. We don't keep much money on the premises and it's in a safe along with any important documents.'

'Is anything missing?'

'Not that I can see. I don't think anyone's been in any of the offices. Everything's in order.'

'OK. That will be all for the moment,' said Oldroyd. He looked around the room. 'If it's alright with you, we'll use this office as our incident room during the investigation. Sorry to displace you.'

Foster's face fell, but he could hardly refuse. 'Fine,' he replied. 'I'll relocate next door.'

∾

'He must be on our list, sir,' said Andy when Foster had left. 'He had at least one clear motive: this beer recipe business.'

'Yes. If that really is knocking around, then it's worth a bit. Wensley Glory Bitter was very famous in its day. It was like no other beer I've ever tasted: smooth, slightly flowery, with great depth of flavour. I remember drinking it with my father in pubs in Harrogate. It was difficult to stop once you'd got started; we rolled home in a merry state more than once . . . much to my mother's annoyance!'

Andy remained sceptical. 'I don't know about all that, sir. I'm not a lager lout like I used to be – you got me drinking proper beer – but I can't always tell much difference between them. It's like wine. Some geezer goes on about how fruity a wine is and how he can taste blackberries, almonds and horseshit. Then a bottle of the stuff costs a hundred quid.'

Oldroyd laughed. 'What a cynic you are! Your palate needs some education! Although you are right. There is a lot of pretentiousness around regarding drinks. It all comes back to branding and capitalism. There was a huge marketing exercise in the seventies to get people to drink mass-produced keg beer. Thank goodness for CAMRA, who started the fight back. Anyway, take it from me, that beer was special and anyone who was able to brew it would make a fortune.'

'There's also the business of Scholes being sacked from here. Maybe Foster nursed some grievance about that.'

'Yes, quite possible.'

'And he was cagey about his alibi, wasn't he?'

'He was, but sometimes that's because someone has been somewhere they shouldn't and doesn't want to say where. Right, let's have a word with this chap who found the body. And then we need to find the sister, Emily. I'm intrigued by this rift between the siblings, although I don't know whether it will have any bearing on the case. She has the same motive as her brother for wanting rid of Scholes. But we'll have to find out more about his other enemies in the town and not just limit ourselves to the breweries.' He moved to the chair behind the desk and sat back with his hands behind his head, much as he was apt to do in his own office at Harrogate Police HQ. He was already making himself at home, and seemed to be enjoying it.

'Well, this case is very intriguing . . . and it seems to be providing us with plenty of promising leads.' He smiled at Andy. 'I must say, though, that all this talk about beer has given me a thirst. What do you say to lunch in one of the town's excellent hostelries?'

Andy grinned. 'Good idea, sir,' he said, though he realised that his boss's old Saab, of which he was very fond, was currently in the garage for its service and MOT, and Andy had driven them out to Markham from Harrogate. He would not be the one drinking.

~

Philip Welbeck was a tall, strong-looking man of about forty, with a sandy beard. He was wearing overalls, and there was a faint odour of the brewery about him.

'I told that other detective,' he began, after Oldroyd requested he explain how he'd found the body. 'I opened the main gate as usual. It was eight o'clock and we were due an early delivery. When I switched the lights on, I noticed the floor around that tank was wet. At first I thought there must be a leak. But as soon as I looked in, I saw him floating there; not a pretty sight.' He screwed up his face as he remembered the unpleasant scene.

'No,' said Oldroyd. 'Quite a shock, I would think. There was no sign of anyone in the building?'

'No. I just called the police and ambulance, and I kept the men out of the building as they arrived for work.'

'Well done,' Oldroyd said. 'You protected the crime scene from contamination.'

Welbeck nodded.

'I take it you knew the victim?' asked Oldroyd.

'Brendan Scholes? Oh, yes. He was a well-known character in this town. If you've spoken to Richard, he'll have told you all about him.'

'Yes, not very popular, we understand, but what we're really interested in is anyone who might have threatened Scholes. Mr Foster told us about the joiner, Norman Smith?'

Welbeck looked uncomfortable. 'Yes, Norman hated Scholes' guts after he was caught messing around with Norman's wife. I'm sure there were a lot of folk who didn't like him . . . But murder? There were rumours that he owed money to people, but I couldn't name anybody who'd kill to reclaim a debt.'

'OK,' said Oldroyd, trying to keep the scepticism out of his voice. In his experience, money was one of the chief motives for violent crimes, and sometimes the sums involved were not even large.

'The funny thing was that Scholes left the town a while ago after he'd been sacked, and we didn't expect him to return. He ended up in Ripon. When his father retired, he went to live with him, I think. I don't know why he came back here, where he was so unpopular. It's funny, really. Doesn't make sense.'

'He claimed he had a copy of the recipe for Wensley Glory Bitter, and tried to sell it to Mr Foster and his sister.'

'What? That's bloody ridiculous!' Welbeck laughed scornfully. 'It's typical of him, though – all bluster and you could never believe anything he said.'

'Do you know anything about the recipe?'

'Only that it was Richard and Emily's father who kept it a secret. When he died there was no trace left of the recipe, or that's what was said.'

Oldroyd looked at him. 'Do you think there could have been a copy?'

Welbeck shrugged. 'I don't know. I worked for old Mr Foster when I was a young lad. Did my apprenticeship as a cooper here. He was a bit of an eccentric, you know. He was always here in the works; he hated sitting around in an office. He got in the way sometimes. When Wensley Glory was being brewed, he put a guard on the door. No one was allowed in when he was adding the hops or whatever else he put in. But it was grand beer, I'll give him that. I just think he wouldn't have wanted it to die with him. He must have written that recipe down. Maybe it just got lost. As I say, he wasn't one for paperwork.'

'Yes, possibly. Thank you, Mr Welbeck, you've been very helpful.'

As Welbeck was leaving, another person appeared at the door. This man was in his sixties, with balding hair, wearing checked trousers, and a jacket and tie. 'Can sumdy tell me what's goin' on?' he said in a broad Yorkshire accent.

'Come in,' said Oldroyd. 'What's the problem?'

The man looked uncertainly from one detective to the other. 'Bert Duffield's the name. Ah do brewery tours; used to work here till ah retired. Then they set me on doin' this job 'cause ah know all abaht brewin' from t'beginnin' to th'end.'

Oldroyd smiled. This was exactly the kind of colourful local character with a story to tell who he enjoyed meeting. 'Well, I'm sorry, but there won't be any brewery tours today. There's been a murder here.'

Duffield frowned as if he didn't believe what Oldroyd was saying. 'A murder? Here at t'brewery? Who?'

'Brendan Scholes.'

Duffield screwed up his eyes. 'Scholes? Wilf's lad?'

Oldroyd nodded.

'Aye, well, ah'm not surprised. He had it comin' to 'im.'

No one seemed surprised by Scholes' death, noted Oldroyd.

28

'Did you know him?' he asked Duffield.

'Aye. Bit of a tearaway, him and his brother, that Frederick.'

'So we hear.'

'Frederick beggared off years ago. He were an odd one. But Brendan, he stayed around and was forever in bother. Anyway.' He shook his head as if he'd had enough of this small talk about murders and wanted to get back to the main point. 'How long is it goin' to be before ah can do me tours again? Ah've got lots of people booked in.'

'When we've done all the forensic work you can start again, but certain parts of the premises will be cordoned off, particularly the murder scene and the walkway above.'

'Mmm,' Duffield growled. 'Ah'd better go and explain to people what's happened. They won't be 'appy, ah can tell thi.'

'I'm sure they won't,' said Oldroyd, amused by the man's seeming indifference to the gravity of the crime, which he clearly treated as a mere inconvenience.

'Ah don't know,' muttered Duffield, shaking his head. 'A murder at t'Yoredale. What would David Foster have thought? It's what comes of unnatural goin's on.'

'What do you mean?' asked Andy.

Duffield pointed at Andy. 'All this business wi' women running a brewery. It's just not reight.'

'That's today's society surely?' replied Andy.

'Aye, well . . . there's more to it than that,' Duffield muttered as he left the office.

Andy laughed. 'He's a grumpy old sod, sir.'

'He is indeed,' replied Oldroyd. 'But it gives you some idea of how Scholes was regarded here and also the hostility those women at the Ewe's Ales Brewery must encounter from some of the locals. It's time we went over and talked to them about it.'

When Philip Welbeck arrived at the works rest area, he found several men waiting to find out if they were able to work that day or if the brewery had been closed due to the investigation. The room was scruffy but comfortable, with a dartboard, sink, microwave and sofas that had seen better days. Several of the staff were lounging around dressed in their work overalls.

'What's happening then, Phil?' asked one man, who was drinking a mug of instant coffee. 'If we can't do owt here, I'd rather go home and get some work done in the allotment.'

'I don't know,' replied Welbeck as he made himself a cup of tea. 'They were just asking me how I found the body and then about Scholes.'

'Did you tell them what a dickhead he was?' called out a thin-faced young man with long hair, who was practising his dart throwing.

'Not in so many words, but I think they got the message. Where's Barry?'

'He's there.' He pointed to a sofa in the corner.

Welbeck went over to a muscly, bald-headed man who was reading a motorbike magazine, and sat beside him.

'Well?' said the man, not looking up from the magazine.

'I didn't say anything, Barry, but it's only a matter of time before someone does. They're going to be talking to anyone who knew anything about Scholes. If you've any sense, you'll go to speak to them yourself, pre-empt it, otherwise it looks bad.'

'Huh!' Barry shook his magazine. 'I bloody hate t'police. They're forever on your back when you're a biker.'

'Well, it's up to you, but I know what I'd do in your position,' said Welbeck, and he got up to begin the task of establishing what work could be done while the crime scene was still closed off. At least he could organise the dispatch of barrels and bottles from the brewery warehouse. The lorries, which had arrived earlier, were still waiting. When they would be able to restart the brewing process was anyone's guess. The whole area had been sealed off by the police. Welbeck frowned as he considered how far they could get behind with their processes and as a result fail to fulfil their orders. Still, it wasn't his problem. It was Richard Foster's.

~

Oldroyd and Andy made their way to the Ewe's Ales Brewery, which was on the opposite side of town to Yoredale Ram. They crossed the now quiet town square; the festival had finished on the Sunday although a few signs of it remained, like the occasional pile of chairs and metal poles. They passed a few visitors sat on benches, and continued down a narrow street until they came to some large gates painted bright green with the words 'Ewe's Ales Brewery' and a white woolly sheep beneath. At the side of the gates was a door, on which Oldroyd knocked.

The door was opened by a curly-haired woman in her thirties, who smiled at the detectives as they presented their warrant cards, and said that Emily was expecting them. She ushered them along a corridor, past a large window which gave a view of the works.

These were similar to the Yoredale brewery: high rooms with large coppers for boiling the wort, steel fermentation tanks and lots of complicated pipework. But it was noticeable that the vast majority of the workforce was female.

They entered an office also not dissimilar to Richard Foster's and were greeted by his sister, who was wearing boyfriend jeans and an olive-green Donegal wool jumper. It appeared that there was no dress code at Ewe's Ales other than that dictated by health and safety for staff involved in the production of the beer.

Oldroyd got the impression that there had been an intention to make this brewery a close copy of the other. He experienced déjà vu as they again sat in chairs before a desk, behind which sat the brewery owner. Except, this time, it was not Richard Foster, but his sister.

'Richard rang earlier and told me about everything that's happened. It's absolutely awful. He said you would be over to talk to me about Brendan Scholes.'

'That's right. But before we do, I'm very intrigued about the relationship between these breweries that you and your brother run. It's well known that you and he are rivals. Does that rivalry get intense?'

Emily laughed rather bitterly. 'You could say that. I suppose all manufacturers who produce the same product are in competition for customers, but I would be misleading you if I didn't say there's more to it than that between me and Richard.'

'Go on.'

Emily paused. 'I'm not sure how relevant this is to what's just happened.'

'Don't worry, we'll decide about that,' said Oldroyd and his penetrating grey eyes were very direct.

'OK. There's only just over a year between Richard and me, he's a little bit older. We were close when we were growing up, and it was only when we reached adulthood that the problems started. Richard had always assumed that he would inherit the family business in that unfair patriarchal way that's been the norm in the past. He trained in the technology of brewing and worked with Dad. I went to university to study business and management and worked in companies in Sheffield and Leeds. It was Dad who wanted me to come back here.' She smiled sadly as she remembered him. 'People thought of Dad as a stuck-in-his-ways Yorkshireman, with his flat cap and everything, but he was a sharp businessman, and he knew Yoredale needed new management and marketing techniques. He appointed me into a senior role within the firm.'

'And that didn't go down well with your brother?'

She laughed. 'No, it didn't. He didn't want to be told what to do by his sister. It revealed a streak of misogyny in him; he saw brewing as a man's job, you know? Men making beer for men.'

Oldroyd found this sibling conflict difficult to understand. He'd always got on very well with his sister and couldn't imagine what it would be like to have such a rift with her.

'So how did you end up here?'

'I stuck at it for a while, and then I read about another family brewing business where a brother had left to start his own brewery . . . and I thought why couldn't a sister do the same? A brewery run by a woman, employing a majority of female workers? It would be a great step forward in terms of equality, and fantastic marketing. These premises were empty, and then I met Janice Anderson – she's our head brewer – at a conference. She was working at a large brewery in Ripon. We had a talk. Janice told me how she faced the same attitudes at her workplace . . . and it had nothing to do with sibling rivalry! It was really hard to be the only woman working in a big brewery; the men didn't take her seriously. She said she would love to come and work for me. So it all came together. I managed to get a bank loan to get the business going. Then Janice and I started a relationship . . . and she's now my partner in both senses.'

'Were you being deliberately provocative with the name of the business?'

'Of course: Ewe's Ales, it's cocking a snook at Yoredale Ram Ales. And it's more elegant, I think.'

'And how have you done? I've had some of your beers, and they're really good. You must be giving your brother a run for his money. That New Lamb Bitter is excellent! What a flavour, and that beautiful classic amber colour.' Oldroyd was becoming quite distracted.

Emily smiled. 'Thanks. Yes, it's gone really well. Much to Richard's annoyance. He scoffed at the idea of me running my own brewery; gave it a year. What he really meant was that he couldn't accept the notion of women running a brewery and making a success out of it. I think Dad was proud of me although he didn't like the fact that his children had fallen out. Then he died quite suddenly of a heart attack. He left the Yoredale to both of us, but I had no intention of going back. So Richard bought me out. That was a great financial boost. We were able to pay off the loan on this place, and since then Ewe's Ales has gone from strength to strength.'

'So relations are still not good between you and your brother?'

'I think the word is "frosty", though it saddens me when I remember how close we used to be. He and his mostly male staff never miss an opportunity to try to diss us in some way.' She told them about the banner at the beer festival. 'That was particularly nasty, as it gave us some poor publicity at an event like that where you want to make a good impression. When I went round to complain, a few of the Yoredale men were sniggering about it. Even Richard was smiling.'

Oldroyd nodded. 'So given that, as you admit, there is bad feeling between yourself and your brother, the possible rediscovery of your father's secret recipe was dynamite, wasn't it?'

'How do you mean?'

'The victim, Brendan Scholes, offered the recipe to you and your brother for money. Whichever one of you got possession of the recipe would gain a massive advantage over the other. You would be able to revive the famous Wensley Glory. The sales and publicity would be enormous.'

Emily shook her head. 'That might have been the case if there was actually any chance that Scholes had the recipe. I didn't believe him, and I'm sure Richard didn't either. And anyway, Chief Inspector, I don't see my main objective as somehow beating the Yoredale Ram Brewery. I just want to make my own business a success. I'm actually glad if other breweries are successful, even my brother's. It leads to more choice and enhances the image of proper beer. Our real enemies are the mass lager and keg beer producers.'

Oldroyd smiled; he agreed with the sentiment. 'Scholes did speak to you, then, at the beer festival?'

'He did, but I hadn't much time for him. I've never liked him. We were in the same class at primary school, and he was a pain then, always telling tales and lies, winding teachers up.'

Andy was writing everything down, as usual, with pen and notepad. Despite his relative youth, he preferred the old method of recording information. 'Where were you last night?' he asked.

'I was at home with Janice. We live up the hill just out of the town. We stayed in all evening watching television and went to bed at about eleven.'

'You used to work at the Yoredale brewery. Do you still have keys for the side door where the murderer and the victim went in?'

Emily looked nonplussed. 'No. I'm sure I turned them in when I left.'

'OK,' said Oldroyd. 'We know that Scholes was unpopular, but do you know of any serious enemies that he had? Anyone who might have been capable of violence?'

'I don't, but like most people round here, I suspect, I'm not surprised this has happened.' She smiled at Oldroyd and Andy and tried to bring the interview to an end. 'And now, if you'll excuse me, I have things I need to be getting on with.'

Oldroyd was happy for the moment and the detectives left.

Emily didn't immediately return to work. She gazed into space for a while reflecting on what was happening in Markham. The chief inspector was right: that recipe was 'dynamite', as he'd described it, and it seemed to have exploded in the town.

~

Andy and Oldroyd adjourned to the Wensley Arms where they settled themselves down in easy chairs and ordered some sandwiches. Oldroyd went to the bar to get himself a pint of Ewe's New Lamb Bitter, which seemed appropriate in the circumstances, and some orange juice and soda water for Andy.

'Are you detectives?' asked the landlord as he pulled Oldroyd's pint.

'Yes.'

'We've heard what's happened; you'll be investigating Brendan Scholes' murder.' He placed the pint on the bar. 'Bill Lawrence, landlord, by the way.'

'Pleased to meet you. Well, news travels fast around here,' replied Oldroyd, taking a drink of his beer.

'Oh, yes. Things like this are round the town in no time and I'm usually one of the first to know. I hear all the gossip. Brendan came in here now and again ever since he reappeared in Markham. Some of us remembered him from the old days.'

'And what was the verdict on him then?'

'He could be good company, though he was very quiet recently. Generally a bit of a rogue, of course. The usual stuff: chasing married women, getting into debt. He had a big row with Barry Green in here a few weeks ago.'

'Who's that?'

'Barry works at the Yoredale. He's a biker, and does a few repairs for people in his spare time. Brendan owed him money and

36

Barry lost his temper with him. Got hold of him by his jacket and threatened all sorts if he didn't pay up. Barry's a big chap, but his bark's worse than his bite; he wouldn't actually do anything.'

'Nevertheless, we need to talk to him. Thanks for the information.'

The barman laughed. 'Well, don't say I told you – I don't want to get on the wrong side of Barry.'

'Or the breweries,' said Oldroyd with a laugh. 'I notice you have both Yoredale and Ewe's beers on draught.'

'Oh, yes.' Lawrence grinned. 'I'd be in serious trouble if I took sides in that argument. Actually, I think they're all damn good beers.'

'I don't suppose you remember Wensley Glory Bitter?'

'Ah, the legendary ale! A bit before my time here, but my father was a publican and he used to say how popular it was. Shame the secret died with old David Foster.'

'So if the recipe for Wensley Glory was rediscovered, do you think it would prove popular?'

'Oh, I think so, yes. Even more than before because it would have that historical feel about it that people love. If anyone got hold of that recipe it would be worth a fortune to a brewer.'

Oldroyd nodded; his assumptions had been confirmed. He went back with the drinks and told Andy what he'd learned about Barry Green.

'Right, sir, I'll note that down. The list of suspects is growing. What did you make of Emily Foster?'

'Same motive as her brother, but more intense, I think. She's clearly angry about how her brother treats her and the Ewe's Ales Brewery, and she'd love to win a big victory over him. That recipe would be the ideal weapon.'

'I didn't buy her denial of having keys for her brother's place. She could have held on to a set, or there are lots of ways she could have got hold of a key to that side door. She must know people who still work there.'

'I agree. Either of the brewery owners could have done it. We need to check their alibis. And I'm also wondering about the relationship between Emily Foster and Janice Anderson. Gay couples are not always accepted in rural communities like this. Did Richard Foster accept that his sister was gay, or did it intensify the rift between them?'

Andy sipped his orange juice and soda water, looking enviously at Oldroyd's pint. 'So, it's brewery wars, sir? A family business face-off, maybe with sexual undertones? In a small town like this, who would have thought it?'

Their ham and cheese sandwiches in granary bread arrived.

Oldroyd took a bite before answering. 'Actually, it's in these rural areas where you often get feuds, usually over land and property; members of a family end up not speaking to each other for forty years, even though they live in the same village or on neighbouring farms.'

'It's those attitudes, that kind of stubbornness, that I would find difficult if I was living in the countryside. Life's too short, isn't it? I'll always be an urban person deep down. Things are less insular in the city.'

'Some would say that in the city the feuds are between criminal gangs and they're a lot nastier,' said Oldroyd mischievously. 'Anyway,' he said, munching his sandwich and taking swigs of his beer, 'who else have we got?'

'In addition to the Fosters, there's Norman Smith, a joiner whose wife – according to Foster – had an affair with Scholes, and Barry Green who was owed money by Scholes and threatened him in front of witnesses. I must say they both sound more like blokes who would lose their temper, maybe even hit Scholes on the spot. Not people who would plan a murder.'

'Maybe. That's all we know yet, but more suspects may come out of the woodwork when we start to probe a bit. We'll find Smith this afternoon and see what he has to say.'

Oldroyd sat back and soaked in the atmosphere of the pub: a group of four men were playing darts in one corner while at other tables walkers with rucksacks were consulting Ordnance Survey maps. The landlord was talking to two people at the bar and cracking the occasional joke.

Oldroyd shook his head and nestled deeper into his soft armchair. 'It's wonderful in here, isn't it? A classic Yorkshire pub. I could stay all afternoon and drink a few of these.' He winked at Andy as he held his pint glass.

Andy laughed. 'Me too, sir. Sometimes work just gets in the way of the good life, doesn't it?'

~

Back at the Yoredale Ram Brewery, Richard Foster was attempting to make himself comfortable in his temporary accommodation, which was in fact a desk in the same room as three office workers who were obviously embarrassed at having their boss in with them. He was in conversation with his finance director, Peter Morgan, who offered to give up his office for Foster.

'That's a kind offer, Peter,' Foster said, 'but there's no point disrupting two of us. I'll be fine here. I'm sure it won't be long.'

'OK.' Morgan nodded. He was very sharp in his job, and much valued by Foster. 'While I'm here, you asked if we could just run through the figures for last month.' He proceeded to explain the Excel spreadsheets that showed that the company was struggling a little with sales down for the third month in a row. 'We need to stop this decline, otherwise we're going to be running a big deficit this year.'

Foster sighed. He'd suspected that this was the situation, but could have done without the problem at the moment. 'Sales are always lower in winter,' he said. 'But you're right, we need to address this. We need to refresh our marketing strategy. Leave it with me; I'll get on to Forman's.' Forman's was the local publicity and promotions consultancy with which the brewery worked.

When Morgan left, Foster looked around the office. The lack of privacy was going to be difficult, especially at moments like this when he urgently needed to make a phone call. He waited until two of the others went out of the office and the remaining person was at a desk on the opposite side of the room. Then he turned away, hiding his phone from view, and dialled a number.

'Yes,' he said, when the person on the other end answered. 'It's all kicked off here – the police have been to talk to me . . . No, they don't waste any time. Look, my alibi for last night is that I was with you and the others. We had a drink and watched a film, OK? I don't want anything to get back to Christine . . . You know why! She'll kill me! . . . Well, I want us to keep to the story I've told her: we had a few drinks and then went back to your place to watch a film. Yes – it's difficult here, the police have taken over my office, there are other people around . . . No, I can't talk for long . . . Yes, just keep to that. Can you tell the others? We all need to say the same to the police if they ask . . . That's great, much appreciated . . . No, it's bad here. No doubt we'll have the reporters soon. OK, thanks again! Bye.'

He ended the call feeling some relief. There were certain things that had to remain a secret. The problem was that Chief Inspector Oldroyd did not look like a man who could be hoodwinked for very long.

Oldroyd and Andy walked down a narrow street off the market-place, passing tiny terraced houses with doors opening straight on to the pavement. At the bottom was a small repair garage where a mechanic in blue overalls was peering under a car bonnet. He directed the detectives to an even narrower and rather overgrown lane at the side of the garage, just wide enough to get a van down. It led to a small workshop. 'Sheep Lane Joiners' announced the board above the door. In a patch of waste ground at the side of the building a goat was tethered to a post. It bleated and walked over to Andy as Oldroyd knocked on the door.

As they waited for a response the goat began to nibble at Andy's jacket.

'Hey!' he cried. 'Get off, you stupid sheep.' He pulled his jacket out of the animal's mouth.

Oldroyd laughed. 'That's a goat, Andy, you can tell from its beard and its bleating. They'll eat anything.'

Andy drew back with revulsion. 'God, sir, it smells!'

'Yes, and it's a good job it's not mating season or it might be peeing on itself and it could spray you with some.'

Andy jumped back a little further from the goat, as it insisted on trying for his jacket again, and Oldroyd laughed. 'I take it you didn't have goats in Croydon?'

'No, sir. And thank goodness, if that's how they behave. Peeing on themselves! That's disgusting. Go away! Shoo! Oh, it stinks!' The goat was still coming forward and nuzzling him.

'I think it likes you.'

At that moment a van came bumping down the lane, coming to a stop by the workshop entrance. A tall man in dirty work clothes and heavy boots got out and looked at the detectives suspiciously.

'Are you Norman Smith?' asked Oldroyd, presenting his warrant card.

'Yes,' replied Smith, watching Andy and the goat. 'Gary, leave him alone!' he called. The goat turned away from Andy, trotted off and started to eat the leaves on a much denuded bush. Andy brushed himself down and swore at the goat under his breath.

'You'd better come in,' said Smith as he unlocked the workshop door. Inside, Smith set out two plastic chairs in a tiny space surrounded by workbenches, shelves and cupboards. He and Oldroyd took a seat.

'I'll come straight to the point,' said Smith, leaning forward in his chair. 'I know Scholes has been found dead and I can't say I'm sad about it. The bastard was messing around with my wife. He took advantage of her; she was feeling down when we were having a difficult time in our marriage. He wouldn't leave her alone. So, yes, I had a good motive for bumping him off, but I didn't.'

Oldroyd had to smile at the forthright bluntness of this. 'Did you ever physically threaten him?'

'Yes, I told him if he came near her again, I'd smash his face in and break his legs.' Smith's hands coiled into fists as he remembered the encounter.

'I see. And how is your marriage now?'

'We're doing all right. Scholes left Markham after I warned him off. That was a while ago and I thought he'd gone for good. Then I heard he'd been back and I walked into him on Saturday in the marketplace when the beer festival was on. He pretended he didn't know me, the bloody rat. I saw red, I can tell you, and I told him to get out of town.'

'And what did he do?'

'He walked away laughing, and that was the last time I saw him.'

'Did anyone witness this encounter?'

'I don't think so. We were just at the side of one of the marquees.'

'And you didn't see him again after that?'

'No.'

'You're absolutely sure you didn't smash him over the head and tip him into a tank of fermenting beer?'

Smith laughed. 'Is that what happened? He got better than he deserved, then. But, no, I didn't.'

'Richard Foster told us you did some jobs at the brewery. Maybe you acquired some keys so you were able to get into the building, lure Scholes inside. Then you could finish him off.'

Smith laughed loudly. 'What an imagination you've got!'

Oldroyd persisted. 'Where were you last night?'

'I was in the Wensley Arms all evening until it closed at eleven. I usually have a night out on Mondays; it gets too crowded at the weekend. There's a group of us – we sit at the bar, talk all evening and down a fair number of pints.'

Sounds good, thought Oldroyd, who would enjoy an evening like that himself. 'So they can verify you were there?' he said.

'Yes.'

'OK, if you can give their names to the sergeant here, we'll be off. Stay around in Markham; an officer will be over to take your statement and fingerprints.'

'OK, bloody hell, seems like a big deal,' said Smith and he went outside to start unloading his van. 'When you find out who did it, send them round to the Wensley and I'll buy them a pint.' He seemed to think this extremely funny and laughed uproariously.

⁓

'Well, sir, this Scholes was not a very popular person, was he?' Andy said when they were outside. 'That bloke seemed to really hate him.'

'He did,' Oldroyd replied. 'He made no attempt to disguise his pleasure that Scholes is dead. Was it bravado or does he have a watertight alibi? Our list of suspects is growing.'

43

'Smith's a big bloke, and he has access to plenty of hammers, sir. He's got a short temper and a clear motive, so he must be a possibility. Maybe that encounter in the marketplace rekindled his hatred of the man, and he killed him as you described back there,' said Andy, as he and Oldroyd made their way back to the Yoredale Ram Brewery. They walked across the big market square, which was still quiet and largely deserted, apart from a single greengrocer's stall that had opened in one corner, selling the usual range of fruit and veg colourfully laid out in straw baskets.

'We're not sure about the murder weapon yet,' replied Oldroyd. 'There was something strange about it. I don't think it was a conventional hammer. And I don't know how strong a suspect Smith is. Sometimes it's a good idea to confront people with things. You can often tell from their reaction if you're somewhere near what happened, even if they deny the details of what you say. I can't say I got that feeling from Smith. He was very upfront about everything, including his intense dislike of Scholes, but that doesn't mean he's not guilty. Let's see how Jeffries has been getting on.' They reached the Yoredale brewery and climbed the steps to the office entrance.

'I think he'll have the whole case solved by now, sir,' said Andy with a laugh. 'He'll certainly have taken statements from everyone in the town.'

'Now, now,' replied Oldroyd, 'don't belittle the lad's enthusiasm. I bet you were like that when you first started, before you got cynical and lazy.'

'Not much chance of that working for you, sir,' replied Andy, still laughing.

When they got to the office, Jeffries was, as expected, waiting for them.

'We've got statements from everyone who had any contact with Scholes, sir. He was universally disliked when he worked here a few years back; people thought he was arrogant and unpleasant – that he'd only got the job because his father was head brewer. And he bothered some of the female employees with his unwanted attentions.'

Oldroyd sat in the easy chair behind the desk and raised his eyebrows. 'Good work, Jeffries. No one seems to have much of a good word for this character. No wonder he ended up in a tank of beer.'

'His place in Ripon is being searched, sir. I'll be able to report back to you tomorrow on that.'

'We've got some more people to follow up,' said Andy to Jeffries and he gave him the names of the people who could verify Smith's alibi.

'I'm on to it, sir,' replied Jeffries with his usual eagerness before leaving the office.

Oldroyd gave Andy an arch look. 'Wonderful, isn't it? The enthusiasm. That's what you need in a young police officer.'

Andy laughed. 'I'm sure it is, sir. I get tired just watching him buzz around.'

'Talking of tired, I think we should call it a day here now. Let's get back to Harrogate. I need to give this case some thought. There are some things about it which intrigue me.'

'Such as, sir?'

Oldroyd sighed and sat back in his chair. 'Was there any truth in Scholes' claim that he had a copy of the recipe?'

'Seems unlikely, sir.'

'If so, it was a very crude attempt at fraud. Did he really think he could get money out of people if he was lying about it? I don't know. He would have to have shown them what he had at some point.' He shook his head. 'Also, why would he arrange to meet someone here in the deserted brewery at night; someone who had reason to kill him? You'd think he'd be a bit more cautious. And if there is a recipe, did he take it with him maybe as proof and then the killer took it after the murder?'

'Maybe, sir, but that would have been risky, wouldn't it?'

Oldroyd shook his head again. 'And then there's the curious fact that he suddenly reappeared here in Markham after several years, peddling this story about having a copy of the recipe. It must have been something to do with his father's death. Did Wilf Scholes have a copy after all, and he gave it to his son? Or did Brendan find it? There's also the business of the unusual wounds to Scholes' head. What does that tell us?'

Andy shrugged. 'I don't know the answers, sir, but certain facts are pretty clear, aren't they? Even if the details aren't. A man with many enemies with different motives has been murdered in a brewery. Surely our main job is to concentrate on finding out which of those enemies is the killer, regardless of whether there really was a copy of the recipe.'

Oldroyd couldn't disagree but on the drive back to Harrogate, he was quiet as he turned the questions over in his mind. Andy's suggestion made sense, but Oldroyd's instincts were telling him that this case would not be as relatively straightforward as it appeared.

Two

Beer was first brewed in Kirkstall, Leeds, by the Cistercian monks of Kirkstall Abbey over eight hundred years ago. Making beer has continued there sporadically since then and the current thriving Kirkstall Brewery occupies a large former dairy in Kirkstall Road. One of the brewery's most prominent beers is Dissolution Extra IPA, a strong India Pale Ale named after Henry VIII's closure of the abbey in 1539.

When Oldroyd arrived back at his flat overlooking the Stray in Harrogate, he found his partner Deborah sitting at her desk-top computer, looking at houses for sale in the neighbourhood. They had decided to sell their apartments (Deborah retained a seldom-used flat in Knaresborough) and buy a house. They both fancied having a garden, although Deborah was the one who was interested in cultivating plants.

'Hi, love,' said Oldroyd. 'Anything good coming up? I'll make some tea.'

'Hi,' she replied, somewhat distracted. 'Not much yet. I've only just started. My last client of the day left a few minutes ago.' Deborah was a psychotherapist with her own practice which she ran from the Harrogate flat. 'How was the investigation?'

'OK,' Oldroyd called from the kitchen, and after a short while he came back into the living room with two mugs of tea. 'Unusual murder method: victim was hit over the head and then drowned in a tank of beer. Andy thought it might be a good way to go. In this job you get somewhat hardened to people being bumped off.'

'So I see,' said Deborah, turning from the computer screen and smiling.

'What I found most interesting was the rivalry between the two breweries in Markham.' Oldroyd sat down on the sofa and drank his tea while he told her about the Yoredale Ram and Ewe's Ales. 'So there we have a brother and sister who have really fallen out and they're competing with each other in these breweries and it seems quite bitter, if you'll pardon the expression.'

'Ha ha,' laughed Deborah sarcastically.

'I just wondered what you thought about it. That kind of sibling hostility is strange to me. I've always been close to Alison, and it would be awful if we didn't get on.' Oldroyd's sister, who was a little older than him, was a vicar in Kirby Underside, a village between Harrogate and Leeds.

'Well, I think a lot depends on how siblings are brought up. If there's a competitive atmosphere in the family, that can intensify rivalries which can then last into adult life. Like you, I've always got on well with my brother, although I did resent the way Sam was treated differently as a boy . . . especially when it came to domestic tasks.'

'Sexism plays a part with the Fosters too. Emily was made to feel by her brother that brewing is not for women and she's on a mission to prove that he's wrong. She employs mostly female staff.'

'Good for her. There's nothing wrong in that. The problems can start if things become obsessional: that the whole venture is about proving a point.'

'Exactly. All this is relevant to the case.' He told her about the recipe for Wensley Glory. 'I'm thinking that one of them could be so determined to win this battle of the breweries that they would do anything to acquire that recipe, which would be a knockout blow in the contest between them.'

'Anything including murder?'

'Maybe.'

'Well, that would certainly be an extreme expression of sibling rivalry.' She returned to the computer while Oldroyd continued to drink his tea and think about the case.

'Oh, this looks interesting,' announced Deborah after a while. 'It's a nice cottage in a village in the Nidd Valley near Killinghall: an end terrace, long garden at the back. I'll book a viewing.'

'Good,' replied Oldroyd, trying to sound as positive as he could. The idea of moving was OK in principle, but when it came to the effort of finding properties and going out to look for them, his enthusiasm waned. He found himself bored and confused by colour schemes, kitchen designs and floor coverings. He was happy to leave the search to Deborah, but there was no way he could avoid the viewing.

'Come and have a look then, show some interest,' said Deborah, in a tone that was part critical and part teasing.

'Yes, yes, I will.' He got up reluctantly and stood behind her. It was the usual collection of kitchen, bedroom, living room, garden. He found it difficult to form an opinion based on photographs.

'You are sure you really want to move, aren't you, Jim?' she asked.

'Yes, yes, of course. It's just my laziness, leaving it all to you. When a case gets going, I find it hard to get my mind off it.'

'Yes, but I want you to be fully involved in this. It's something I want us to do together. And don't use the job as an excuse. We've talked about this before; you've got workaholic tendencies and they can shut out other things in life and affect relationships.'

'I know.' Oldroyd reflected on how his overwork had led to his separation from his wife Julia. He was determined that such a thing would not happen again. 'Well, I quite like the colour scheme in that kitchen . . . but do you think it's a bit gloomy?'

~

Emily Foster and Janice Anderson lived in a barn conversion in a field accessed up a narrow lane out of Markham. It meant they were close enough to walk to work, but they were also out in the countryside. From the large window in their kitchen they looked across a small patch of garden, in which daffodils and anemones were blooming, to a field that contained grazing ewes with small white newly born lambs. In the distance were the fells of Upper Wensleydale.

They sat together at the table eating their evening meal and gazed out on this beautiful scene as the spring day came to an end and the light slanted over the freshly green fields.

'We're so lucky to have this to retreat to, especially after a day like today,' said Emily with a sigh of contentment. She scooped up the last of her spaghetti with prawns in a tomato, chilli and white wine sauce and took a sip of her wine. It was a lovely end to what had been a difficult day.

'Yes,' replied Janice, who put her fork and spoon down as she had already finished. She had long black hair, and brown eyes that looked into the face of her partner. 'Were the police difficult?'

Emily shrugged. 'No, just doing their job. They're a sharp team, especially that chief inspector. I don't think it'll take them long to get to the bottom of it.'

'So they think either you or Richard could have killed Brendan to get your hands on the recipe for Wensley Glory?'

'That's about it, yes. And it doesn't help that they know Richard and I are not on good terms. I'm sure they think that adds to the motive: the one who got possession of the recipe would get ahead of the other in terms of the business.'

'Surely they don't think either of you could be so ruthless?'

'Well, they don't know what nice people we really are, do they?' said Emily with an ironic smile. 'It's what I would be thinking if I was them.' She got up, collected the empty plates and took them over to the dishwasher. 'Do you want some of that strawberry yoghurt?'

'Oh, yes, please.'

Emily got two bowls out of the cupboard and a tub of yoghurt from the fridge.

'You know,' continued Janice as she played with her wine glass, 'I was there when Brendan came into the tent at the beer festival, and I thought there was something odd about him.'

'Really? What? You didn't say anything on Saturday.'

'No. I didn't think about it at the time, but after today and he's been found murdered, I started to think. I used to see Brendan in the town and at folk gigs in pubs round here. He liked the same music as me.'

'And?'

'He just seemed a little off.'

'Can't say I noticed, but I've not had much to do with him since we were in primary school.'

'No. I'm probably imagining it. He didn't say much to me and seemed eager to get away, which I thought was strange, you know? It was a while ago when we last talked, but we were good mates. Anyway, none of us will be seeing him again.' She paused and looked out on the bucolic scene. 'I know he was, like, the local villain and a terrible womaniser, but I'm sad about it. He didn't deserve to be murdered.'

Emily looked at her curiously. 'Well, if you weren't gay, I'd be feeling jealous. Sounds like you were quite fond of him.'

Janice laughed. 'Not really, he was just part of a group who used to meet in the pubs and have a bit of fun. Then we all got older, some got families, and it sort of fizzled out. Brendan never changed, though. There was even a rumour that he had something going with a woman up at the manor.'

'He was a pain when we were at school,' said Emily. 'He was in my class. The teachers had a hell of a time with him, though I did learn later that his mum died when he was quite young. That must have had an effect.'

'Yes, you could see that mischievousness in him. I suppose I only saw him at social events, though. He could be quite entertaining.'

'Yes, there are always plenty of charming rogues around. Funny how he never got married, did he?'

'I don't think he would have been capable of fidelity to anyone, and I think women sensed that.' She broke off suddenly. 'Oh! Look at those lambs!' Two very young lambs had appeared with their mother. Their fluffy white tails wagged vigorously as they dived under the ewe and sucked on a teat. 'New life! Isn't it wonderful?'

'Absolutely, and we're so lucky to see it from our kitchen window.'

They ate their yoghurt and watched the lambs for a while in peaceful silence.

Finally Emily said, 'I've been busy with the police today and didn't get the chance to talk to the team much. How are they feeling about what happened on Saturday?'

'You mean the nasty banner?'

'Yes.'

'No one was really surprised. We've come to expect it. Not that that makes it any better.'

'Of course not.' Emily frowned. 'The problem is my darling brother won't come down hard on whoever's behind all this abuse. I don't think he instigates it, but he sort of half condones it because he's got sexist attitudes himself.'

'That makes things difficult.' Janice collected the empty bowls and put the coffee on to brew.

Emily continued to stare out of the window, but she was not really looking at the scene any more. 'It does,' she said. 'The last thing you want to do is let them think they're getting to you. The police know about it, but they're too busy to do anything. If it goes on, I shall take it further. Even if he is my brother. But I do feel sorry for him, with that body in the fermentation tank. On top of everything, it's not good publicity for his brewery, is it?'

'No. Well, maybe it's a judgement on the Yoredale for their attitudes towards our brewery,' said Janice half seriously. 'They might think carefully before they do it again.'

~

'How lucky are you, then, working with the boss at a brewery? Don't drink too much or you'll never solve the case.'

Andy was relaxing with his partner, Steph, in their Leeds flat. Her blue eyes sparkled as she teased him.

'Not much chance of that. He'll have me driving so that he can fit in the odd pint,' laughed Andy. 'Chief inspector's privilege, I suppose.'

'And you say the brother and sister are rivals?'

'Yeah, both running breweries in the same town. And the sister is in a relationship with her head brewer. The boss thinks that might be a factor, too, so there's a lot going on there: homophobia and misogyny as well as a competition about who can brew the best beer.'

Steph raised her eyebrows. 'Well, best of luck to Ewe's Ales, I say. It's great to hear about pioneering women in areas that have been exclusively male.' She grinned at him for a moment. 'Oh, I forgot to tell you, Dad rang; he's coming up again in a couple of months.'

'OK.'

'He's going to stay at the First Choice Inn.'

'Good. I'm happy about it if you are. I think you're being very sensible taking it steady.'

After being estranged for many years from her alcoholic and abusive father who had left the family and gone back to London when they were quite young, Steph and her sister Lisa had seen him twice in the past year after he had contacted their mother and expressed a desire to see his daughters again.

'You know, I've never thought about it before,' said Andy. 'Maybe it's the breweries in this case that have made me think, but you seem to have kept a very balanced view of drinking, even though it was alcohol that broke up your family.'

Steph thought for a moment. 'Have you ever seen me drunk?'

'Actually, no.'

'Exactly. I don't think I could do it after the things I saw when I was little. I'm acutely aware of the dangers of drinking, so I set myself strict limits. Drink destroyed our family life until he left and then it deprived me of a father.'

She recalled how shocked she'd been when she and Lisa had met up with their father in Leeds. It was the first time they'd seen him since they were young girls. Not only was he much older but also smaller than she remembered, and he seemed thin and frail. His receding hair was now grey. Alcohol had devastated his body, though he was dry now for the first time in many years and managing to hold down a job in customer services. He lived in a shared rented house in Barking with no partner, no family, and few friends.

'I used to worry about you a bit when we first met,' she continued. 'You were a bit of a binge drinker under the influence of Jason.' Jason Harris was one of Andy's oldest London friends; a rather wild character until he had reformed a little in recent years. He'd left the financial world to become a maths teacher in a deprived area.

'I know, but you soon got me under control. Anyway, I couldn't do it now, I'm too old. I feel full up after a couple of pints.'

'Good. It's probably safe for you to investigate a case in a brewery, then.'

'Yeah. I can't see this one lasting that long. There are a number of suspects with a motive; it's just a matter of finding the right one.'

Steph laughed. 'Well, I wouldn't count your chickens on that. You know how often with the boss things turn out to be more complicated than they appear.' Suddenly there was the sound of a kitchen timer going off.

'True! Anyway, that means dinner's ready.' Andy had made a beef chilli.

'Great, I'm looking forward to it.'

~

Back in Markham, Bert Duffield was sitting at the bar in the Wensley Arms. He was feeling rather grumpy after a frustrating day. He enjoyed his retirement job conducting brewery tours; it gave him scope to parade his knowledge about all things related to brewing. He was a bit of what Steph would have called a mansplainer, often submitting the people on the tour to long and detailed technical accounts of various processes. Today he had been thwarted as all tours had been cancelled until further notice.

'It's a damn nuisance, Bill. Ah had to ring up t'people who were supposed to be comin' on t'tour and tell 'em it were cancelled,' he said as he fiddled with his beer glass.

'Did you?' asked Lawrence sceptically, half listening to Duffield as he dried some glasses.

'Well, I got that young lass in th'office to do it for me. I'm not reight good on t'phone, you know. But I had to deal with those who she couldn't get in touch wi', and they weren't best pleased, ah can tell thi.'

Lawrence finished drying the glasses and placed them back on hooks above the bar. He found Old Bert, as he thought of Duffield, an amusing character. He seemed tone deaf to the seriousness of the situation, saying nothing about the fact that someone had been killed.

Lawrence liked to tease Duffield and sometimes wind him up. Now was the perfect opportunity. 'You do know that someone was murdered at the brewery, Bert? And here you are going on about your tours.'

Duffield frowned and took a drink of his beer. 'Aye, well, ah'm sorry about that, it's a bad do somebody bein' drowned in a fermentation tank. But it's t'police who are messing it up for me, cancelling t'tours.'

'Well, they've got to do their investigations, Bert. They can't have you and a lot of visitors trampling over the murder scene and destroying forensic evidence.'

'Aye, ah suppose not.' He mumbled for a while and then carried on. 'It would be that blasted Scholes, wouldn't it? Ah don't know how poor Wilf put up wi' those lads.'

'Hey, that's a bit of what they call "victim blaming", isn't it, Bert? It wasn't Scholes' fault that he was murdered in the brewery.'

'Well, ah don't know . . .' Duffield grumbled to himself again.

'Never mind; you'll be able to show the visitors where the body was found. And you could even create a story about how that part of the building is haunted by a ghost dripping in beer.'

'Get on wi' yer,' said Bert with a laugh.

Lawrence decided to move the conversation on. 'Anyway, they're saying that Scholes was going round offering to sell a copy of the recipe for Wensley Glory. Do you know anything about that?'

Duffield looked up sharply. 'Wensley Glory? Aye, those were t'days. It were a great brewery when Mr Foster were in charge; everybody worked together and we made t'best beer in Yorkshire – nay, the world.'

'Same thing, isn't it?' said Lawrence, smiling.

'Aye, you're reight there. But Mr Foster never let anybody know t'secret o' Wensley Glory, oh no!' Duffield spoke with enthusiasm now as he reminisced about his time at the brewery. 'He used to say, "Nub'dy in here now, lads," and we all had to go outside while he added his secret ingredients.'

'Did you have any idea what they were?'

'Not really, but we all thought it was summat to do with th' 'ops. He got some special 'ops from somewhere.'

'Surely Wilf Scholes must have known something about it?'

Duffield shook his head. 'Well, ah don't know; he never said owt abaht it.' He had another drink of his beer and noticed a group of women sitting at a table nearby, all of them drinking pints. 'Things aren't the same nowadays,' he said, lowering his voice as if he knew what he was about to say was unacceptable to most people. 'Women runnin' a brewery, whatever next!'

'Now then, Bert, don't start on that. All you're doing is showing your age,' said Lawrence, grinning. He pointed to the pumps at the bar. 'Look, we have their beers – and they're popular. You should try them.'

Duffield had a sneer on his face as if he would never believe that women could produce good beer. He got down from the bar stool.

'Right, ah'm off,' he announced. ''Night, Bill.'

''Night, Bert. Have a pint of Ewe's Ales New Lamb Bitter next time. It's very good,' said Lawrence, laughing as he raised a glass.

Duffield flapped his hand at Lawrence and went out of the bar. He was in a thoughtful mood as he walked home. He hadn't told Lawrence all he knew or suspected about the recipe for Wensley Glory. The truth was, he was pretty sure a copy of the recipe really did exist, and he had a good idea where it might be.

～

Swinfield Hall was a majestic late-eighteenth-century house built for Peter Langford, Lord Markham, who owned a vast estate near the town and up on to the fells. His family were originally called the de Langfords and the land had been granted to them by William the Conqueror. Over the years the land around the house had been landscaped and the moorlands converted to a grouse moor.

Jeremy Langford, the present Lord Markham, had grasped the necessity for aristocratic landowners to earn money and in addition to the grouse moor and opening the house to the public, he used the large and splendid eighteenth-century stable block to run a riding school and to breed racehorses. To be precise, it was his daughter Sophie who ran the riding school, which she'd done ever since she left boarding school in England and a finishing school in Switzerland.

The next morning was bright and cheerful, but Sophie Langford looked worried as she entered the stable block dressed in jodhpurs and riding jacket. She had a number of girls working for her, and she called one over from where she was brushing a handsome grey horse.

'Melanie, can I have a word, please?' Her voice contained no trace of a Yorkshire accent; the stables could have been in Hampshire.

The girl walked over obediently.

'I've heard that there's been a murder down in Markham,' Sophie said. 'I can't believe it. Is that right?'

'Yes, the whole town was buzzing with it yesterday.'

'And is it true the victim was Brendan Scholes?'

'I think so, that's the name I heard. He was found dead in a tank at the Yoredale brewery.'

'Oh my God!' Sophie put her hand to her face.

'Did you know him?'

Sophie turned away, tears in her eyes. 'Yes,' she said, wiping her eyes with a tissue, but gave no details. 'Do the police know who did it?'

'I've no idea. My uncle works at the Yoredale and he told my dad that the police were all over the building so they couldn't do any work. But I've not heard that they've arrested anybody.' Melanie paused, clearly concerned about Sophie's emotional reaction to the news. 'Are you OK?'

'Yes, I'll be fine. Just carry on.' She turned away from Melanie, walked out of the yard and found a quiet spot on a bench by some trees. She got out her phone and made a call to someone local, who confirmed that Brendan Scholes was the victim.

She sat and slowly pulled herself together before she called a friend who lived on the outskirts of Ripon. 'Amelia, hi . . . Oh my God, you'll never believe what's happened. Apparently Brendan's dead – yes – he was murdered here in Markham at the brewery . . . No, there's no word about who did it . . . I'm feeling awful, obviously, but look, when Dad learns about this, he'll be hopping about.

The last thing he wants is Scholes' past to be investigated. He thinks it would damage my reputation like I'm some nineteen-fifties debutante . . . I know, it's absolutely ludicrous . . . What? Oh my God, I never thought of it like that, but you're right, the police will.' She ended the call, which had only succeeded in making her feel worse. Amelia had pointed out that she and her father could be suspects. What on earth could she do next?

~

The same morning, DC Jeffries was at work early overseeing other officers as they conducted a search of the small, terraced house in Ripon that Scholes had recently inherited from his father. Jeffries had been given charge of the task by Oldroyd, who he was keen to impress, but the search had so far yielded disappointingly little in terms of significant discoveries.

The flat was furnished in a basic fashion. It was untidy and didn't look as if it had been thoroughly cleaned for a long time. In fact, it looked like what it was: a flat that had been lived in for some time by men who were not in the least house-proud.

Jeffries walked around looking at the pictures on the walls – mostly framed photographs connected with beer and brewing in the area. There was an old black and white image of the Yoredale Ram Brewery dating from Edwardian times, showing workers lined up outside the gate sporting long, droopy moustaches. Another, more recent, depicted Wilfred Scholes smiling at the camera while he supervised the men inside the big brewhouse.

Brendan's father had clearly loved his job at the brewery and was very proud of its achievements. In a sideboard drawer, Jeffries found a large bag full of medals, certificates and small trophies, all of which had been won at beer festivals and competitions going back to the 1960s. Above the sideboard was a photograph showing

David Foster holding a trophy. At his side was Wilfred Scholes, both men flanked presumably by other people from the brewery. A caption at the bottom of the frame stated, 'Wensley Glory Bitter, Beer of the Year 1995'.

Jeffries knitted his brow together thoughtfully as he examined the photograph. Clearly those two men had been very close. Maybe Brendan Scholes wasn't lying after all: perhaps David Foster really had entrusted the recipe to Scholes' father, and the son had found it after his death.

There was another photograph, more recent but still a while ago, showing Wilf with his two sons, Brendan and Frederick. Jeffries removed this, thinking it might prove useful in his investigation.

The room upstairs, which had obviously been Brendan's bedroom, was even more untidy than the rest of the house. It was impossible to sort through things on the spot, so the detectives bagged up a computer and some folders of papers in the hope that they might yield something of interest when they were analysed back at the station.

The only concrete piece of evidence they had discovered was some payslips that confirmed Scholes had had a job in Ripon as an estate agent's clerk. That employment seemed to have ceased at the time his father died, as there were no payslips after that date. Jeffries made a mental note that this would have to be followed up.

When the search ended, Jeffries left immediately for Markham. He was eager to report back to DCI Oldroyd, as he had some news on another matter to relay to the chief inspector.

~

'It's the usual carry-on, Jim. He doesn't take any interest in a case unless it has some significance for him and his bloody cronies in the Lodge, or it's affecting some bigwig in the area that he wants to impress. He was on the bloody phone first thing this morning asking how the investigation's going into the murder in Markham. I don't think he has any idea where Markham is, but he must know somebody who's involved in the town or something. I don't know. Anyway, how are you doing with it?'

Oldroyd was at Harrogate HQ in the office of his superior Detective Chief Superintendent Tom Walker. It was the kind of austere office of someone who would have preferred to be out in the field. This summed up Walker exactly. He and Oldroyd had worked with each other for many years and were on first-name terms in private. They liked to throw in the occasional bits of Yorkshire dialect into their conversation.

Walker was complaining to Oldroyd about Matthew Watkins, the relatively young, trendy, managerial chief constable of West Riding Police for whom Walker – with forty years of service behind him, mostly out in the field – had the utmost contempt.

'Well, it's only the second day, Tom,' Oldroyd said. 'We've already got a line of suspects, but no front runner yet.'

Walker grunted and stroked his moustache: something he always did when Watkins was winding him up. 'Good. Nothing wrong with that. What the bloody hell does he expect? He hasn't a clue what real policing is about: hard work, persistence, patience. You can't expect results in two minutes. There wouldn't be any results at all if we were like him, sitting in an office, gazing into space and thinking up his next bit of meaningless jargon.'

Oldroyd was used to Walker going on about Watkins and had found that the best course of action was to sit it out. Replying just fuelled his anger, extended his rants and then it was very difficult to get away.

'Who've you got with you?' continued Walker.

'Carter, and a young DC from Ripon branch called Jeffries. He's a good lad, gets on wi t'job, as we say.'

'Aye, well, that's what we want to see. He'll be doing more good than his bloody chief constable. Anyway, I won't keep you. No doubt the press will be wanting a statement soon. Let me know if you want any more help. The sooner we get Watkins off our backs, the better.'

Oldroyd smiled to himself as he made his way to his own office briefly before setting off with Andy for Markham. Walker was a very supportive boss to have, and it was worth putting up with his sometimes curmudgeonly nature. Despite their personality differences, they shared the same view of what policing was all about. And that, Oldroyd had found over the years, was extremely valuable.

Oldroyd was intrigued by Watkins' interest which, as Walker had pointed out, was not usual. What angle did the chief constable have on the case? And who did he know who was involved?

∼

Richard Foster owned a large, detached house on the outskirts of Markham. He was sitting with his wife Christine in the dining room. Their two children, Phoebe and Tim, had already departed for their school in Ripon, catching the chartered bus which stopped almost directly outside the house.

There was a white tablecloth on their long dining table. On one side of the room was a sideboard containing a lot of glassware. The walls were adorned with rather second-rate landscape pictures of the Dales painted by a local artist.

Richard and his wife sat at opposite ends of the table, eating breakfast.

'Will the police be at the brewery again today?' asked Christine. She didn't like anything that disturbed their cosy life in Markham, and she wasn't feeling very secure at the moment. It had always been her ambition to marry into money and she'd done it. She didn't need to work, but she didn't want to stay at home all the time so had continued part-time in her job as a doctor's receptionist. She was also a very proud housekeeper.

Richard looked at her with irritation. Sometimes she really annoyed him with her silly questions. 'Of course,' he said. 'They've only just begun their investigation. I told you they've set up an incident room in my office. I expect they'll be around until they catch the killer.'

'Oh. Will you be able to carry on with your work?'

'Yes, I'm sure we'll manage once they give us the go-ahead to start the brewing process again. I can manage without my office for a while; I'm working in the general office.'

Christine drank her tea and finished eating a piece of toast. She looked at Richard, and her brow furrowed. 'You say Scholes was killed on Monday evening when you were with Alistair at his place?'

'Yes. Roger and Dennis were there, too. I told you.'

'And you watched a film?'

'Yes.' Richard got up from the table and put his jacket on.

'Which film?'

He looked at her and then away. 'It was some French thing, with subtitles, you know. I found it hard to follow. There were a few of us there. Can't remember the title. Something French, obviously. Why do you ask?'

'Just interested. You don't normally watch French films.'

'No. But you know what Dennis is like with his arty stuff.' He stood up. 'Anyway, I must be off. See you tonight.' He gave her a peck on the cheek and hurriedly left the house feeling unsettled. His wife might sometimes ask silly questions but she could also be disturbingly perceptive about what he might be up to.

Christine watched from the window as he got into the car for the short drive to the brewery. She was always encouraging him to walk. It would do him good. But of course, he kept refusing to do so. The same as the other damaging bad habits that he had promised her he would stop.

She took a deep breath as he drove away. If he'd not kept his promise, he would be short of money and maybe that had . . . No, it was a ridiculous idea. She took the breakfast dishes through to the kitchen where she began to stack the dishwasher. When she'd done that, there was someone she had to call. And after that, there was another problem she had to face. Something very serious.

~

Tom Walker was right. When Oldroyd arrived at the Yoredale, there was a small group of reporters outside waiting for him. He gave them the usual spiel describing what had happened and that the police were following a number of lines of enquiry, etc. before asking for questions.

'Nice way to go, Chief Inspector . . . in a tank of beer!' observed one of the group, grinning at Oldroyd who was tiring of this joke and did not respond.

'We've heard that there's some bad feeling between the two breweries in the town. Do you think that has anything to do with the murder?' asked another.

Oldroyd smiled. Although, as usual, they were looking for a dramatic angle on the story, this was actually a pertinent question.

'You may be right about the rivalry between the breweries, but there is no evidence so far to suggest that this has any connection with the murder.' He wasn't going to mention the missing recipe. That would provoke all manner of time-wasting and sensational speculation. In similar situations in the past, newspapers had offered rewards for members of the public to come forward with documents sought by the police only to find that it led to forgery on a grand scale.

'The victim's name was Brendan Scholes,' said a reporter, reading from his notes. 'He was a bit of a local rogue, wasn't he? Is his murder the work of a jealous husband, Chief Inspector? Or someone he owed money to?' This was quite perceptive, if sensationalist in tone.

'You're right about the character of the victim and it may turn out that you're also correct about the motive. As I said, we are pursuing a number of lines of enquiry.'

'Surely the killer must have some connection with the brewery or how would they have got into the building?'

'Good question, but we all know that acquiring keys and opening doors is not too difficult for the determined person. Also, Scholes himself worked at the brewery at one time so may have stolen a set of keys.'

'Is anyone else in danger, Chief Inspector?'

This was a standard question and always difficult to answer. It was important to be neither too complacent nor too alarmist.

Oldroyd gave them his stock response. 'We have no evidence that anyone else might be attacked. But clearly there is a dangerous person on the loose, so I would counsel everyone in the town and the surrounding area to be cautious and to report anything unusual to the police, particularly if they are suspicious about someone's whereabouts on Monday evening.' Oldroyd paused for these warnings and requests to register. 'Now,' he continued, 'if there are no more questions, I would like to reiterate that it is vitally important that anyone who knew the victim or has any information about the events leading to his death comes forward without delay.'

After this, Oldroyd brought the proceedings to an abrupt ending. He didn't have time to indulge the press. He had to meet with

Andy and together they were going to interview another suspect: Barry Green, the man to whom Scholes owed a rather large debt.

~

'Bloody hell, sir, what a place this is!' Andy said, sounding almost in awe.

Green worked at the Yoredale brewery, but the detectives were told that it was his day off as he normally did a weekend shift. They were given his address, which was at the end of another of the narrow lanes that led off the big main square in Markham.

'Good Lord!' exclaimed Oldroyd with a laugh.

They were standing in front of a run-down, detached 1960s bungalow. There were St George's flags and posters with biker slogans adorning almost every window. The house was surrounded by what must have once been well-tended gardens, but which were now completely overgrown with brambles, grass and weeds. Almost every available space was filled with motorbikes in various states of assembly. Some near the house were in good condition, others were rusty and dilapidated with flat tyres and missing lights. There was a large garage at one side of the house and the battered old wooden doors were open. The noise of tinkering and hammering came from the dark interior.

The detectives went in past a shiny and powerful Harley-Davidson which was parked alongside some vintage bikes. Clearly, Green kept the cream of his collection sheltered and locked up.

'Mr Green!' called Oldroyd. The hammering stopped and a burly figure appeared out of the gloom. The brows were furrowed above the oil-stained face. He clearly didn't welcome being interrupted in his work.

'Who are you?' he said suspiciously. The detectives showed their warrant cards, with which Green was not impressed. 'I don't like you lot. You never leave us bikers alone. What do you want?' he growled.

'We need to ask you about the death of Brendan Scholes,' replied Oldroyd, ignoring the accusation of police harassment.

'I know nowt about it.'

'We hear that he owed you money.'

'Who told you that?'

'Never mind. Is it true?'

Green frowned and said nothing.

Oldroyd turned a little more insistent, his tone becoming much firmer. 'Look, this is a murder inquiry and we're not going away. It's going to be a lot easier if you cooperate.'

Green scowled at Oldroyd. 'Yes, he did owe me. He had an old Honda, and I did some work on it for him. I do jobs in my spare time . . . but not for nowt! He never paid me, and then he buggered off. Went to Ripon, so they said. He was trying to avoid the folk he owed money to. I wasn't the only one.'

'But we have a report that you had a confrontation with Scholes in the Wensley Arms a few weeks ago,' said Andy.

'I was just making it clear that I wanted my money.'

'And what were you prepared to do if you didn't get it?'

Green looked at Andy with contempt. 'Not bump him off, if that's what you mean. How would that get me the money?'

'Maybe you'd just had enough of him,' said Oldroyd. 'And you're obviously someone who can put it around a bit.'

'Well, I didn't.'

'Where were you on Monday night?'

'Here. I was working on the Harley, then I watched some telly and went to bed.'

'Can anyone corroborate that?'

'No. I live by myself. My ex went off with a publican in Leyburn a couple of years ago.'

I'll bet she was sick of coming second to the bikes, thought Oldroyd, but kept it to himself.

'You weren't at the Yoredale Ram Brewery?'

'No, I wasn't. I spend enough time working there.'

'I see. Well, stick around. An officer will be over to take a statement. And don't leave the area.'

'Does that mean I'm a suspect?'

'You and a number of others.'

Green scowled at Oldroyd again but the detective was not in the least intimidated. 'It's always much better,' he continued, 'if you cooperate.' He looked into Green's face with his fierce expression and the latter looked away. 'And by the way, I've nothing against bikers. I used to have one myself for a while. It's a great way of getting round the Dales.'

Green's face lost its scowl, but he didn't say anything.

The interview having concluded, Andy and Oldroyd walked back to the Yoredale.

'He clearly is a suspect, sir,' Andy said. 'He had the motive, no alibi . . . and, as he worked at the brewery, he would have been able to access the building. I can just imagine him slamming the victim over the head with something from that workshop and tipping him into that tank.'

'Yes, very suspicious, but, like Smith, I'm not sure he's the type to plan a murder. And how would he have got Scholes to meet him at the brewery? Scholes would have avoided that man at all costs.'

'True, sir. Maybe more than one person was involved in this murder. Someone else lured Scholes there and Green did him in.'

They arrived back at the brewery and went in by the door through which Scholes and his killer had entered on the night of the murder.

'It's possible,' replied Oldroyd. 'But as yet we've no evidence for it. We've got a lot more work to do.'

The resourceful Jeffries had acquired a cafetiere from somewhere, and had coffee ready when the two detectives returned to the incident room. He also provided a plate of chocolate biscuits.

Andy and Oldroyd looked at each other and smiled before taking a biscuit. Steph and Deborah were conducting long campaigns to try to get the two men to lose some weight, but little indulgences like this, so they thought, could remain a secret.

Jeffries was looking very pleased with himself as he updated them on his own investigation. 'The forensic team have completed the examination of the murder scene and they found a fingerprint on one of those railings where Scholes was bundled over. Lots of people will have held that rail, but this was a very fresh print so it will be recent.'

'Good,' Oldroyd said. 'That's an important lead, so follow that up with our suspects. We've been to interview Barry Green who is a top suspect. I want you to get forensics to examine the tools in his workshop and also those of Norman Smith, the joiner. Let's see if we can find the murder weapon.'

'Yes, sir.' Jeffries was feverishly making notes. When he was done, he continued, 'Sir, we've done a preliminary search of Scholes' house. We found payslips that showed he'd been working in Ripon up until his father died two months ago and we've confirmed that with the estate agents' where he was a clerk. They said he left abruptly one day not long after his father died. He rang in, said he was leaving, and they never saw him again. Other than his payslips we found nothing else in the house that was immediately identifiable as something important but we took away some files of documents which need to be examined.'

'Good. Well, let us know if you find anything.'

'Yes, sir. To be honest there was more stuff connected to his father, which you would expect. The walls were full of pictures of the brewery and of him with David Foster. I'm beginning to wonder, sir, if Scholes was telling the truth and his father did have a copy of that recipe.'

'Yes,' said Oldroyd, sipping his coffee and crunching a biscuit. 'Why do you think that?'

'It's like you or the sarge said. It would be strange if he was happy to allow the recipe to die with him.'

Oldroyd nodded. 'We need to get to the bottom of that if we can. If it exists and Scholes showed it to anyone, that person would have had a solid motive to kill him. But you didn't find anything to suggest it was there?'

'No, sir. But it wasn't a very detailed search.'

'Hmm. Well, we'll leave that for the moment. I want you to get on with taking statements and checking alibis as well as trying to match that fingerprint and checking the tools. There's plenty to do. Do you have enough officers to help you?'

'Yes, sir. Plenty from the Ripon station,' replied Jeffries before he promptly left the office.

'Wow, he's a bundle of energy, sir, as ever,' said Andy.

'I know,' laughed Oldroyd. 'There's nothing like the keenness of the young.'

'Especially when you want to impress someone.'

'I suppose so. You certainly wanted to impress me when you first came to Harrogate.'

'Oh, I still do, sir,' said Andy.

'Anyway,' continued Oldroyd, 'can you find out where Scholes senior died and in what circumstances? That might prove interesting. The death of his father seems to have triggered a number of things for Scholes. I wonder why he left his job so suddenly? Did his father leave him some money? Find out about that, too.'

'OK, sir.'

'Meanwhile, I'm going to have another talk with Richard Foster. There are one or two things about him that I find suspicious, and he hasn't responded to our requests for information.' He stopped speaking as he caught sight of the chocolate biscuits on the plate. He looked at Andy, who frowned and shook his head.

～

It was late morning, and the Wensley Arms was quiet. Bill Lawrence, the landlord, was chatting to a regular – a retired farmer – when Barry Green came into the bar with a thunderous look on his face.

'Bill,' he said. 'Someone in here's been blabbing to the police about me.'

'What do you mean?' replied Lawrence with a half-smile on his face.

'Two coppers came round this morning saying they've heard that Scholes owed me money and so they've got me down as a bloody suspect.' He leaned over the bar and spoke conspiratorially. 'I think it was someone who saw me have that row with him in here a few weeks back. They want to mind their own bloody business.'

'Right,' said Lawrence, trying to prevent the smile from spreading across his face.

'If I find out who it is I'll drop him one,' declared Green, clenching his fists.

'Calm down, Barry, there's no point. Look, what're you drinking?'

'Pint of bitter.'

'OK.' Lawrence pulled the pint while he continued speaking. 'The police aren't daft. They find all this stuff out sooner or later. It's well known you and Scholes weren't getting on; you talked about it enough in here. Just forget it, if you really did have nowt to do with it.' He put the pint on the bar.

'Bugger off, you cheeky sod,' said Green and took a long swig at his beer.

'Are you talking about the bloke who was drowned in a fermentation tank over at the brewery?' asked the farmer.

'Aye, and I'd like to put whoever's been talking about me to the police in there as well.'

'Watch it, Barry. You're incriminating yourself. We might ring up the police and tell them what you've said. That you've threatened violence.'

'Eh? Piss off, you wouldn't dare!'

Lawrence laughed. Green took another long swig of his beer and virtually finished the pint. He put the glass back down on the bar. 'That bastard, Scholes,' he continued. 'He's died still owing me money. I'll never bloody get it now.'

'You could try to register yourself as a creditor,' said the farmer. 'You might get something out of whatever Scholes left. The house might be sold.'

Green frowned. 'He lived in Ripon, didn't he?'

'Yes. Down that road behind the Minster, Church Street. There's a row of small terraces.'

'I know it.' Green finished the last bit of his beer and looked at the glass as he considered something. 'Right! I'm off.'

'Bye, then,' called out Lawrence as Green exited by the same door through which he'd entered not long before. It was unusual for him to only have one pint.

Green walked across the square, which was bright with April sunlight, with a spring in his step. The conversation in the pub had given him an idea.

∾

Oldroyd sat in the incident room facing Richard Foster, his grey eyes searching his face.

'Can you tell me a little more about Frederick Scholes, who you said was in your year at school?' asked Oldroyd.

'I didn't know him very well. He was mostly quiet and sullen. But I remember he had a reputation as someone you didn't want to cross. And I think he left; yes, he left before the end of our time there. He must have gone to another school. I don't remember seeing him again in Markham, but that's not unusual – lots of young people leave the towns and villages in the Dales; there's never enough work. I think he may have gone into the forces.'

'I presume you went to Wilfred Scholes' funeral?'

'Yes, it was a couple of months ago.'

'And did Frederick turn up?'

'Not that I recall. I saw Brendan at a distance. It was mostly old people who worked with Wilfred at the Yoredale in my father's time. People like Bert Duffield, who does our brewery tours.'

'Right.' Oldroyd continued to look at Foster. 'I've also called you in because we still need that information about your alibi for Monday night.'

Foster clapped his hand to his head. 'Oh, sorry! I forgot with all that's happening. I'll get it for you now.' He left the room and returned promptly with a sheet of paper containing names and addresses with telephone numbers.

Oldroyd looked at the paper for a moment.

'So, these people can verify you were with them all evening?'

'Yes.'

'And what were you doing?'

Oldroyd noticed that, for a moment, Foster looked uncomfortable again.

'It was just a social get-together. We had a drink and watched a film.'

'I see.' Oldroyd put the sheet of paper on the desk. 'What film was it?'

'Oh, it was some French thing. I can't remember the title. One of my friends is into arty films.'

'OK. Tell me more about your relationship with your sister and the Ewe's Ales Brewery. She seems to think you harbour sexist attitudes towards the idea of women being involved in the brewing industry.'

Foster laughed scornfully. 'I don't, Inspector. It's true that I wasn't happy that my father brought Emily straight into the company in a senior role. She hadn't studied brewing like I had. All she knew about was marketing.'

'So, you resented her presence?'

'I suppose I did.'

'And you were keen to buy her out and take sole control of this company?'

'Yes. I've always thought of myself as my father's successor.'

'But you didn't expect her to be so successful in her own business.'

'To be honest, no. But all credit to her and to Janice. They've worked hard.'

'I expect it rankles, though, doesn't it? Your little sister equalling your success at your own specialism. Is that why you are tolerant of the abuse they get over there?'

Foster's face darkened. 'Is that what she said? That's not fair. I don't condone it, but I think she overreacts to a bit of fun.'

Oldroyd looked at his notes. 'I understand there was a banner at the beer festival that said, "Ewe's Beer: Made by Girls for Girls". That was quite insulting, wasn't it? Hardly a bit of fun.'

'I suppose so.' Foster shuffled uncomfortably.

Oldroyd tilted his head to one side and then spoke very directly. 'You see, I'm wondering how you really feel about this rivalry and whether it's strongly enough to motivate you to kill Scholes in order to get that recipe so that you can get ahead of your sister. Did you arrange for Scholes to bring it to the brewery that night, then murder him and take it?' It was a blunt accusation; a shock tactic to unsettle the interviewee.

Foster shook his head. 'No, Inspector, it wasn't me. And would Scholes have brought the recipe to the brewery? That would have been risky, wouldn't it?'

Oldroyd shrugged. 'Maybe he didn't but you were trying to negotiate with him, and it got acrimonious. You got into a fight and killed him accidentally.'

'No, Inspector.'

Oldroyd looked at him again and then said, 'Very well. I won't keep you . . . but stick around in Markham. We may need to talk to you again. An officer will take a statement from you and fingerprints.'

Foster said nothing and left the room looking relieved that the ordeal was over.

Oldroyd sat alone deep in thought until his phone rang. It was Deborah.

'I've arranged a viewing of that house near Killinghall. Can you meet me there at six o'clock?'

'That could be awkward if I'm still tied up here.'

Deborah was having none of it. 'Look, Jim, unless it's an emergency make it wait until tomorrow. You've got to say no sometimes, and call it a day. Remember what we said. You are in charge, after all! We need to do this otherwise it will just drag on and we'll never find anywhere.'

'I know. Yes, I'll be there. Text me the address.'

'Good, I will. See you later.'

After the call, Oldroyd thought about the past and how his being a workaholic had ruined his marriage to Julia, who he'd met while still at university, and who was the mother of his son, Robert, and daughter, Louise.

Oldroyd felt that Deborah was much more understanding of his work than Julia had ever been, but at the same time she was more assertive in insisting that he didn't place everything second to the demands of the job. He had to admit she was right. And he wasn't going to make the same mistake and damage another relationship.

A little later Andy came in. 'I've had HQ working on things, sir, and it hasn't taken them long.' He consulted his notes. 'Wilfred Scholes died in Harrogate Hospital on the twenty-fifth of February at the age of eighty-two from heart failure. The funeral took place in Ripon a week later.'

'What about Frederick, the eldest son? He seems to have disappeared from the face of the earth. No one seems to have seen him since he was at primary school. Is he still alive?'

Andy grinned. 'I thought you might ask about that, sir, so I consulted the records of deaths. There's no record of someone by that name which correlates with the age he would have been at the time. Also, the ones recorded are all in distant parts of the country. Of course, he could have moved somewhere far away and probably did, as no one has had any contact with him, but the dates aren't right.'

'So he's probably still alive, but he might have emigrated or who knows? I think we need to find out more about him. Get HQ to delve into it in more detail: follow up every person with that name. There must be some trace of him after he left primary school. Richard Foster said that he didn't come to his father's funeral.'

'Do you think there was some rift with the family?'

'Maybe.'

Andy was unconvinced. 'I'm not sure this has much bearing on the case, sir. I mean, we've got the victim and some pretty good suspects. Where would the brother come in?'

Oldroyd shook his head. 'I'm not sure, but as I said yesterday, there are some odd things about this case. My instincts are telling me to look deeper into events, even if they don't appear to be immediately relevant.' Oldroyd's procedural doctrine of combining a ruthlessness in following the evidence with a willingness to listen to instincts and hunches was legendary. 'Anyway, there's not much more to do today. You might as well go in to HQ tomorrow, and you and Steph can get on with the research together.'

'OK, sir.' Andy was always disappointed when he had to stay in the office. He preferred to be out in the field with his boss. At least he would be with Steph, however. It was nice to occasionally spend time together professionally as well as personally.

'I've got to call at a house on the way back for a viewing. Deborah and I are considering moving out of Harrogate.'

'Right, sir.'

'Yes. We want a bit more space and a garden.'

'Sounds nice, sir, but it wouldn't do for me and Steph. We like being in the city and an apartment is fine for us.'

'You might change your mind if you get a family.'

Andy grinned. 'I don't think that will happen for a while yet, sir.'

'You never know,' replied his boss, with a twinkle in his eye. 'The attractions of parenthood might suddenly grab you.'

When his boss had left, Andy received some information by email. A colleague at Harrogate HQ had sent him details about vacant inspector jobs going in other branches of the West Riding Police. The truth was that Andy was not desperate to leave Harrogate HQ and cease working with Oldroyd, but his boss's recent remarks about his potential – and that of Steph – had made him think. Was it indeed time to move? He'd discussed it briefly with an experienced detective inspector at Harrogate HQ who'd told Andy that he considered him ready for promotion. He'd offered to look out for vacancies at police stations where he knew the senior people would be good to work for.

Andy knew that DC Jeffries would leap at the chance of replacing him and he would make a good detective sergeant. He frowned to himself. It was a difficult decision, and he would need to talk it over with Steph.

~

At the Ewe's Ales Brewery, another working day was coming to an end. Janice Anderson had just finished supervising the fermentation process of the latest brew, and had returned to her small office just beside the cavernous works area. As always, there was a strong smell of barley and hops, but she liked this; it was part of the job she loved.

She completed the data on the current batch of beer. Everything was recorded: times of the processes, the hops and barley used and the quantities. As she did this she was looking forward to the weekend and hoped that the good weather would continue. She and Emily had motorbikes and enjoyed going off on long outings and meeting up with groups of bikers at rendezvous points such as the Devil's Bridge just outside Kirkby Lonsdale on the way to the Lakes, where there were reserved parking spaces for bikers – and a van that sold excellent bacon sandwiches and big slices of cake.

Thinking about bikes made her remember Brendan Scholes. He'd been a biker, too, and a group of them had gone on classic trips up the Dales in summer. She had fond memories of those fun times with a happy group of people cycling through the gorgeous landscape.

She looked up from the screen as something occurred to her. Hadn't Brendan had some kind of argument with Barry Green, the part-time mechanic? There was a suspect for the murder, at least in her mind. She shrugged; no doubt the police were already on to it. There was no point in her saying anything.

She carried on working for a little while, but still couldn't get recent events out of her mind.

She sighed and sat back in her chair. Why did she keep thinking about Brendan? It was quite a while since they'd been part of the same social circle. It was because there was something strange about the whole thing: him turning up like that, claiming to have the recipe for Wensley Glory. He'd changed in some way she couldn't quite put her finger on. And he'd seemed to hardly remember her, which she'd tried not to take personally. Then almost immediately he'd been murdered. It was weird, but she had this feeling the two events were connected in some fashion. But she was no detective. Again, she told herself she'd be better leaving it to the police.

Suddenly there was a loud banging on the frosted glass window of the office which opened on to an alleyway. This was followed by the sound of laughter and scampering feet. It was a group of local kids again. They enjoyed making a nuisance of themselves and they probably thought the Ewe's brewery was a soft touch because it was owned and mostly operated by women. In small communities there was often a price to be paid for being different. But it was a price they were prepared to pay for what they represented, and most people in the little town were very supportive.

The office door opened and Emily came in. As they were alone, they had a brief embrace. They tended to tone down their affection in the workplace.

'Have you nearly finished?' asked Emily. 'It's a lovely evening, I thought we could go for a walk by the river before tea.'

'That's a nice idea. And, yes, I'm ready to go.' She started to shut down her computer. 'Those kids have been banging on the window again.'

'Oh, just ignore them. I'm less concerned about them than the so-called grown-ups who harass us and should know better.'

'I know. I'm just worried that the glass is quite old and if they punch it, they're going to break through and get badly cut.'

'Right. We'll have to get it reinforced somehow. I'll call those window people in Ripon.'

'Have the police been round today?' asked Janice.

'Nope. Which is a good sign, I think. I can't be high on the suspect list.'

'Actually, I got a call from an officer in Ripon this afternoon asking me to confirm where you were on the night of the murder.'

'Good.'

'I told him you were out all evening and didn't come back until late. And that I was worried.'

'Get lost!'

Janice laughed. 'No. I told him we had a cosy evening in together and went to bed early.'

'Did you make it sound sexy? I bet he was embarrassed.'

'I think he was. He ended the call quickly after that. Anyway, let's go.'

The two women continued laughing as they left the brewery.

∼

Driving up the bottom part of Nidderdale, Deborah couldn't contain her excitement as they approached the house in the small village. Oldroyd was less enthusiastic. The house looked as if it might need quite a bit of work done to it and he was not keen on DIY.

'Well, this has definitely got kerb appeal, Jim,' she said. 'I love the sash windows.'

'Looks like they might be the originals,' observed Oldroyd, thinking it would cost a fortune to replace them if they were rotten.

'Even better,' said Deborah. 'Hard wood rather than plastic.'

'They certainly look good, but I doubt that they're double glazed. They'll be very draughty.'

Deborah decided to ignore this and walked to the front door to introduce herself to the smartly dressed young estate agent who was waiting to show them around.

'I'll take you into the kitchen first. It's full of potential,' he said. 'You can really stamp your own taste in here.' Deborah and Oldroyd surveyed the shabby faux dark-oak units in the galley kitchen.

'Isn't it a bit small? I thought we'd decided we want a kitchen we can eat in?' said Oldroyd.

The estate agent was quick to jump in and suggest a knock-through.

'Well, I don't think we want to do a lot of work. Do we, love?'

Again, Deborah ignored Oldroyd. He wondered if he was annoying her with comments that sounded negative.

'Knock through to the dining room and put in French doors . . . Oh, Jim, this is perfect. We'd be able to cook and eat looking out on that fabulous garden and the hills beyond it.'

Oldroyd gazed out of the window. 'But the garden . . . it's just a lawn; you like lots of plants. What are those borders you like at Beningbrough Hall?'

'Herbaceous borders,' said Deborah. 'And we can create them here; we can go to that lovely new garden centre near Harrogate and—'

'Oh, yes. I've heard they've got a nice restaurant there. And of course, I will help with the plants,' he hastened to add.

Deborah rolled her eyes and shook her head, and the estate agent tactfully led them into the living room.

'Before you come up with another problem,' said Deborah, 'we can easily get someone in to remove the Artex. Try to focus on the positives . . . like the size of the rooms, and that lovely marble fireplace.'

'Not very green to have an open fire.'

'Jim, shut up! We don't have to light a fire. We can put flowers in the grate.'

They continued through the rest of the rooms and the bathroom.

'As you can see, the bathroom has been modernised in a tasteful way. It's a new suite and recessed light fittings, tiled with underfloor heating.'

Oldroyd looked around the room sceptically as the estate agent delivered his patter. 'Tasteful' was very subjective. He wasn't at all attracted to the minimalist design of the sink and bath; it was all a bit too square and functional for him. He preferred old-fashioned curves and hadn't Deborah once said she liked free-standing baths?

He peered into the boiler cupboard. 'How old's the boiler?' he asked.

'Recently replaced,' said Deborah. 'We've already established that. Weren't you listening? There's nothing to do in this room. Look at the size of the bath and that heated towel rail; no more damp towels lying around and it's so light and spacious.' Deborah was full of enthusiasm.

'No, I suppose not, but don't you think it's almost too bright and too white?' replied Oldroyd.

'Maybe, but we could contrast it with a few plants and dark towels.'

When they were walking back to the car Oldroyd had to admit that it was a very attractive, characterful house. Added to this the proximity to the village pub, which he knew always had a good selection of cask ales, was making him warm to it a little.

'You're right. It is a lovely house but, apart from the bathroom, a bit more of a doer-upper than I was thinking we'd go for.'

'But liveable. We can do it up gradually to my – I mean, our – taste.'

They both laughed at this.

'OK,' said Oldroyd, relaxing and thinking maybe he'd been wrong about how annoyed she was earlier. 'But let's at least look at one more.' He glanced around the village again. It was full of chocolate box cottages with carefully tended spring gardens, but there was no one about. 'The other thing that concerns me is living in a small village.'

'Why's that?'

'Well, don't you think you might feel isolated and a bit that the village was all on top of you? I've never lived in a small place like this. I might find it a bit narrow. I suppose I'm used to the anonymity of a larger place; you know, somewhere with a bit more of an urban vibe.'

Deborah laughed. 'I'd hardly say that Harrogate was a big multicultural metropolitan area, and you don't go out much anyway.'

'I know . . . but . . .'

'I think it would be relaxing here and great to be so close to the countryside. The only problem I would have is keeping you out of that pub.'

'Maybe. Actually, do you fancy a quick drink in there? If it's going to be our local, then we should check it out to see if it's any good.'

'Oh, all right, then,' said Deborah, sounding a little weary. They'd made it through the viewing, but it had seemed like heavy weather.

~

Back in Markham, the local cricket team was gathering for a net practice at their ground near the river. It was an idyllic place for cricket, and a much photographed scene. The flat green playing area with its white boundary line, manicured wicket and white wooden pavilion with attached clubhouse was backed by tall trees including a magnificent copper beech. Beyond, there were views of the church spire in the distance and the river flowing nearby lined by more trees. Beside the pavilion was a huge and ancient metal roller used to keep the surface of the wicket smooth and level. It took several people to pull it.

The season was just about to start, and the players were keen to impress in their first match, which was at home. The fabled smack of willow against leather could be heard from the nets behind the pavilion along with much laughter and banter. Excitement was in the air after the long winter lay-off and the prospect of playing again.

The current captain was Philip Welbeck from the Yoredale Ram Brewery. It was his, often thankless, task to crack the whip and get team members to come on time to these important practice sessions. He looked at his watch. There were still some people missing.

'Where's Barry?' he called to a player who was just padding up.

'Said he's not coming tonight. He's got to go into Ripon for something.'

Welbeck grimaced. Barry Green was the first-choice wicket keeper, but, like everyone else, he needed practice, especially after the long break. There were only two days left before the match. 'What's he bloody playing at? He knows we've got North Tanfield here on Saturday.'

'Don't know, skipper.' The player shrugged and made his way over to the nets. Two young men arrived cycling at speed down the lane at the side of the clubhouse. They dumped their bikes and ran to the nets.

'Where the hell have you been?' called Welbeck. He shook his head and went over to where a group of young players were gathered. He was going to do some coaching with them tonight:

line and length in bowling, taking guard and defensive positions in batting.

'OK, lads!' he shouted as he rubbed his hands together. It was getting a bit cold now that the sun was going down. 'Let's get moving. Half of you get padded up, the other half do some loosening-up exercises, and then pick up a cricket ball and get bowling.'

The session continued with the same enthusiasm. A number of evening walkers paused for a while to watch. It was one of those unmistakable English signs that spring had arrived, and that summer was not far behind.

Emily and Janice appeared on the path by the river as they neared the end of their pre-meal stroll. They sat down on one of the benches set along part of the boundary to watch the session.

'I've always enjoyed cricket,' observed Janice.

'I've always fancied it, too,' replied Emily. She turned to her partner. 'Maybe as our next venture into modernising rural village life we could establish a women's cricket team. Then we could apply to merge with the men. That would stir things up a bit.'

Janice laughed. 'It would. If we're not careful we'll get such a reputation for subversion we'll get run out of Markham.'

There were sudden shouts of 'Watch out!' and 'Catch it!' A batsman had lofted a ball high up out of the net, and it was heading straight towards them.

'Oh!' exclaimed Emily. She stood up uncertainly, watching the ball, and hastily placed herself in position as it dropped towards her. It landed firmly in her hands and she held the catch. There were cheers and applause from the players. Grinning with satisfaction, Emily threw the ball back to the bowler as Janice clapped.

'Good catch!' she said. 'You know, I think we should go for the cricket team idea. And I want you on my side.'

Later in the evening when it was dark, Barry Green was walking slowly through the narrow streets of Ripon carrying a rucksack. The streets were mostly deserted, but he still checked his surroundings regularly, as it was important that no one he knew saw him and asked what he was doing.

He was heading for Scholes' house, and he was going to break in. He knew the police would have already searched the place, but even if they'd removed any money, documents and maybe the computer, there might still be a few things inside worth stealing.

Green was not a thief or burglar, but he felt he'd been cheated out of the money he was owed. He knew that people claimed debts from estates, but the work he'd done for Scholes was all casual. He had no paperwork, and he didn't want to go to a solicitor anyway and end up paying fees that would probably be more than whatever he wound up getting. This way was much simpler.

He walked quietly down a lane with the dark mass of the cathedral on one side, where a few ancient-looking streetlamps provided a dim light. He reached the terrace of small houses at the far end of the lane. Here, the lighting was a little better, and he found the right house with no trouble. It was the only one that was completely dark and in which no curtains were drawn.

He paused for a moment to search out an access route to the rear of the house and found a ginnel running between the houses at one end. He bent down to avoid being seen and shuffled along the path to the darkness at the back of the terrace.

He pulled out a small torch, keeping the light down as much as possible. There were no gardens to the rear, just a series of backyards with various walls, sheds and fences. Each house had a one-storey kitchen extension that covered part of the yard. He counted the houses until he had located the back of Scholes' house. There was a substantial wooden door, which was locked, into a little yard, so he climbed up and over the brick wall at the side as quickly and as agilely as he could for a man of his stature.

A cat meowed at him, and he froze for a moment with fright. But there were no humans about.

His knew this type of house and his plan was to enter through a window in the kitchen extension. This would be relatively easy and less noisy than forcing a door or a large window. He stood quietly for a moment and looked around again. He could hear the faint noise of a television. Someone walked across the end of the street and Green ducked to avoid being seen. He set to work and it didn't take him long with the tools he'd brought in the rucksack to force the window catch and climb into the narrow kitchen area.

It was very dark inside. He shone the torch around the room to get his bearings before proceeding carefully so as not to trip over anything. He reached the hall – he could see the back of the front door and the dark shapes of coats hung on the wall. It was eerie, and felt as if people were still living there.

He went into the front room, where some light came through the curtainless windows from the streetlights. He kept to the edge of the room and looked around for anything that might be valuable: a painting or some items of pottery or glassware – something that he could sell on.

He saw an old-fashioned display cabinet, which looked very promising. He opened the door and examined various items including a china dog and a coffee pot. There were some medals which had been awarded to Wilf Scholes at beer competitions over the years. He wouldn't take those; he had a great deal of respect for Scholes senior. He became so engrossed that he failed to hear the faint sound of footsteps coming stealthily down the staircase and along the hallway.

He had just decided to remove a silver candle holder when he heard a noise behind him. He looked up and felt a jolt of shock.

He was facing the fireplace, which had a mirror above it. In the ghostly light from the street, he could see the reflection of a figure standing behind him at the door. He recognised who it was and turned quickly to face them.

'What the hell are you doing here?'

There was no reply. The second intruder was carrying a weapon, which they quickly raised and smashed down on to Green's head. He fell heavily to the floor. Two more heavy blows followed, which ensured Green's death.

$$\sim$$

Green's fatal break-in at Scholes' house was not the only clandestine activity being undertaken that night. Back in Markham at some time past midnight, a figure slouched quietly down a back lane to the Ewe's Ales Brewery. Like Green, they were carrying a small rucksack. They stopped at the main gates, took off the rucksack and looked around to see if they were alone. They weren't wearing a hood over their face but there were no CCTV cameras. Then, from the rucksack, they took a can of paint and began to spray a message over the gates. When they had finished, they stood back to admire their work and smiled before turning to the brewery building, putting up two fingers, and slinking off into the shadows, walking rather unsteadily. They didn't realise that they had been watched by people passing at the top of the lane.

Three

Sam Smith's in Tadcaster, between Leeds and York, is England's oldest brewery – founded in 1758. It is a family business still run on very traditional lines. It uses water from the original eighteenth-century well and a slate 'Yorkshire Squares' system of fermentation using the same strain of yeast as in Victorian times. Local deliveries of beer are still made by a horse-drawn dray. Sam Smith's most famous beer is Old Brewery Bitter, which has a creamy texture and a malty flavour.

Blue and white incident tape barred the front and back entrances of the Scholes family's terraced house in Ripon. A uniformed officer had been stationed by the door and there was the usual crackle of police radios emanating from inside the building.

In the rather crowded living room, Oldroyd, Andy, and Jeffries watched Tim Groves examine the body of Barry Green.

'Trauma to the head – looks like hammer blows – death pretty much instant. Been dead for about ten hours. It looks as if someone discovered him at his burglary work and decided they didn't approve, wouldn't you say?'

'It certainly seems like it,' agreed Oldroyd.

'What you will find interesting is that there are the same markings on the head as with the previous victim: narrow indentation and the small ridge. It suggests the same murder weapon and so probably the same murderer.'

'Thank you,' replied Oldroyd with a smile. 'It sounds like you won't be needing us.'

Groves laughed. He liked to tease his old friend Oldroyd by transgressing on his area and offering solutions to the murders they investigated.

Green's body was sprawled on the floor near to the display cabinet, which was still open. The items he had attempted to remove were on the floor, some spattered with blood. There was a large pool of congealed blood on the carpet.

A neighbour had noticed the open window in the kitchen and called the police earlier that morning. Jeffries and another DC attended, and Jeffries – recognising Green as one of the suspects in the brewery murder – had called Oldroyd and Andy.

'What do you think he was doing here, sir?' asked Jeffries.

'Trying to find things that were worth stealing, I should think. It's clear that he was determined to get back some of the money Scholes owed him.'

'I don't think he would have got much for this junk, sir,' remarked Andy, looking at the objects near the body.

'Maybe not, but it's the principle: he would have got something towards the debt.' Oldroyd looked at the body. 'Clearly he had no idea how dangerous that would be.'

Tim Groves was packing up his equipment. 'OK, Jim. I'll send you the report as normal. Pretty straightforward this one, like the last. Don't you go in for impossible crimes any more? You know, locked rooms and puzzling murders?' He smiled as he gathered his things together.

'This case is not as straightforward as it appears, Tim, I can assure you.'

'Right.' Groves sounded unconvinced. 'I'd better let you get on with it then. Bye for now.'

As Groves left, Oldroyd turned to Andy and Jeffries. 'OK. We need to get this place examined in minute detail for any clues. That means not just in here, but all over the house. Is there any evidence of forced entry other than the kitchen window?'

'I don't think so, sir,' replied Jeffries.

Oldroyd frowned. 'Then unless Green let this person into the house, that suggests his killer was the same person who killed Scholes.'

'You mean they had keys for the house, which they'd taken from Scholes' body before they dumped him in the tank, sir?' ventured Andy.

'Exactly. They didn't have to break in. They just waited until the police weren't around.'

Andy smiled to himself. He was glad to have worked this out and suggested it to his boss in front of Jeffries, who was looking a little downcast.

'But why were they here? What were they looking for? Surely not just money or valuables like Green was?' continued Oldroyd.

'That recipe, sir?' suggested Jeffries.

'Possibly, but maybe it was something else, something the killer wanted to retrieve – something incriminating.'

'Do you have any idea what it could be, sir?'

Oldroyd shook his head. 'Also, it was obviously too incriminating for the killer to be seen here by someone who knew him. For Green it was unfortunately a case of MOTP.'

Jeffries looked puzzled.

'Malignancy of Time and Place,' said Andy. He was familiar with Oldroyd's habit of creating acronyms to summarise murder situations. 'He chose the wrong night to break in.'

'Correct,' said Oldroyd.

Jeffries had received a text message and was now on his laptop. 'Sir, we've had a result with that fingerprint in the brewery at the first murder scene. A team have been examining the print with those taken from the suspects. It's a perfect match for Norman Smith.'

Oldroyd raised his eyebrows. 'Is it now? OK, well done. Andy, we'll get over there straight away. Everything seems to be happening today. Too late to save poor Barry Green, though.'

Oldroyd and Andy left, leaving Jeffries again beaming from the effects of Oldroyd's praise.

∼

When Emily and Janice arrived at Ewe's Ales that morning, they were surprised to find a group of their workers standing outside the gate. Some were talking and one was crying and being comforted. When they saw their bosses, some went quiet, while others looked away almost as if they were embarrassed.

As soon as Emily and Janice read what had been spraypainted on the gates they understood why. The large, ragged letters in pink paint read 'Ewe Beer is Dyke Piss'. The irony was that the clumsy letters looked like a child's writing, but no child could have written something so calculatedly horrible.

Emily's stomach lurched with shock as she stood gazing at the message. Janice murmured, 'Oh no!' and put her hand to her mouth as a tear ran down her face. Emily's shock was quickly replaced by anger. She put her arm round Janice's shoulder.

'It's OK, don't let them get to you.' She turned to address the assembled employees. 'Right, everyone. This has gone on long enough. I'm as disgusted as I know you are. I shall be reporting this to the police, and I shall speak to my brother as well. We strongly suspect that all this harassment is the work of someone from the

Yoredale. On this point, though, be careful. We don't know for certain that this is the case so don't make accusations you can't prove, especially if the press get hold of this story and start asking questions. If that happens, say nothing. They'll only twist things.' She paused and looked round. The women were downcast. This latest act of derision had hit them hard, and they knew their bosses' relationship was also being attacked.

Emily continued, 'This is an awful thing, but I don't think it represents what most people in Markham think about gay people or an enterprise like this run by women. We are not going to let anyone stop us. We are successful; our beers are popular. We believe in ourselves and in what we are doing!'

'Hear, hear!' called someone and there was enthusiastic applause and some cheering.

Emily grinned and then shouted, 'OK, then let's get to work making the best beer in Yorkshire!'

There was a chorus of 'Hooray!' and everyone went through the gates. Emily and Janice stayed behind to look again at the graffiti and see if there were any clues as to who might have done it. There was nothing.

'First job is to get that cleaned off,' said Janice as she frowned at the spraypainted message. 'They've got some stuff that'll get it off in the cleaner's cupboard. I'll come out with a brush and do it.'

'Great. But wait until I've taken photos and talked to the police; they may want to come and look at it.'

'OK.'

'We're going to have to install some CCTV round the site. I never thought it would be necessary, but I was being naïve.' She took a deep breath. 'Anyway, I've got some calls to make. The air is going to be blue in that office.'

News of Barry Green's murder soon reached the Yoredale Ram Brewery and was received with stunned shock. The death of the unpopular Scholes was bad enough, but Green was one of their own. A group stood around in the break room, talking quietly. Nobody had the energy or desire to start work.

'I thought it was funny he didn't turn up to cricket practice last night,' said Philip Welbeck. 'We're going to miss him badly. Who the hell will go behind the stumps now? He was a bloody good worker too; he'll be hard to replace here.'

'He could knock a few runs up as well if he got his eye in,' observed another workman and cricketer.

'It won't be the same round here without him and his bikes,' said a third. 'He did a lot of repairs for me and we had some good trips.'

'Aye.'

Things went quiet for a while; people were shaking their heads and looking uncomfortable.

'Do the coppers think it was the same person who killed Scholes?'

'I've no idea,' replied Welbeck.

Richard Foster appeared on the platform above – the same one from which Scholes had been pushed. 'Right, lads,' he said, getting everyone's attention. 'I know it's hard, but we'd better make a start, or we'll get behind with the schedule. We'll talk about Barry later and see if we want to create some sort of memorial to him, OK?'

There were a few mutters of agreement before everyone reluctantly set about their various tasks.

Foster returned to the main office and found Peter Morgan at his desk looking rather harassed, clearly also finding it difficult to focus on work.

'Two murders of people connected to Markham. I suppose they must be linked,' he said, echoing the point made by one of the

95

workmen. 'It's too much of a coincidence. I wonder if the police have any theories?'

'I'm sure they do. And they'll be back wanting more information about Green soon. Was he a good employee? Did he have any enemies apart from Scholes? And so on.' He sat back in his chair and took a deep breath. 'This is driving me nuts. It's hard enough running a business without dealing with murders and a full-scale police investigation as well.'

'Just answer their questions and then put it to one side. Try not to let it get to you.'

'Yes, it's easier said than done, I—' Foster's phone rang and he looked at the number. 'Damn! What does she want? Hello?'

Morgan watched as Foster's face fell, and his eyes closed in what was clearly frustration.

'Are you serious? Of course it's unacceptable, and I'm very sorry, but how do you know it was someone from here who did it? . . . I know, I know. I will. I'll get to the bottom of it . . . Well, that's not necessary, it'll just put more pressure on us all . . . OK, well, it's up to you. We've got a lot on here . . . Have you heard about Barry Green? He worked for us – found this morning murdered in Scholes' house in Ripon . . . Yes, another one. It's really kicking off here. I think the town is going mad and the police will be swarming all over the place again. Anyway, I must go.'

Foster ended the call and swore.

'What's going on?' asked Morgan.

His boss was drumming his fingers on the table, looking angry and agitated.

'It was my sister. There's some graffiti written on the gates of her brewery. It's nasty. Far worse than that banner at the festival. She's going to the police about it. I can't say I blame her.' He slammed his fist on to the desk. 'When I find out who's done this, if they work here, they'll be straight down the road. It's gone far beyond a joke. I'm going to find those two who put up the banner. If it was them again, they've had it.'

He stomped out of the office, red-faced with rage. Morgan shook his head and went quietly back to his work.

~

Andy and Oldroyd's second visit to Norman Smith's workshop proved less fruitful. When they'd made their way down the lanes it was only to find the workshop locked up. Luckily for Andy, the goat wasn't there either.

'Let's see if they know where he is at the garage,' said Oldroyd and they retraced their steps to a small forecourt where someone was leaning under the bonnet of an old Volvo.

'He's at a job up on Meadow Lane, fixing some bookshelves, I think,' said the oily-faced mechanic in reply to Oldroyd's question. He pointed down the lane. 'Back up to t'main square and it's on t'far side on t'left. T'post office is on t'corner, you can't miss it.'

'Hope he hasn't done a runner, sir. It sounds like this could be our man,' said Andy as they walked on.

'I don't think he will, but I'm going to play it safe and bring him in when we find him. Can you call Jeffries and get him to send a car to meet us in Meadow Lane? We'll walk down there and check if Smith is around, then we'll get a lift back.'

'OK, sir.'

~

At Swinfield Hall, Jeremy Langford called his daughter, Sophie, to his study. The old-fashioned formality of this was typical of the way he behaved. He was a very conservative character, who dressed mostly in the country manner with tweedy shirts, ties and jackets.

Outdoors he wore green rubber boots and a flat cap. He spent most of his time on his estate, of which he was extremely proud. He enjoyed playing the role of local dignitary in the surrounding area.

He saw the conservation and enhancement of the estate that had been in his family for generations as part of his duty. Another part was ensuring the best future for his family. This responsibility had fallen entirely to him after the premature death of his wife from cancer several years ago.

He was very satisfied with his son, Hugo, who had progressed from Marlborough to Oxford, and then to a firm in the city. He was more concerned about his daughter Sophie who, unfortunately, had not exhibited any particularly academic abilities. Her achievements at school were mediocre and she had now returned home and was running the estate riding school. Langford saw this arrangement as temporary. His main aspiration for Sophie was to get her to make a good marriage. To this end he had sent her to finishing school to sharpen her husband-attracting talents and features. He was working on getting her some kind of position in London, maybe as a nanny or as a secretarial assistant at some niche publisher – a position from which she could enter London society and make a catch.

His study was an oak-panelled room with floor-to-ceiling bookshelves crammed with attractive volumes largely unread by their owner, who lacked intellectual curiosity. He frowned as he sat at his desk waiting for Sophie. The news was unpleasant and threatened his ambitions for his daughter. At least he had access to influential people in high places. There was a knock on the door.

'Come in, my dear,' he called.

Sophie came in with the look of a defiant, naughty schoolgirl on her face.

'Daddy, if this is about Brendan, I've heard all about it. I'm sure you're delighted that he's dead.'

Langford raised his eyebrows. 'No need for that, my girl. Sit down, please.'

Sophie sat without another word. She folded her arms.

'But have you heard the latest?' continued her father.

'No.'

'There's been another murder. This time at the house in Ripon where Scholes lived.'

'What?'

'Yes. It was a man called Green who worked at the brewery. It appears he broke into the house.'

'So, he was a burglar? What's that got to do with Brendan's death?'

'Well, we've been lucky so far. We seem to be off the radar as far as the police are concerned. But that's not going to last very long. As this latest killing was in Scholes' house, they're almost certainly going to link it with the previous murder in some way. The bigger the investigation gets, the more likely it is that we – or *you*, I should say – could get drawn in. The possible results for your reputation could be very serious.'

Sophie looked exasperated. 'Daddy, can you please try to live in the twenty-first century? Nobody cares about virginity and chastity and all that stuff any more! Everybody has a history. Nobody holds it against you if you've had relationships in the past.'

'I should think it rather depends on who with. Are you telling me that an eligible young man in the City of London from a good family wouldn't mind the fact that you've messed around in the past with a ruffian like Brendan Scholes, let alone what we had to deal with?'

Sophie ignored this indirect reference to her abortion and laughed scornfully. 'A "ruffian"? Oh my God, Daddy, sometimes you speak like a character from a Dickens novel! You really are a ter-rible snob, aren't you? Brendan was much too lower class for you.'

Langford shook his head and continued in the same vein. 'I think it's very important that your name does not crop up in any media reports of these murders and especially not linked to Scholes. You don't seem to realise the social implications were that to happen. The kind of families I have in mind don't want to be contaminated by association with nasty crimes and undesirable people.'

'You make these "families", as you call them, sound absolutely awful. And you expect me to marry into one of them? Why don't you just arrange a marriage for me and let's pretend we're living in the time of Jane Austen?'

Langford shrugged. 'I'm assuming you want to get the best outcome for yourself. You're clearly not going to make an impact in public life like Hugo has, so your best bet is to make what they used to call a "good marriage".'

'In other words, marry some rich banker wanker who's as boring as hell, live in St John's Wood, produce a lot of babies, and go to coffee mornings and lunches with empty-headed yummy mummies.'

'Isn't that better than what you've got now? Running the riding school here? Where's the future in that? I could easily get a young woman from the town to replace you. Don't you aspire to improve yourself? After that finishing school I paid for, you're in an excellent position to make a good catch. We just need to get you back into London society. I'm not fond of it, but I don't need to establish myself.'

Sophie looked at him with incomprehension as she slowly shook her head. 'I wish Mummy was still alive,' she said. 'She would have understood how I feel.'

Langford smiled. 'Are you sure about that? Anyway, she's not here, so you'll have to put up with me looking after your best interests.'

Sophie was about to say something, but he held up his hand. 'The important thing is: don't say anything to anyone about Scholes and your involvement with him, especially not to the media.'

She was looking down, and appeared to be beyond words. He couldn't be sure if she was angry or upset. Or both. Not that it mattered to him.

'I'm monitoring the situation and using a contact I have in the West Riding Police. Right at the top, actually,' he said with a self-satisfied chuckle. 'Watkins is the chief constable. After the latest news, I need to get back to him again.' He frowned at his daughter. 'So carry on playing with your horses, but remember what I've said. I'm doing it all for your benefit.'

Sophie got up and left without another word. As she returned to the stables, she felt like crying. Her father was so callous about Brendan, so dismissive of what she did working with horses and so determined to control her life that she was full of frustration and anger. She was also frightened of a possibility that had occurred to her. Her father had seen her involvement with Brendan as a real threat to her future. To what lengths would her father have gone to get rid of him, especially if he'd found out what had been going on recently?

~

Back at the incident room, Norman Smith, who had been interrupted in the process of drilling a wall and bundled into a police car, faced Oldroyd and Andy with a scowl on his face.

'What's this all about?' he demanded. 'I've told you all I know about Scholes.'

'Have you?' replied Oldroyd. 'I'm not so sure about that. You don't work at the Yoredale Ram Brewery, right?'

'Of course I don't! You know that.'

'But have you been into those works recently, maybe to do a job?'

'No, I'm not sure I've ever been in.'

'Then can you explain how a fresh fingerprint of yours has been found on the railings by the platform where Scholes was pushed off into the tank on Monday night?'

Oldroyd looked straight into Smith's face after delivering this torpedo of a question. Smith's expression immediately changed, fear and uncertainty suddenly moving across his face. His eyes flitted from side to side, and he didn't reply for some time. He seemed to be thinking hard about how to respond.

'OK,' he said at last, in a subdued voice drained of anger and arrogance. 'This is what happened. I did go to the pub that night, as I said. When I left, I walked past the brewery and I saw there was a light on. When I got to the side door, it had been left open and was moving about in the wind. I thought I'd better go in to investigate. Thought maybe someone had broken in. The light was on in the works area. I walked up the corridor and out on to that platform. I looked over and I saw there was a body in the tank. It was a shock. That's probably when I grabbed the railing. I went down the steps to see if I could get them out, if it wasn't too late. I thought it was some kind of accident. I reached in and forced the body round. I saw his head was smashed in at the back and when I pulled the head towards me, I saw it was Scholes. Somebody had killed him.' Smith took a deep breath.

'I panicked. People knew I'd had arguments with him about my wife. If anybody saw me there, they'd think I'd done him in. So I let the body sink into the beer and ran out of the building, checking before I left that nobody was around. I didn't know I'd left a trace behind.' He gave Oldroyd a look of defiance. 'That's exactly what happened. I didn't kill him.'

Oldroyd returned Smith's look with a stern one of his own. 'You realise there is nothing to confirm your story. You had a motive for luring Scholes into the brewery and smashing him over the head.'

'How would I get into the place? I don't have a key.'

Oldroyd shrugged. 'Doors can be opened in many ways. Locks can be picked. You're a joiner; I'm sure you know how to do it. And you've got a nice set of hammers to finish him off with. And where were you last night when Barry Green was murdered in Ripon?'

'What? I don't know anything about that. Barry Green? Murdered?'

'Yes. Killed in Scholes' house.'

'What was he doing there?'

'He'd broken in for some reason, but the killer was already in there.'

'Bloody hell. Well, that definitely wasn't me either. I was at home all evening.'

'Can anyone confirm that?'

Smith shook his head.

'OK.' Oldroyd looked up at Jeffries. 'Take him to Ripon. We're detaining him on suspicion of the murder of Brendan Scholes and Barry Green.'

'It wasn't me – I'm telling the truth,' Smith protested as he was handcuffed and taken away.

'You mustn't be sure about his guilt, sir, or you would have charged him by now,' said Andy when Smith had been removed.

Oldroyd was drumming his fingers on the table and was considering what to do next with Smith.

'Well, he's the chief suspect at the moment . . . but you're right, I do have doubts. I was bluffing a bit about the door. I'm not sure how he would have got into the brewery. The other thing is that his alibi is sound up to when he left the pub when it was quite late. How would he have persuaded Scholes to meet him at the brewery at that time

103

of night? And why the brewery anyway? He also sounded genuinely surprised and shocked to hear about Green.'

'Maybe he wanted to make it look as if it was someone who worked at the brewery who was the killer.'

'Perhaps,' said Oldroyd, sounding unconvinced. 'Anyway, he lied to us and there's a lot of evidence against him, so he deserves his time in custody. We'll need more evidence before we can charge him.'

Oldroyd's phone rang. It was Emily Foster. Oldroyd frowned as he listened.

'It says what? Good Lord – OK. You're right; it's much more serious – it's a homophobic hate crime. Could it be someone else not connected with your brother's brewery? . . . Fine, you've done the right thing to report it to us. I'll be taking it up with your brother very soon. I'll send an officer round to take a statement so don't clean the gates until we've examined them and taken photographs . . . Yes, you're welcome.'

He ended the call and explained to Andy about the graffiti at the Ewe's Ales Brewery.

'That's not a joke, sir. It's a hate crime, as you said.'

'I agree. I'm wondering if the graffiti and the murders are connected in some way?'

'How, sir?'

'If people at the Yoredale hate Ewe's Ales so intensely, maybe they would have killed Scholes to get that recipe so that they could get ahead. On the other hand, what if people at Ewe's Ales are responsible for the murder and are conducting a clever campaign to smear the Yoredale? Has it occurred to you that the graffiti could have been daubed by someone from Ewe's Ales to suggest that the Yoredale hate them?'

'Emily Foster said that some men at the Yoredale found putting up that banner funny.'

'Yes, but they would, wouldn't they? It doesn't necessarily mean the same people graffitied the gates. That might be what we're meant to believe. Yes, I know it sounds a bit convoluted, but we have to consider all possibilities. Emily Foster seems tougher and more capable than her brother. She may, for a number of reasons, be so possessed with a desire to outperform the Yoredale that she will resort to anything to get that recipe. The hostility to her brewery could be a useful misdirection, as the illusionists say. We need to get her alibi for last night too.'

'The problem is we've no evidence either way, have we, sir?'

'No, you're right.' Oldroyd sat back in the chair with his arms behind his head, contemplating the next move.

'OK,' he said finally. 'Get Richard Foster in. Let's see what he has to say about the latest developments.'

'Sir.'

~

Christine Foster drove her SUV along the quiet country lanes outside Markham. The day before, she'd phoned a friend of hers whose husband was a farmer, and today she was driving round to see her. The news of Barry Green's death was particularly shocking coming after the murder of Scholes, but much worse was the added anxiety it had provoked in her about other matters.

She looked at the hedgerows beginning to sprout green. The blackthorn was still flowering white, and the fields were lush in the bright sunlight, which shone powerfully through the still leafless trees. She enjoyed her comfortable life in these beautiful surroundings and was afraid to think about anything that could take it away from her. Such a thing would not happen without a fight.

She arrived at the brick farmhouse surrounded by large trees and turned up the drive, parking in front of the house. A woman came to the door looking very serious.

'Mary?' she said, getting out of the car.

'Come in, Chris. I've made some coffee. It's not good news. We need to sit down and decide what we're going to do.'

Christine's heart sank, but she took a deep breath and followed her friend into the house.

~

'Ladies and gentlemen, my name is Bert Duffield. Ah worked for many years here at t'Yoredale Ram Brewery. T'brewery itself is very old, dating back to th'eighteen-forties, but although my service was long, ah weren't around at that time.'

There was some polite laughter at this, the first of Duffield's little jokes that he always delivered on his brewery tours. Duffield had received permission to restart the tours earlier that morning. Oldroyd believed that things should be returned to normal as soon as possible near the scene of a murder once the police and forensic teams had done their work. He thought that this tended to calm the community of people who had suffered the shock of a murder being committed in their midst.

Of course, the actual scene of the murder was still taped off, but Duffield could work round that.

The tour was well attended. Maybe there was, as Bill Lawrence had suggested to Duffield in the pub, an added fascination due to recent events. But Duffield was not, if he was honest with himself, on top form. The news had come through earlier about the death of Barry Green in Ripon and he was wondering if this was the moment when he should finally speak to the police about what he knew.

It was at the back of his mind throughout the tour, which began with a short film about the history of the brewery. Duffield then spoke about the raw ingredients of brewing and persuaded the audience to eat a grain of roasted barley and rub some hop leaves between their fingers to release the fragrant oil.

The next stage was a – presently restricted – walking tour of the works, up staircases and around galleries, outlining the different processes and indicating the giant pipes, coppers and tanks. Duffield always gave knowledgeable, if over-detailed, answers to any questions from the guests, and tended to give more attention to those who showed the most interest.

Nevertheless, the visitors were happy with the tour experience, which always included a visit to a small museum and ended in the gift shop where they could buy a variety of tourist-style gifts and bottles and cans of beer. Each person also received a token to spend in the nearby bar where they could sample the Yoredale beers.

When all the tourists had departed, Duffield sat down in the little bar with half a pint of bitter and thought about what he should do. He'd seen the police arriving earlier and they were presumably still around. If he spoke to them now, he might be able to help the investigation. Yes, that was what he had to do.

He finished his beer and left the bar, his mind made up.

~

'This harassment of the Ewe's Ales Brewery is getting much more serious, isn't it? If it was ever a joke at all, which is an idea I reject. Things like that are not funny if you're on the receiving end.'

Oldroyd was speaking to Richard Foster, who sat facing the detectives looking very uncomfortable.

'Look,' Foster began, 'I'm sorry about it all. My sister rang, and I apologised to her. If it was anyone at the Yoredale, I'll punish them. I know I've been too lax with this. I've spoken to the two who put up that banner and they vehemently denied graffitiing the gates.'

Oldroyd fixed Foster with his grey eyes. 'It strikes me that you were happy about unpleasant slogans and the like when you thought they might damage the image of your sister's brewery. But now it's got nasty and homophobic, you realise it's getting out of hand.'

Foster shook his head. 'Yes, I know. And I've said I'm sorry.'

'Who do you suspect, anyway? We need to interview them. Not only is it a crime to deface property like that, but they may well have committed a hate crime.'

Foster sighed. 'I don't have any proof and surely we don't know if it was the same person who put up the banner and defaced the gate.'

'No, we don't, but we'll find out when it's all been properly investigated.'

Foster paused, as if he really didn't want to implicate anyone.

'There's a bloke called Tony Handley,' Foster said reluctantly. 'He works in the warehouse; strong bloke, good at his job moving barrels around, but he's a bit of a loudmouth and he comes out with some nasty stuff – borderline racism and misogyny that he thinks is amusing. Of course a lot of the others do find it funny, though I think they know he goes over the top. He likes practical jokes too. I've had a word with him before but I'm not sure he takes any notice.'

'OK. Sergeant Carter will take the details. I also need to ask you where you were last night.'

'Last night? You surely don't suspect me of killing Barry Green? He's one of my best employees. He's worked for me for years. And why the hell would I be in a house in Ripon late at night?'

'It wasn't any house, it was Brendan Scholes' house and formerly his father's. Whoever killed Brendan Scholes probably took a set of house keys from him. You could have been there searching for that recipe.'

Foster laughed derisively. 'Not that again, Chief Inspector. Anyone searching for that recipe is on a wild goose chase. It's gone forever.'

'Nevertheless, someone was there looking for something and we believe Barry Green disturbed them. So, where were you last night?' Oldroyd repeated and fixed Foster with an implacable look.

Foster sighed. 'I was at home all evening. My wife can verify that.'

'Very good, we will be following that up.' Oldroyd leaned towards Foster. 'Now, a word of advice. Don't you think it's time that you mended all the fences with your sister? Otherwise, things are going to continue to be nasty. Do you want your relationship with her to be permanently damaged and your breweries to be constantly at war?'

Foster did not reply. He looked flustered and sheepish.

'I didn't think so,' continued Oldroyd. 'Anyway, it's up to you. But take it from me: life's too short.'

'I think you're probably right,' said Foster with a sigh.

'Yes, I am,' said Oldroyd. 'Anyway, that's all for now.'

'You got him wriggling, sir,' said Andy with a laugh after Foster had left the office. 'But if he's got a solid alibi, he may not be our main suspect after all. Assuming the same person committed both murders.'

Oldroyd had picked up a pen and was fiddling with it absent-mindedly. 'No. I have to admit I've never thought he could be the killer. He strikes me as quite a weak character, hardly capable of one brutal murder, never mind two.' He looked at Andy. 'What do you make of this graffiti business?'

'I'm not sure it's got anything to do with the case, sir. It's just some homophobic yob who can't take women being successful. Sometimes those attitudes are worse in small places than in the towns and cities.'

There was a knock on the door and Jeffries came in.

'There's quite a gathering of reporters outside, sir,' the young DC said. 'I think the second murder has made the investigation more newsworthy.'

Oldroyd sighed. 'Yes, it's to be expected. I'll be out in a moment. It'll be a matter of trying to prevent their imaginations going wild and producing the lurid headlines and awful puns: "Did Bitter Row at Breweries Lead to Second Death?"; "More Trouble Brewing in Dales Beer Town". But we'll see. I'm hoping to keep this short. We've got a lot of work to do. While I'm talking to them, go and have another word with Emily Foster and find out what her alibi is for last night. Then track down this Handley character and the best of luck with him.'

'OK, sir.' Andy grinned. He'd had plenty of experience during his time at the Met of dealing with thugs who thought they were tough. They usually backed down when they saw a strong and determined police officer like himself.

Oldroyd had got up and was about to go out to face the press when Bert Duffield appeared at the door and came straight in.

'Now then,' he began. 'Ah've got summat to tell thi.'

Oldroyd had to smile. 'OK, have a seat. I've got to go out and speak to the press soon so I haven't a lot of time, but my sergeant here will speak to you.'

Duffield sat down. 'It won't take long. You see, I worked wi' Mr Foster and Wilf Scholes for many years and it were a good carry-on in those days before we had all this nonsense of women runnin' a brewery.'

Oldroyd raised his eyebrows, glanced at Andy, but decided to ignore this comment.

'In those days, as you know, we made this beer called Wensley Glory, and it won a lot o' prizes.'

'Yes, we know all about that,' said Oldroyd, looking at his watch.

'Well, Mr Foster ordered everybody out from where the fermentation tanks were when he was adding stuff to Wensley Glory. Wilf knew a bit abaht it but he were always very secretive. He were always very close to Mr Foster and he'd never tell us owt. Just once, when he'd had a few drinks, he did let slip to me and a few others that Mr Foster had written down a recipe for Wensley Glory and he sort of led us to believe that he had a copy of it.'

Oldroyd and Andy both looked up, their interest piqued. Oldroyd sat down again.

'When was this?' asked Oldroyd.

'Oh, it's a while since. He never mentioned it again but now Wilf's dead ah wondered if Brendan had found it and that wa' causing all this trouble. You see, it'd be worth a lot o' brass to sumdy if they could make that beer age'an. There's never been owt lahk it. And that Brendan, well, he were a wrong 'un; he's got himself into a right mess and sumdy's bumped him off to get that recipe.'

Oldroyd glanced at Andy again. This was a very perceptive analysis.

'Yes, you're right. I was fortunate to have drunk some of that beer many years ago. Thank you for coming forward. We'd already considered whether this recipe was the motive for the murders but there was no evidence that a written copy existed, and most people seemed sceptical about the idea. This is very useful information which suggests that it really did exist.'

'Aye, now there was one more thing that Wilf said, but ah don't know what he meant, and he was a bit drunk at t'time and laughing as if it wa' a kind of joke.'

'What was that?'

Duffield leaned forward conspiratorially, as if he had something mysterious to impart. 'He said t'recipe was behind him.' He nodded and repeated the phrase. 'That's right: "behind him".'

'Have you any idea what he meant?'

'Naw, and it could have just been t'beer talking, yer know, but ah thought ah'd come and tell thi.'

111

'Quite right and thank you again.' He looked at the time. 'Unfortunately, I must be off now, but my sergeant will take your details and a statement from you.'

Duffield nodded, looking satisfied with himself as Oldroyd left.

~

'This is getting more interesting, isn't it, Chief Inspector? Two murders now.'

Oldroyd was holding his second press conference, which was much better attended than the first. It wasn't just that two crimes were better than one; another murder held out the possibility of that holy grail of crime reporters: the elusive serial killer who kept evading the police and striking again. This allowed all kinds of stories and speculations to flourish in the press and be greedily absorbed by a fascinated and frightened public. After many years of experience he knew exactly how to handle them.

'I suppose it depends on your definition of interesting,' Oldroyd replied, stern-faced, to the grinning reporter. He hated how some of the press positively welcomed stories of human suffering. 'I wouldn't get too excited, if I were you. The victim, Barry Green, had broken into the house belonging to the recently murdered Brendan Scholes. We believe he disturbed another intruder who killed him.'

'You're sure that the crimes are connected, then?' asked another reporter.

'Not necessarily. The first intruder may have panicked and hit Green, not intending to kill him. However, the fact that the killer had not broken into the house suggests that he may have had keys stolen from his first victim.'

'Why had the victim broken into the house, Chief Inspector? Did he have a record of burglary?'

'No. We believe that he was looking to remove money or valuable objects that he could sell because he was owed money by Brendan Scholes and presumably saw no way of getting it back as his debtor was now dead. Of course he believed that the house would be empty.'

'And why was the killer there?'

Oldroyd was still inclined not to reveal the business of the beer recipe. 'We're not sure,' he replied. 'It may have been for the same reason as the victim. We won't know until we work out if anything has been removed. That's difficult because the recent occupants are both dead. Other than that, they may have been looking for something connected to the murder of Brendan Scholes, but we don't know what that might be at this stage.'

'We understand this second victim worked at the Yoredale brewery, Chief Inspector, where the first body was found. Is that just a coincidence? Did he recognise his killer? And was that why he was murdered? Maybe they were both in it together and had a disagreement.'

There were nods of approval from some of the other journalists, who were clearly thinking the same thing.

'Hold on,' stated Oldroyd firmly, and held up his hand. 'That's a lot of questions and a great deal of speculation. Some of the things you mentioned may turn out to be true, but we have no evidence for them. Can I remind you that we are still in the early stages of the investigation? We have to proceed carefully in relation to what we find and not according to what might make the best story.'

'Have the breweries got anything to do with these murders, Chief Inspector? We hear that they're at war with each other, and the Ewe's Ales Brewery has been the victim of malicious graffiti.'

Again Oldroyd admired the swiftness with which they found things out, but deplored the hype.

'That's correct about the graffiti,' he said, 'and we are investigating who might be responsible. Whether it has any connection with the murders we don't know at this stage. I think it's an exaggeration to say that the breweries are at war although there is clearly bad feeling between them.'

'It's getting bitter, isn't it, Chief Inspector?' said the same grinning reporter, who clearly thought he was funny.

Oldroyd shook his head and refused to reply to this predictable, and increasingly tasteless, joke. He certainly wasn't going to play their game and make lame puns.

'Could this killer strike again, Chief Inspector?' This was a much more sensible question and Oldroyd had been waiting for someone to ask it.

'As I said before, clearly there is a dangerous person at large and people should take care. Two people have now been murdered, but I still don't think we've got a deranged random killer on our hands. To help us catch this person, it is important that anyone comes forward who saw anything around the house in Ripon last evening or has any information relevant to this case.'

Some of the reporters nodded and, with this, Oldroyd brought the session to an end. He made his way back to the office feeling rather downbeat. The press conference had reminded him that they lacked a really clear lead after two people had been murdered. His instincts were still telling him that there was a twist somewhere in this case, but what was it?

~

Andy frowned as he looked at the ugly graffiti on the gates of the Ewe's Ales Brewery. A SOCO had just finished taking photographs. Emily Foster was standing next to him.

'That's nasty,' he said, turning away from the hate-filled words. 'As a minimum we'll get them for defacing property. And they should be done for hate crime.'

'Why "should be"? Isn't it obviously homophobic?'

'Yes, the wording tells against them. But with hate crime you have to prove intent. You could get some clever lawyer arguing that the accused person only intended it as a joke. Or, in this case, that it was part of the spat between your breweries and so on.'

Emily shook her head. Andy continued as they walked back into the building. 'If the person has a history of associating with homophobic groups, and has committed similar acts before, then it will be easier to prove that this was an intended slur.'

Emily sighed. 'OK. Well, if this is what we can expect, we're going to have to install CCTV. We could really do without the expense of that. I still believe that our brewery and our set-up is accepted here by most people.'

Andy hated having to ask her about the latest developments at this difficult time. He admired her optimism and fortitude. They reached Emily's office and sat down.

'I'm also here concerning the murder of Barry Green,' began Andy.

Emily looked at him with a puzzled weariness. 'We heard about that – in Scholes' house, wasn't it? What has that got to do with me?'

'I'm sure you realise that you and your brother are still suspects in the first murder because of your rivalry, and this business about the secret recipe gives you a motive. We believe Barry Green was probably killed by the same person who murdered Brendan Scholes, so I have to ask where you were last night.'

Emily looked shocked, then angry and finally she laughed. 'I feel sorry for you and your colleagues, Sergeant. You have to pursue all lines of enquiry, don't you? However tenuous. Why on earth would I be in Scholes' house in the first place and then murder someone who broke in? Do I look like a tough and ruthless criminal?' Andy had to admit that she didn't, but he said nothing. 'Anyway, I was at home all evening with my partner Janice. We watched television and went to bed at about eleven o'clock.'

'Did you know Barry Green?'

'Only vaguely from my time working at the Yoredale.'

'And you've never been to Scholes' house?'

She laughed again. 'No, I've no idea where it is.'

'Not even in an attempt to search for the lost recipe?' Andy looked straight at her. This was a technique he'd learned from his boss. Often the interviewee would react to a direct, unexpected question in a manner that could be – however fleetingly – revealing.

But in this instance, Andy could see nothing significant in her response.

'No, Sergeant. Not even for that. As I've said before, I'm not sure that a copy of that recipe even exists, and I'm sure my brother believes the same. You're on the wrong track if you think that our rivalry and the hope of finding that recipe is behind all this.'

There was a knock on the door, and Janice entered. She gave Andy a suspicious look and asked, rather abruptly, 'Can we start on the work of removing that disgusting graffiti now? Every minute it stays there is an affront to people like us.'

'Yes, we've done everything we need to do. While you're here, I just need to ask you if it is true that the two of you spent yesterday evening at home together.' He indicated Emily.

'Yes,' replied Janice. 'I'm not even going to get into why you're asking me that.'

'OK, that's fine,' said Andy.

Without another word, Janice turned and left the room, slightly banging the door behind her. Andy frowned. The assault on the gate might have only been of words, but the hurt had gone very deep, and the anger was raw.

116

When Oldroyd returned from speaking to the press, he decided to take a stroll into the brewery and look at the crime scene again, hoping it would stimulate some new ideas about the case. As he entered the works, his senses were assailed by the aromas of yeast and hops, the hiss of steam and the whirring and clanking of machinery. The brewing process was now largely mechanised, and everything was made of metal. Even the classic wooden casks, made for centuries by coopers, had been replaced by ones made of steel. Nevertheless, all brewing still used simple, natural ingredients: water, barley, hops, yeast. Cask ale was a great drink that didn't need chemical additives.

Philip Welbeck was operating the control board by the fermentation tanks. It was noticeable that the one in which Scholes' body had been found was still empty. It might be some time before they used that one again, mused Oldroyd, if ever.

'Can I help you, Chief Inspector?' asked Welbeck.

'Not particularly, I was just taking a break. But I must say I'm interested in what goes on here. Can you tell me a bit more about it?'

Welbeck smiled; he was always keen to talk about his work. 'Of course. I'll just finish off here, and we'll take a walk round.' He pressed a few more buttons and consulted the dials before leading Oldroyd on a guided tour.

As they walked, he explained about roasting barley, milling it into grist and then heating it up with water in a huge container called a mash tun to make wort. Hops were added when this wort, the liquid extracted from the grain, was boiled up in a massive round copper. The cooled liquid was placed in fermentation tanks and yeast added. After conditioning, the beer was placed in casks and was ready to be distributed throughout Yorkshire and the world. The process took days and, although simple in outline, took great skill to achieve the desired result. It was a process that had changed little over two hundred years, even if there was more steel and electronics and less wood and slate than in former times.

Oldroyd was fascinated by both the equipment and the ingredients. He already knew about the basics of brewing but had never actually been on a brewery tour before. Welbeck gave him some malty grains of barley to chew and some hops to rub between his hands to release the oil and aromas. Then he got him to turn a metal wheel to release the flow of wort into a fermentation tank.

'Brewing has a lot of pride attached to it, hasn't it?' observed Oldroyd as he was drinking a few small samples of the different beers that the Yoredale produced.

'Oh, yes,' admitted Welbeck, laughing. 'We all think our beers are the best, and that our method of brewing is how it should be done. Every aspect of the process is important: we take our water from an old artesian well; we only use certain types of barley, hops and yeast and in just the right quantities. All this is very precious to us and jealously guarded.'

Oldroyd looked at Welbeck. Something he'd just said had somehow resonated with him. The head brewer had taken a small drink himself and wiped his beard before continuing.

'None of that justifies all these goings-on between the breweries here,' he continued. 'I think all that stuff that was said about Ewe's Ales was right out of order. And writing stuff on their gates – things about their private life – is disgusting. They do a good job over there. And it's a very decent beer!'

'I take it you don't approve of the rift between your boss and his sister, then?'

Welbeck drew back cautiously. 'Well, that's not really any of my business, Chief Inspector. But I will say that I think it would be better if we were all on good terms. Then we could work together in a sort of friendly rivalry, you know. This town is a great centre for brewing, and we could make it even better.'

Oldroyd felt like clapping. 'A fine speech and very judicious,' he said.

'Let me show you this while we're down here,' Welbeck said. 'Although this is Bert's domain, really. He takes all the tour visitors in here.'

Welbeck led Oldroyd through a small door into a room that had been fitted out as a brewery museum. The walls were lined with black and white photographs of the brewery, showing men with droopy Victorian moustaches. Horse-drawn drays stood in the yard which had changed very little over the years. Old workbenches contained displays of tools used in the brewing process and by the coopers who made the traditional wooden barrels. There was an original 'Yorkshire Squares' fermentation tank made out of slabs of slate.

Oldroyd wandered around showing a keen interest and then he saw something that really grabbed his attention, and answered an important question in the case.

~

After his traumatic day at work, Richard Foster drove the short distance home in his BMW, parked in the driveway of his house, got out and scrunched his way slowly across the gravel, past pots of daffodils that had finished flowering and were now looking droopy and forlorn. He made a mental note to replace the bulbs with pelargoniums for the summer when he had the energy. He went in by the side door, hoping to have a restful evening. It was not to be. He found the kitchen quiet and deserted.

'Hi, darling, I'm home,' he called.

'In here,' came the reply from the living room. She did not sound cheery. Foster found her sitting in an armchair with its back to the door. She did not get up to greet him. 'Sit down,' she said abruptly. She had a glass of gin on a small table next to her chair.

Foster sat in an armchair opposite and saw that she had a face like thunder.

'What's wrong, darling? You look angry.'

She looked at him with contempt. 'Don't "darling" me, you . . . you liar!' That last phrase was shouted. Her words were slightly slurred. How much had she had to drink?

'What? I—'

'You've been gambling again! After all your promises. And you lied to me about the other night! Watching a French film at Alistair's? Like hell you were. You were doing online gambling with Alistair, Roger, and that Dennis Bratley – he's always trouble – and I don't know who else. Probably a whole roomful of idiots throwing their money away.'

Foster's face had gone white. 'But . . . how did you know?'

'Joy was suspicious. They've been short of money and Roger's been blaming poor business. But he's weak like the rest of you and she got it out of him. So how much have you lost?'

Foster turned away. He couldn't face her. 'Look, it's only a bit of fun. We just meet up for a laugh. I swear it's not like it was before when I was going online by myself. We try to—'

Christine picked up a paperback she'd been reading and threw it at Foster, hitting him on the head.

'A bit of fun!' she shouted. 'How many times have we been through this? Answer me! How much have you lost?' She picked up her glass and gulped the gin.

Foster was scared of what she might do next. 'Just a couple of thousand,' he blurted.

'Oh my God!' She buried her face in her hands and started to cry.

'Don't worry, love. I'll get it back. You'll see.'

She looked at him with tear-filled eyes. 'That's exactly what I am worried about: you trying to win it back and then losing more. Haven't you learned anything from the last few years? How are we going to pay the school fees and the mortgage if you throw money away like this? The brewery doesn't make that much these days, as you well know, and we're still in debt from paying off your previous losses.'

Foster tried to laugh and pass it off. 'No . . . Look, darling, the guys and I just meet and consider the odds and stuff. We're in a group and we stop each other from betting too much.'

'Huh!' she shouted in contempt. 'More like dare each other to increase the bet, like the bunch of fools you are.' She tried to pick up her glass again, but her arm was unsteady and she knocked it over on the table. Luckily there was not much left in it and none dripped on to the floor. 'Now look what you've made me do!'

Foster got up, and attempted to put his arm around her. 'I promise—'

She shrank away from him. 'Don't touch me! I'll never forgive you if you put our family life in jeopardy.' She flung her head into the back of the armchair in a gesture of despair. 'You had that counselling, and everything seemed OK. I thought we were through it and now . . .' She shook her head.

Foster struggled as to how to reply. 'Look, I swear to you, it's not serious, not like it was before.'

She shot him a glance. 'Then why didn't you tell me about it? Because you knew I wouldn't approve. You're just a bunch of self-deluded chancers who—'

She stopped at the sound of the outside door opening, followed by the voices of the children as they came in.

'Be quiet! They're back from school – don't you dare say anything,' continued Christine and went into the kitchen to greet them, although she was a little unsteady on her feet.

Foster sat dispirited and ashamed, cursing the fact that he'd allowed himself to be persuaded into joining that group. His wife was right: they were tricking themselves into thinking that they could control their gambling together, whereas in fact they just encouraged each other. The problem was that things were even worse than she thought. He could hear Christine and the children in the kitchen.

Furtively, he called a number on his phone. 'It's me. Yes, they know we've been playing again, but how much did Roger tell Joy? Not everything, I hope . . . Good. Well, he wouldn't dare tell her the full truth, would he? . . . Yes, yes, I think we can contain it to this. Tell everyone to hold their nerve or we really will be in trouble.'

He sat back in his chair and closed his eyes, wanting this awful day to end now. He hadn't even told her about all the bad things that had happened today at work.

∼

Janice Anderson was finding it hard to concentrate after what had happened at the brewery and in Ripon. She had delegated supervision of the processes to her deputy and was sitting in her small office at her desk, gazing at her monitor with a frown on her face. She looked at her hands, which retained some smears of colour from when she had removed the graffiti from the gates after Andy had given permission. The situation was getting worse. There were things that had to be done and she couldn't take Emily into her confidence.

Suddenly she came to a decision, got up and went to the door that led outside into the works.

'Paula!' she called. Moments later a stocky woman with short hair and wearing overalls came into the office. 'Just come in and sit down, will you?' She indicated a chair.

'What's all this about, boss?' Paula said, taking the seat she'd been offered. 'We were just about to start pumping the wort into the copper.'

Janice sat down across from the other woman. 'OK, Paula, this won't take long. Now, I know you've lived in Markham all your life, and you know everybody in town.'

'Well, yeah, quite a lot of people. I went to school round here and everything.'

'Good. Well, there are certain things I need to know . . . and I think you can help me.'

'About people?'

'Yes.'

Paula looked uncomfortable. 'What? I don't go round saying things about folk, boss; it gets you into trouble.'

'Yes, but you might get into trouble with me if you don't help. If you see what I mean.' She stared at the woman and her eyes were icy. Paula shuffled uneasily in her chair. 'I think you have a good idea who was behind that graffiti on the gates.'

'Ms Foster told us not to accuse people of anything, in case we were wrong.'

'Is that why you won't tell me? Or is it because you're afraid of them?'

This remark made Paula perk up. 'I'm not scared of anybody, boss.'

'OK, so look – are we going to take this lying down or do something about it? I don't know about you, but I'm not prepared to wait for the police to tell that person to be good in future and not do it again. There's a lot at stake here and we need to defend ourselves by sending out a clear message.' Janice could tell that Paula was impressed by this speech, so she continued. 'Tell me who did it. And, then, this is what we're going to do.'

Andy found Tony Handley outside the Yoredale brewery moving casks and barrels with a heavy trolley. He was solidly built with a pronounced beer belly and a shaved head. He wore a short-sleeved T-shirt, and his arms were tattooed with a variety of symbols – skulls, Union Jacks, dragons, and eagles. There was something on the back of his neck that looked like a swastika.

'Good afternoon, I need a word with you,' he said and showed his warrant card.

'Bloody copper!' snarled Handley. 'What do you want? You can see I'm busy. It's not about the van again, is it? I've had it MOTed and insured.'

'It'll be better if you're not so hostile,' returned Andy. 'It creates a bad impression.' Handley growled like a threatening dog but said nothing. Andy continued. 'I'm sure you know that there was an act of vandalism last night. The gates of the Ewe's Ales Brewery were defaced with a homophobic slogan.'

Andy saw the ghost of a smile on Handley's face. 'What's that got to do with me?'

'I understand that you have a record of making homophobic and misogynistic statements,' Andy said.

'Mis-what?' replied Handley, looking puzzled.

'Statements showing hatred for women.'

'I don't hate women. If they stay in women's places.'

'So you wouldn't be in favour of women running a brewery?'

Handley laughed. 'No, and I'm not the only one round here. It's daft, isn't it? As if women can brew beer like men.'

'Well, they seem to be making a success of it.'

Handley scoffed. 'Have you tasted their beers?'

'No.'

'You're lucky.'

Andy ignored this; he wasn't going to be drawn into a discussion about beer, never mind the question of whether women could or couldn't brew it. 'So did you paint that slogan on the gate, saying what you thought of the beer and slurring the owner and her partner?'

Handley's face darkened. 'Couple of lesbians. We don't want them round here. It's bloody unnatural.'

'It sounds to me as if you're admitting doing it.'

'Huh, you prove it, then,' said Handley contemptuously.

'We might well do that. Let me warn you.' Andy looked the man straight in the face. 'Putting up that slogan was not only damage to property, but it was also a hate crime. That's a serious offence and you could go down for it.'

Handley spluttered for a moment with inarticulate anger and finally blurted, 'Hate crime! What a load of crap!'

'OK. Well, I've warned you and my advice is to keep your nasty views to yourself and leave other people alone. You might find out that you've less support in this town than you think you have.'

Handley scowled and grunted but didn't say anything else. Andy left him to his work trundling barrels around the brewery.

~

Before returning home that evening, Oldroyd drove to the village of Kirby Underside, between Leeds and Harrogate, to pay his sister a visit. She was the Anglican vicar of the parish, and very dear to him. She was a little older, and he regarded her as a person of deep wisdom, although he didn't share her religious faith any more. She could always be relied upon to provide some insight into the behaviour and motives of the people involved in the cases he was investigating. In his fanciful moments he sometimes thought of her as a Mycroft Holmes to his Sherlock, although she had none of the fictional Mycroft's laziness.

He entered the pretty village with its long main street and daffodils blooming in the grass verges, and turned on to the drive that led to what he called the 'Jane Austen' vicarage: a large Regency period building redolent of a different era.

The large, leggy rhododendrons in the rather overgrown and neglected garden were heavy with buds and one or two early flowers poked through the undergrowth. The vicarage was absurdly too big for his sister who lived alone after the death of her husband from cancer.

She had always been a cheerful and optimistic character, but Oldroyd worried about her living by herself, especially after the traumatic experiences she had undergone a while ago when she had become unwillingly involved in one of his cases. He had gently suggested once or twice that she might consider retiring, or moving to a parish with a smaller vicarage, but she seemed intent on staying at Kirby Underside for the time being.

She was there to meet him when his car drew up. Her hair was a little greyer these days, but she was still tall, upright, energetic, and smiling.

'Jim! It's great to see you!' she exclaimed as they hugged. 'It's been too long. Come in.'

'I know,' replied Oldroyd as he followed her into the echoing hallway of the house. 'We've been so busy with one thing and another. We spent nearly a week down in London with Louise, and then I've been straight into this case up in Markham.' They reached the large, homely kitchen with its Aga cooker, spacious pine table and comfortable chairs.

'Tell me about both,' said Alison as she put the kettle on and produced a plate of homemade chocolate brownies. Oldroyd sank into a deep armchair with a contented sigh. He always found the vicarage and his sister's company very relaxing.

'Louise is doing fine. She's practically running that women's refuge now and she's getting noticed by people in the council and by the local MP. She was full of the problems they face – the lack of funding and so on – but you can tell she finds the work very fulfilling.'

'Good. You know, I could see Louise going into politics some day; she's got the feisty energy you need and causes that she believes in.'

'I know. She's got a new partner, too. Sean. An Irish lad. Seems very nice.'

'That's good news after what happened over that Whitby business.' She shuddered.

'Yes.' They were both quiet for a moment as they reflected on the terrible experience that Louise had gone through with a man she had been about to enter into a relationship with. Oldroyd had been worried she might find it hard to trust anyone again, so he was glad to know she'd found someone she seemed to be comfortable with.

'And the case?' asked Alison. She, like Deborah, was always interested in his work, especially the psychological and spiritual issues involved.

'Well, it's interesting . . . Happened up at Markham. Two murders. Both with some similarities. One of the bodies was found in a tank of partially fermented beer.'

Alison shook her head. 'Oh dear, I bet there's been a lot of joking about a nice way to go and so on, so I won't add to it.'

'You're right. Anyway, we've got some suspects and motives, but we can't pin it down yet. I must say, it's a very pleasant working environment. It's absolutely beautiful in Markham at the moment.'

Alison nodded as she poured out the tea. 'Yes, it is wonderful up there. I love those towns and villages in Lower Wensleydale. There's a lot of religious history, too, with Jervaulx Abbey, and the Knights Templar graves.'

'The case does have some curious features.' He told her about the rivalry between the breweries and the lost beer recipe. Alison drank her tea as she listened carefully.

'It's a shame that their relationship seems to have broken down over business rivalry. How often that seems to happen! I wonder if they were brought up to be competitive with each other?'

'I don't get that impression. I think it's more to do with lingering attitudes towards women. The brother and other men in the industry didn't take kindly to a woman being prominent in their world. There's been some nastiness towards the Ewe's Ales Brewery.' He took a bite from a brownie and told her about the banner and the graffiti.

'That's awful! But I bet it's only made the women more determined.'

'I'm sure it has.'

'And you say the first victim claimed to have a copy of this long-lost recipe?'

'Yes.'

'That's very intriguing. I can see why you might think that it would be a motive for murder. Such a thing would be extremely precious. I suppose it's like the holy grail of brewing: to be able to bring a famous beer back to life.'

Oldroyd didn't reply. He was looking into the distance.

'Jim?'

'Oh, yes, sorry. I was just thinking. A chap was showing me round the brewery today and he used a word you've just used: "precious".'

'What about it?'

Oldroyd shrugged. 'I don't know, but it's rung a bell with me.'

'Ah, the old subconscious is working, is it? You've always told me how reason and instinct work together in detective investigations.'

'Yes, but I can't always interpret the message straight away.' He sat back in the chair as he thought about the case. 'You see, there were some odd aspects of the first murder and I think that word is telling me something about it. But I can't work out what it is.'

'People will go to terrible lengths to retain or acquire things that are precious to them – whatever it is that gives them their special value.'

'Yes, I've seen that many times. Especially with what happened in Whitby.' Oldroyd was still remembering the terrible murder case which, in the end, had revolved around the possession of something valuable, which people had been willing to kill for. 'Anyway, I must get off – Deborah's making one of her spicy cheese and vegetable pies so I want to be there on time.'

'You don't want to miss that,' laughed Alison.

They walked out to the car together and Oldroyd looked at the garden. 'We should be living here,' he said. 'Deborah would welcome a challenge like this garden.'

'I think it would be beyond even her.'

Oldroyd paused before he got into the car and thought again. 'This thing will come to me in time.'

'Of course it will, Jim – it always does, doesn't it? And let me know how things work out. I hope it all comes to a reasonable conclusion and the breweries can get along together. It's always particularly sad when close relatives fall out with each other.'

'Yes,' replied Oldroyd somewhat absentmindedly. Alison had just said something that had sparked another theory in his mind.

~

The spring evening was clear and rather chilly, with a nearly full moon appearing in the sky. The interior of the Wensley Arms was warm and bustling with people and some were eating in the restaurant section. Philip Welbeck sat on a stool at the bar talking to Bill Lawrence. There were some members of the cricket team sitting around and others were playing darts.

'No cricket practice tonight, then, Phil?' asked the barman.

'No, we didn't think it was right after what happened to Barry. Mark of respect, you know. He was part of the club for so long and a good player. He was brilliant behind those stumps. And to think I was mad with him for not turning up last night.' He shook his head and took a drink of beer. 'I feel terrible now.'

'You weren't to know what was going on,' said Lawrence, as he pulled a pint for a customer. 'Are you going to cancel Saturday's match?'

'We've thought about it, but I don't think it's what Barry would have wanted. He would rather we beat North Tanfield. They've been our closest rivals over the years. We're going to try our best to do it. We're going to have a practice tomorrow night.'

'Good. I think you're right. Barry would have hated to think that he was stopping cricket being played. He loved the game.'

'He did,' said Welbeck with a sigh. 'He'll be hard to replace.'

'What do you think about all this business at the women's brewery?' asked Lawrence.

'I think it's disgusting,' replied Welbeck, finishing his pint. 'Another one, Bill, please.' He handed his glass over. 'That chief inspector was in the works today, and I told him what I think about it.'

'Have you got any idea who did it?' asked Bill.

Welbeck glanced around before answering. 'I think it was that bloke Handley. You know, big man, works in transport for us. It's round the works that people saw him there by the gates.'

'Yes, I wouldn't be surprised. He comes in here sometimes, throwing his weight about.'

'Exactly. He's a bit of an oddball; comes out with some crap stuff, you know. Racist nonsense, and things about gay people. He's got some weird tattoos. I think the boss has put the police on to him. So it seems he's got to be a suspect given all that.'

'Right.'

Welbeck lowered his voice. 'To be honest, I think it was a person like him behind these murders. You never know with someone like that. They think and do some weird stuff.'

'Did he know Scholes?'

'Highly likely in this small town.'

There was a great roar at the far end of the room where the dartboard was located. 'Sounds like that game's ended,' continued Welbeck. 'I'd better go over and see. I'm on soon. Cheers, Bill.' He picked up his replenished glass and went to join the darts players, leaving Lawrence to think about their conversation.

Suddenly the door was flung open, and Tony Handley strode into the bar. His face, normally reddish from beer drinking, was a darker tone than usual due to his anger. He caught sight of Welbeck and strode across to him.

'Oi,' he called. Welbeck was talking to the darts players and turned to see Handley, who pointed at him and raised his voice. 'Have you been saying stuff to t'coppers about me?'

Welbeck looked at him impassively; Handley was strong but overweight and Welbeck was powerful too and taller. He could handle him if necessary. 'Calm down, Tony. No, I haven't.'

Handley was not pacified. 'Somebody bloody has. I've had that young detective round – sounded like a bloody cockney, he did – talking about hate crime and being kind to bloody lesbians. He just about accused me of putting that stuff on their gates.'

Bill Lawrence was watching from behind the beer pumps and the sound of Handley's voice had drawn the attention of other people in the bar, which had fallen quiet.

Welbeck shrugged. 'Well, the way you carry on and the things you say, do you wonder that the police think it was you?'

Handley came up closer to Welbeck. Lawrence walked over from the bar.

'What the hell do you mean?'

Welbeck stood his ground. 'You've never made any secret of the fact that you hate gay people and women who don't behave as you think they should.'

'You . . . !' Handley spluttered with rage and lurched towards Welbeck. One of the darts players came forward and stood between the two men as Lawrence grabbed Handley from behind.

'That's enough, Tony!' said the publican. 'Out you go, and don't come back unless you can behave yourself.'

Handley looked round and saw that he was outnumbered. Without a word, he pulled himself free from Lawrence's grasp and stamped out of the bar, slamming the door behind him.

'Phew!' said Lawrence. 'I thought he was going to go for you then.'

Welbeck was unruffled. 'I could have dealt with him. Anyway, it's time we let people like him know what we think of them. I don't know whether he scrawled that stuff on the gates or not, but there's no doubt he agrees with it. It's not acceptable.'

This little speech was met with some nodding of heads and murmurs of, 'Aye.'

'He was drinking in here last night, and went out fairly plastered. Goodness knows what he got up to. Has anyone here told the police about him?' asked Lawrence.

People shook their heads. No one admitted to it.

'They must have got a tip-off from somewhere. I wouldn't be surprised if it was Richard Foster. He knows what Handley is like, and the police are on his back about these murders. They think the rivalry between the breweries has something to do with the crimes.

Foster wants to deflect suspicion away from himself. He doesn't want the police thinking that he had that graffiti put on the gates.'

Things in the bar had returned to normal after Handley's departure and there was a hum of conversation. The players picked up their darts again.

'I see,' replied Lawrence and shook his head. 'Stuff like this going on. I never thought I'd see such things in this town: murders, threatening messages, confrontations. It's like gangsters in America in the nineteen-twenties.'

Welbeck laughed. 'Start worrying when they rake this bar with machine guns. I can't see it, somehow. Anyway, it's my turn to play, I think.' He handed his empty glass to Lawrence and went to join the darts game.

Four

Theakston's Brewery, located in the market town of Masham in Lower Wensleydale, was founded in 1827 by Robert Theakston and his business partner John Wood, who started brewing in the cellar of the Black Bull Inn. A new brewery, still in use today, was built in 1875. Old Peculier is a strong, dark, ruby-red ale. Its name is a reference to the time when the Archbishop of York granted Masham its own independent Peculier Court which presided over religious matters.

'This is promising, Jim.'

It was Friday morning, and Deborah had been up for a while, looking at properties for sale online. Oldroyd was sitting opposite eating his muesli with semi-skimmed milk, yawning and gathering his energy. He'd never been an early morning person, and when he had a particularly difficult case, he tended to lie in bed thinking about it far into the night. At this moment he was not feeling receptive to details about houses, bathrooms, gardens and such. In fact, he was even less in the mood than last time.

'I've found another house, Jim,' said Deborah, 'not far from the last one we looked at – village location again, nice pub and closer to Harrogate.'

Jim admired Deborah's enthusiasm, and wished he could feel more interest. Maybe a slice of buttered toast with thick-cut marmalade would help.

'Just popping a slice of bread in the toaster, love,' he said. 'It'll help me concentrate. Do you want one?'

'Not for me, thanks.' She thought that Jim shouldn't be having one either but worried that she was becoming a bit controlling on the diet front and decided not to comment. After all she wouldn't like it if he told her not to eat toast.

The house in question was detached and only thirty years old.

'"This super property has been updated and modernised by the current owners to a high standard",' read Oldroyd. 'Definitely not a doer-upper. I like the sound of that.'

The toast popped and Oldroyd's mood improved as he spread it generously with butter and marmalade.

'Good, I'll see what times they have available, then.' Deborah read through the estate agent's details and called to make a viewing appointment for the following day, which was Saturday, much to Oldroyd's secret disappointment; he'd been hoping for a free weekend in which to relax. Deborah gave him a searching look and he smiled back at her.

'Is that OK?' she asked.

'Of course, love. We need to get on with it, don't we?'

'Yes, and eleven thirty is a good time. We can do parkrun first.'

'Ah, yes, of course.' The Saturday parkrun was an important part of Oldroyd's fitness routine, but he couldn't honestly say that he looked forward to it. He glanced away and frowned; parkrun and house viewing. It was not his ideal Saturday.

∾

Tony Handley woke up, scratched his head and got up quietly, so as not to wake his wife Pam. They lived in a rented former council house on the outskirts of Markham. It was a sunny day and the light streamed on to the landing as he went to the bathroom. As he brushed his teeth, he remembered the events of the day before and was still simmering with anger. Someone had dobbed him in to the police and he thought about who it might be as he got dressed. Philip Welbeck had denied it. Maybe it was the gaffer, Richard Foster. Handley's lip curled. Never mind; he would tell him what he thought and also to stuff his bloody job if it came to it. There were lots of jobs to be had for a strong bloke like him.

When he went downstairs, he sensed that something was not right. The living room door was open, but no light seemed to be coming through. He was sure the curtains had not been drawn the previous night. He went into the room and saw that what was blocking the light was paint, in zigzags, across the windows!

He quickly went to the outside door and unfastened it. He looked around to see if anyone was watching from the other houses and then stood in the little garden reading what had been sprayed in large, garish red letters over the windows and front of the house. 'Homophobic Bastard! Nobody's Scared of You!' There was also paint all over his garden gnomes.

He was about to bellow with rage, but controlled himself. He had to move quickly and remove the paint from the walls and windows before the neighbours or Pam saw what it said. He couldn't get rid of it completely, but if he could blur the message, then he might be able to blame the graffiti on hooligans. He could make up a story about telling some kids off for climbing up the walls at the brewery.

'Somebody's got it in for you, Tony!' He turned to see the grinning face of his neighbour Dave Broadbent, who was standing outside his front door across the road. 'What've you been up to?'

'Nothing. Damn kids,' Handley mumbled and went back inside to get some cleaning stuff as he heard Broadbent laugh and beckon to his wife to come and have a look. He would have to work quickly. He heard his wife calling down.

'What's going on, Tony? Was that Dave calling over?'

'Yes, it's nowt, love, don't get up. I'll bring you a cup of tea.'

'All right, thanks.'

Shit! This was going to be impossible, he thought, and his faced snarled. Yes, he'd put the graffiti on the Ewe's Ales Brewery gates. He'd been a bit drunk at the time, and no one could take a joke these days. Those disgusting women deserved it, anyway. And this was obviously revenge; it must be the work of someone at the Ewe's Ales Brewery, meaning that he'd been dobbed in for a second time! Was it the same person as the one who'd told the police? His hands curled into fists. If only he could find out who it was.

He scrubbed frantically at the windows, but he wasn't quick enough and then the worst thing happened: his wife appeared in her dressing gown. She looked around and her brow furrowed.

'Tony!' she said sharply. 'Where's my tea? And what the hell are you doing?'

Handley was red-faced with the effort of cleaning the paint off.

'Bloody kids, love!' he blustered. 'Look what a mess they've made.'

His wife was immediately sceptical. She knew about her husband's unsavoury views on certain matters and his habit of being provocative. She went into the garden and turned to look at what had been written. Despite her husband's efforts it was still easy to make out the words. She pointed to the window.

'That said "homophobic". Hardly a word that kids would use, is it? Do you think I'm stupid?' A realisation came over her. 'Oh, right, I know what's going on! I heard about what happened at the Ewe's brewery. You put that graffiti on the brewery gates, didn't you, you idiot? And you were drunk! Someone's found out it was you and got their own back.' She stood with her hands on her hips with a look of amused contempt.

Handley's embarrassment made him even redder in the face.

'It serves you right,' his wife said. 'You're a bloody dinosaur, Tony Handley. You can not only get all that off the walls and windows, but you can go and apologise to the Ewe's brewery. Those women are doing a great job, and their private life is their own affair.'

Handley, looking sheepish, carried on scrubbing while muttering to himself. Unfortunately he'd come up against the only person he was frightened of: his wife.

～

At Ripon police station, Jeffries brought Norman Smith out of the cells and questioned him for a final time. He was very suspicious of Smith's account of how he stumbled on to the murder scene with Scholes in the fermentation tank and would have liked to have charged him with the murder, but the evidence against him was inconclusive and DCI Oldroyd didn't want to proceed. Smith was eventually released, and Jeffries prepared to leave for Markham where he and a number of other DCs continued to work on the – now double – murder case.

He got into the police car with his colleagues, feeling disgruntled. It was exciting to be working for DCI Oldroyd again, but he felt like an opportunity was slipping away. He wanted to be able to shine in the admired detective's presence.

Jeffries was ambitious and he envied Carter his rank and his close working relationship with Oldroyd. He was weary of the mundane drudgery which was the lot of a detective constable: taking statements, checking alibis, tracking phone calls. As a detective sergeant he would be more involved in the front line of the investigation. He felt that his talents were being wasted. He sat in the back of the car in silence, looking out at the gorgeous scenery. The case was not progressing well. If only he could uncover something important that would really catch DCI Oldroyd's attention.

Jeffries closed his eyes and fantasised about being transferred to Harrogate station, promoted to the rank of detective sergeant, and working with the famous detective.

He had to be nudged by one of his colleagues when the car arrived in Markham as he was deeply engrossed in his daydream. Reality beckoned: more slog through paperwork and boring interviews.

∼

Steph arrived at Harrogate HQ. Now that there were two murders to investigate, Andy had been spared the disappointment of having to return to the office, so she was going to do some research by herself into the mystery of the elder Scholes brother.

She settled into her workstation, making sure she had a cup of coffee. Although, like Andy, she preferred to be out in the field with the boss, she also enjoyed finding out information about people. In this case, she was looking for more on Frederick Scholes, the missing brother. She had a photograph of Scholes which Jeffries and his team had found at the house in Ripon.

Once she was set up, she got to work using all the resources of the police data systems. It wasn't long before information started to emerge. The trail concerning Frederick's early years was not too difficult to follow. It made for a very interesting story.

The elder Scholes brother had attended a high school in Ripon but had been suspended at the age of fourteen for three months for provoking and being involved in fights. He left at sixteen and went to a nearby Army Apprentice Training Centre. After a year he had been suspended for persistent trouble-making and insubordination, but he had returned and finished the course. He left the army, and that was where the trail went cold as he didn't appear to have returned to Ripon.

Steph had long ago discovered that all names were more common than was generally assumed. There were many people in the records named Frederick Scholes although the name sounded unusual. Researching each one to find out if he was the one from Ripon could take a long time. At least she had some interesting information to pass on to Andy and her boss about Frederick Scholes' character, although she was not sure how relevant it was to the case.

'Morning, Sarge! How's it going?'

Steph looked up to see the smiling face of Sharon Warner – a young detective constable who Steph had been mentoring since she'd joined the force almost straight from school.

'Very well, thank you, Sharon.' She explained what she'd been doing to the young DC who was always alert and keen to learn. She had worked with Steph on a number of cases, and was already proving to be very good at researching and hunting down information.

Sharon looked at the photograph. 'So, to get any further you would have to go through the list of people called Frederick Scholes and eliminate them until you found the right one?'

'Yes. But even then we might not track him down because people often use assumed names, especially if they're trying to escape their past.'

'It could be worth trying, Sarge. If you need me, I could help. I can quickly finish off what I'm doing at the moment.'

'Thank you, Sharon. That would great. But I warn you it will be a bit of a slog . . . Possibly with no solid outcome.'

Sharon smiled. 'Never mind, Sarge. I like a challenge. You know what DCI Oldroyd says: we have to accept the hard grind of police work as well as the more exciting bits.'

Steph laughed. 'Yes, he does say that,' she said and thought how well her own protégée was coming on.

∾

Oldroyd was on his way to Markham when he received a call on his car phone. It was Tom Walker.

'Sorry about this, Jim. I know things are hotting up, and you've got another murder on your hands, but I've had you-know-who on the blower again. Jumping up and down, as usual, but I've managed to get it out of him what's behind him getting worked up. Apparently, he's well in with some bloody minor aristocrat who's Lord High Sheriff of the North Riding or something – you know, one of those ridiculous ceremonial things straight out of Gilbert and Sullivan. So, this bloke, Lord Markham, lives at Swinfield Hall. It's a stately pile near Markham and he's been on to Watkins asking what's going on as it's damaging the reputation of the area, and bad for tourism and so on. It's unbelievable, isn't it? Never mind that people have died, oh no, they don't give a bugger about that! It's the fact that it's creating a bad impression of their patch. Do you know I was the closest I've ever come to losing it with him?

'Anyway, the upshot is that this Lord Whatsit wants to speak to the "officer in charge of the investigation" – that's how Watkins put it, like the pompous fool he is. And, of course, that's you.' Walker chuckled. 'I think this bloke knows Watkins is a bloody lightweight who knows nothing, and he's saying he wants to talk to a real police officer. So, can you give him a call and arrange to go over? I've got the number here.'

'Of course, Tom.'

'Anyway, as I said, I know you're under pressure. How's it going? Are these two murders connected?'

Oldroyd was pleased that Walker's rant had only lasted as long as it had. He was starting to think he would be listening to him sound off all the way to Markham.

'Yes, we're pretty sure about that, Tom, and we're narrowing the suspects down. We've got some useful forensic evidence to go on.'

'Good. Well, keep at it. You know I've got faith in you and your team, whatever other people think, and if you need more help just let me know.'

The call ended. Oldroyd had deliberately put a positive gloss on how the investigation was progressing, to keep Walker happy, but in reality, he thought they were floundering.

∾

Andy was already in the incident room office at the Yoredale brewery when Oldroyd arrived.

'Morning, sir.'

'And to you,' replied Oldroyd. 'Any coffee going?'

'Yes, sir. I brought a packet in with me and some of these.' He pointed to some chocolate digestives beside the cafetiere.

'Oh, that's very naughty,' said Oldroyd. 'I suppose we can allow ourselves just one a day.'

'I'm sure we can, sir,' said Andy with a grin. 'I won't say anything if you don't.'

Oldroyd found the coffee and biscuit soothing and he drank and ate silently. Progress in the case was slow and he looked downhearted.

Andy sensed his boss's mood and decided to talk about something more light-hearted.

'I forgot to ask, sir, with all that happened yesterday – how did the house viewing go?'

'Oh, not too bad. I don't think it's the right place for us, but we enjoyed looking round. At least Deborah did. We've got another one on Saturday. Can't say I'm looking forward to it.'

Andy laughed. 'I'd be the same as you, sir. I can't get interested in stuff like that, but you have to try to show some enthusiasm, don't you?'

Oldroyd smiled. 'Yes, but it's not always easy. Especially after a long day at work. It's . . .' His phone rang. It was Steph, who explained what she'd found concerning Frederick Scholes. 'I see – so no recent information about his activities and whereabouts? No? OK, well done for what you've found.' The call ended and Oldroyd passed on the information to Andy. 'She's got young Sharon Warner with her. They're continuing to follow up on people of that name to see if they can track him down. That won't be easy.'

'They're a great researching team, those two, sir. I wouldn't put it past them to come up with something.'

'Maybe.'

'So, it's as we thought, sir. Frederick disappeared. Not surprising was it, really, with a record like that? He sounds a very unpleasant character. His father had probably had enough of him and banned him from the house. Do you think he is relevant to the case, sir? I mean, he's been out of the picture for so long.'

Oldroyd had sat down and was thinking. 'I don't know,' he said at last. 'It's strange, though, isn't it? All this kicks off not long after his father dies. Is that just coincidence?'

Andy sat up. 'You think he came back then, sir? And could he even have been the murderer? Pushed his brother into that tank?'

'Whoa, hold on!' said Oldroyd. 'Let's not jump to conclusions. I think what we need to do is find out where Wilfred Scholes, the father, and his two sons lived when they were in Markham. It's a while ago but I'd like to speak to the neighbours and see if any of them were around at that time. They might be able to tell us something interesting.'

Jeffries arrived. He had shaken off his daydreaming lethargy and presented himself as keen and dynamic in front of the chief inspector.

'Good morning, sir. I can report that we made excellent progress yesterday with the statements and alibis. Everything seems sound, no discrepancies. Smith was released this morning, sir. I questioned him again, but he didn't change his story.'

'Excellent work,' replied Oldroyd. 'In that case, we're going to have to look beyond our current suspects.' He finished his coffee and looked at Jeffries. 'I have a job for you and you can use your local knowledge.' Jeffries beamed. 'Find out where the elder Scholes and his two sons lived when they were here in Markham. We need to find out more about the family.'

'Of course, sir. I can track them back from Ripon. The schools will have information and other people I know from this area. I'll find out everything I can.'

'Good. Do you fancy a coffee before you go?'

'No, thank you, sir. I'll be off and get cracking on it.'

'Fine.'

'Before I go, sir, we've had a tip-off that someone has graffitied the wall of Tony Handley's house. It looks like revenge to me.'

'I'm sure you're right and it's exactly what he deserves. We're far too busy with important things to waste time investigating that.'

'Exactly, sir. But I think he would be too embarrassed to report it, anyway. Sir, Sarge.' Jeffries nodded, smiled at both of them and left the office at a smart pace.

Andy laughed. 'I thought he was going to salute you then, sir. If you asked him to jump in the river and search for the murder weapon, he'd be straight in.'

'Well, I hope you would, too,' replied Oldroyd, smiling. 'There's nothing wrong with a bit of youthful enthusiasm. You were like that when you first arrived from the Met. Now you're just old, cynical and going through the motions like the rest of us.'

'Not at all, sir. We always get there in the end.'

'Well, we have so far,' replied Oldroyd, whose mood had suddenly darkened again. 'But there's always a first time.'

~

Although it wasn't yet eleven o'clock in the morning, Christine Foster was drinking gin. She drank it every day, and in increasing quantities, but had so far managed to conceal the fact that it was out of control.

She had started several months ago with a mid-morning gin and tonic, then progressed to two. Now she was drinking half a bottle of gin a day and neat. She always drank it quite early in the morning and alone. This gave her time to sober up and get rid of any smell before she went to work or saw anybody in the afternoon, and then her husband came home from work. She was very careful in how she disposed of the bottles, and she bought the gin at a supermarket in Ripon so there was less chance that she would be recognised.

She blamed Richard for what she accepted was now an addiction. His gambling had caused her so much stress that she had turned to drink to calm herself down. She was terrified that he would gamble all their money away, bankrupt the business, maybe lose the house and they would be unable to afford the school fees. Their lives would be ruined. She had thought that he was avoiding the temptation and she had begun to feel better. She had even started trying to cut down on the alcohol. Now the latest revelation had thrown her back into turmoil. She didn't know whether she would ever be able to believe what he said again.

She sloshed some more gin into her glass, knocked it back, sat in the armchair and groaned. The double irony of her situation was not lost on her. Here she was with an addiction of her own after lambasting her husband about his; a husband who produced alcoholic drinks for a living. What would become of their poor children with parents like this? The thought upset her deeply, and she started to cry.

A knock on the door made her jump. Damn! She'd forgotten it was the cleaner's day! That was another luxury that would have to be foregone if their finances collapsed.

But her more immediate problem was how to conceal the drinking. She grabbed the gin bottle and went into the hall.

'Come in, Julie, the door's open. I'm just going upstairs for a while.' She ran up to their bedroom. Julie always began with the downstairs rooms and hopefully the smell of polish and disinfectant would disguise any odour from the gin. She lay on the bed for a while, resisting the urge to drink more. She needed to appear sober in front of Julie at some point. After a few minutes of despair wondering how she and Richard had ever got to this point, she ate some mints which she kept in her bedside cabinet to freshen her breath. Then she undressed and got into the shower with the water on cool. Hopefully this would sober her up.

Afterwards she lay on the bed, trying desperately to recover so that she could go down to speak to Julie. She now realised that this couldn't go on any longer. She would have to tell her husband.

~

Oldroyd and Andy walked through the streets of Markham again. It was a sunny day and birds sang in the trees on which the leaf buds were bright green and ready to burst. The car park in the square was filling up with visitors to the picturesque town, some to embark on trips around the breweries. It wasn't an official market day, but there were stalls selling ice cream and postcards.

Jeffries had been super quick in finding out where the Scholes family had lived in Markham. He'd had a stroke of luck because one of his team of junior detectives came from the town and knew the family slightly. It gave him great satisfaction to be able to give DCI Oldroyd the information he needed; it created such a good impression of efficiency.

The Scholes family had lived in a cottage belonging to the Yoredale brewery, behind some bigger houses on the square. Oldroyd admired the neat row of dwellings, each with a tiny garden at the front. Jeffries' informant believed it was the third house down the street. Andy knocked on the door, which looked newly painted. There were tubs of daffodils at either side.

The door was opened by a woman in her forties with ginger hair and freckles. 'Can I help you?'

Oldroyd explained why they were there.

'Oh, yes,' the woman said. 'We moved in here after Mr Scholes left. He retired from the brewery. My husband Simon works there; that's how we got this house.'

'I see. So, you didn't know the Scholes family then?'

'No, we moved here from York when Simon got the job. But Mr and Mrs Butterworth next door will remember them – they've lived here for more than forty years.'

Oldroyd's face lit up. 'Ah, thank you. We'll call on them.'

'OK. I'll just go in and explain. They're getting on a bit now and I don't want them to have a shock when they see the police outside their door.'

'That's fine.'

She knocked on the door and called out as she went in. A few minutes later she came back. 'It's OK to come in. They said they'd been expecting that you might come round.'

Oldroyd and Andy followed her into a sitting room that was stiflingly hot. The gas fire was on even though the day was warm. An elderly man and woman sat in armchairs on either side of the fireplace. Oldroyd introduced himself and Andy, and they showed their warrant cards. They were offered tea, but declined, not wanting to put the old couple to any trouble.

'I'm Ada Butterworth and this is my husband Joe,' said the woman. She had silvery hair and wore glasses and a flowery dress. Joe, wearing woollen trousers and a cardigan, didn't say anything. It soon transpired that he was rather deaf but responded when his wife raised her voice to ask him a question.

'Thank you for seeing us,' began Oldroyd. 'We understand that you've lived here a long time and you knew the Scholes family.'

'Oh, yes,' said Ada. 'Wilfred was a nice man, wasn't he, Joe?'

'Eh?'

She shouted. 'Wilfred Scholes was a nice man.'

'Oh, yes. Grand chap.'

'He worked for the brewery all those years. It was such a shame about Marjorie. It was breast cancer, you know. She was only in her forties. She was a lovely woman. She loved those boys, and she kept them in order. It's sad, really. They were typical boisterous little lads and happy enough in those days.'

'What happened after she died?'

Ada shook her head. 'Well, poor Wilfred, he couldn't cope. Men weren't really expected to be able to look after children in those days, and he must have been devastated by losing his wife. Those two boys went off the rails. I don't know whether it was because they missed their mother, or Wilfred couldn't deal with them or what . . . probably both. We used to hear him shouting

148

at them, but it didn't seem to make any difference. Brendan, the youngest, was always in bother at school and he was a rogue after he left. Mind you, he didn't deserve to be murdered like that. It's absolutely shocking. I've never known anything like it in this town. Poor Marjorie must be turning in her grave.'

'What do you remember about the older son, Frederick?'

Ada frowned and turned to Joe. 'He's asking about Frederick.' Joe shook his head but said nothing. Ada turned back to Oldroyd. 'He was a very unpleasant boy, Inspector. I don't like saying it, but it's the truth. Brendan was naughty, but I don't think he would ever have harmed anybody. Frederick was a different matter. The two boys were very alike to look at, there wasn't much in age between them, but Frederick could be violent. He got into fights and really hurt people. I think he was suspended from school for a while.'

Oldroyd nodded.

'He was quiet, but it wasn't because he was shy. He had a surly look. You could never really talk to him and you didn't know what he was thinking. He was once sitting on the step with a radio on loud. I told him to turn it down and he gave me such a look. It was quite chilling.'

'Do you remember what happened to him after he left school?'

'Wilfred was at the end of his tether with them both. He got Brendan a job at the brewery, though it didn't last, but Frederick left Markham and went to that army training college. I think he got thrown out of there. I don't know what happened after that. He never came back here. I think his father was pleased he'd gone.'

'So you never saw him again after he left home as a teenager?'

'No. Wilfred retired and moved to a house in Ripon. I used to see Brendan now and again. I think he was living with his father. The last time I saw him was at Wilfred's funeral. There was no sign of Frederick.' She turned to Oldroyd. 'I was quite glad. I didn't want to see him again. There was something very dark about him, Inspector. I think he would have been capable of anything.'

'Did you see much of Wilfred after he moved to Ripon?'

'Not a lot, but he always popped in to see us if he was in Markham. Brendan was living with him, but I don't think he'd changed his ways much.'

'Did Wilfred ever mention the recipe for Wensley Glory – you know, that famous beer?'

She turned to her husband and raised her voice. 'Did Wilf ever mention that recipe for Wensley Glory?'

'Naw.' He shook his head.

'That beer was very famous round here, Chief Inspector, and when Mr Foster died there were all sorts of rumours about where the recipe might be. Mr Foster and Wilf were always close, and a lot of people thought a copy must have been passed on to Wilf if anybody saw it at all. But he never said anything to us about it.'

'Well, thank you very much,' said Oldroyd, bringing the interview to a close. 'You've been very helpful.' He was glad that Ada's memory of the Scholes family was so clear. Her recollections had been very helpful in creating a more detailed picture of the Scholes family and its problems, and it had corroborated what Steph had discovered about Brendan's mysterious brother.

～

'What did you make of that, sir?' asked Andy as they made their way back to the Yoredale brewery.

'Very interesting and it confirms what we've been starting to think.'

'That this brother, Frederick, could be the murderer?'

'Exactly. He appears to have had a rough and violent side to his personality.'

150

'Even to killing his own brother?'

'If the stakes were high enough. I think we may be back to that recipe again, and—' He stopped and clapped a hand to his head. 'Of course, that's what's been at the back of my mind: "precious"!'

'What, sir?'

'Have you read *Lord of the Rings*?'

'No, sir, but I've seen the films.'

'You remember that creature Gollum who wanted the ring?'

'Yeah, he fell into that fiery mountain at the end, didn't he? And everything Sauron had built collapsed. I liked that bit.'

'Yes. Do you remember how Gollum got the ring in the first place?'

Andy shook his head. 'No, sir.'

'Gandalf tells Frodo the story. Sméagol, as he was called then, was fishing with his cousin Déagol – who found the ring. Gollum murdered him and took the ring for himself. He began calling the ring his "precious". That word has been resonating with me for a few days. So, let's say Frederick finds out about his father's death and turns up at the house in Ripon hoping to benefit in some way. Brendan has got possession of the recipe, which is worth a great deal of money, and tells Frederick to get lost. Maybe Wilfred left nothing to Frederick, and Brendan tries to palm him off with a bit of furniture. Frederick, overcome by anger, jealousy and maybe his brother's taunts, decides to kill his brother and then take the recipe for himself; his "precious", if you like.'

'It's plausible, sir. But why would Frederick be in the house a few days later when Green broke in . . . still assuming it was the same killer?'

'Brendan could have refused to tell him where the recipe was hidden so he had to search for it under cover of darkness.'

'And is he still in hiding somewhere around here or did he find the recipe and clear off?'

Oldroyd shrugged. 'I don't know. It's all speculation. There's no actual evidence that Frederick has been anywhere near Ripon and Markham, but, as I say, he sounds like the kind of person who could have committed those two brutal murders.'

They arrived back at the brewery and climbed the stairs up to the side entrance.

'There are some other things that puzzle me about that scenario, sir,' said Andy as they reached the office. 'How did Frederick get his brother to meet him at the brewery on the night of the murder? And why go to all that trouble anyway? He could have bumped him off somewhere much less public and risky. There might have been some noise and a bit of a struggle in the brewery. Someone could have heard it and walked in on him.'

Oldroyd sat down. He was always pleased when one of his young detective sergeants questioned his theories; it showed that they were thinking about a case in the way he was training them to do.

'Maybe he was trying to deflect attention away from himself. Murder in the brewery might draw suspicion on people who worked there. Brendan had been employed there and left under a cloud. He could have made enemies. Anyway, get the coffee on, will you?' He frowned. 'And we'd better stay off the biscuits. We've already had one this morning.'

'Never mind, sir . . . they can't see us out here.'

'In theory, but in practice . . . women always seem to know. I don't know whether there's anything in this female intuition thing.' He chuckled.

'I'd be careful with that, sir. It's not a very progressive attitude,' laughed Andy. 'It's probably just that we can't hide our guilt.'

'Or we leave crumbs on our clothes. Anyway, we'll get off for a bit of lunch soon, so we don't want to spoil our appetites.' He sat back in his chair. 'Now, get on to Steph to do a search of wills.

It would be interesting to know the contents of Wilfred Scholes' will, if he left one.'

'OK, sir.'

'I wonder if he left anything to Frederick? If not, that would have made things worse.'

'It would, sir. Frederick would not have been at all pleased about it.'

'Hmm. Anyway, we'll have to see what Steph finds out.' He tapped the table with his fingers. 'If only we could find out the truth about this blasted recipe. That house in Ripon has been searched without success, but if the murderer was Frederick Scholes, I'm starting to think that Jeffries could be right: he was looking for the recipe.'

Andy smiled. 'Tell Jeffries you agree with him, sir – it'll make his day.'

'Yes, I'm sure it would. But we need to get back to that house and do another search. It might be very revealing.'

Later, as they got up to go, Andy reflected on how much he had enjoyed this analysis of the case. It was one of the things he most valued about working with Oldroyd. He regarded you as an equal in the task of solving the puzzles and mysteries of an investigation. It was stimulating to engage with him in an interchange of ideas and theories. He would miss it a great deal. The mention of Jeffries had reminded him that there was someone who stood ready to replace him. But was he ready himself to make the move?

~

Tony Handley sloped into work a bit late that morning after removing the graffiti from his windows and walls, hoping no one would comment. But his arrival was noticed by Philip Welbeck, the foreman. To Handley's surprise, as he came through the main works entrance where the workers clocked on and off, Welbeck was standing there almost as if he was waiting for him and smiling.

'Not like you to be late, Tony. Had a few problems, did you?' said Welbeck, grinning.

Handley noticed that other workers were looking towards him and also smiling. Then he spotted a certain person and knew what had happened. This man lived close to him. He must have seen the graffiti on the house and told everybody at the brewery!

'Shit!' he exclaimed.

'What did Pam think about it, then?' called one mocking voice. 'I'll bet she gave you a bollocking, and made you clean it off! Is that why you're late?'

'You daft sod,' said Welbeck. 'We know it was you who graffitied those gates at the Ewe's. More than one person saw you drunk as a pig, daubing the paint on. They didn't waste any time getting their own back, did they? Why can't you live and let live like the rest of us?'

'Oh, bugger off, the lot of you!' growled Handley. 'Was it one of you lot that dobbed me in to the police? That was a nasty bloody trick.'

'No, was it 'ell! And what're you going to do about it, anyway?' came the reply, half joking and half threatening.

Handley slunk off into the back of the warehouse where it was darker, followed by derisive hoots of laughter. It was going to be a difficult day. Later on, he had to summon up the courage to go to the Ewe's brewery and apologise for putting the graffiti on the gates. Otherwise, he knew he would get the sharp end of Pam's tongue again when he got home.

~

Down the short corridor from his office now commandeered by the police, Richard Foster remained in a state of anxiety about a number of things but chiefly the state of his finances and how to deal with his current crisis. He had decided that he would try to take more money out of the company, maybe as a loan, which he would find hard to ever pay back. He knew this would be difficult because the profit margins were very narrow, and Peter Morgan had already explained that they were in line to run a deficit. However, Morgan was also the person he needed to advise him if he was going to find a way to squeeze some money out of the system. The man was very clever with figures. He checked that there was no one around who could listen in and then called Morgan over. He tried to explain his problem as judiciously as he could while the accountant sat beside his boss and gave him his full attention.

'You see, I'm in a bit of a difficult situation, Peter, with money. I have bills to pay, and I've got a bit of a shortfall.'

Morgan looked at him sharply from behind his glasses and said quietly, 'Have you been playing and losing again?'

Foster was surprised. 'Yes,' he whispered, glancing round to double check that no one could hear him. 'How did you know?'

'I didn't. I just wondered. It's a hard habit to kick and you inevitably get into difficulties.'

'Yes, I almost forgot that you know all about it.' Morgan had once been part of the same gambling group as Foster, but had dropped out some time ago. He had showed more self-control, reflected Foster ruefully. 'Anyway, can we analyse the figures again and see if there's any way that the company could pay me a bonus, or loan me money? Let's look at everything, all the funds we have, all the incomes and expenditures, you know.'

Morgan frowned. 'Of course we can, but if you want to go into that depth of detail, I'll have to prepare a report for you. I'm rather busy at the moment. Would Tuesday be OK?'

'Oh, yes, it's not that urgent, but I really would appreciate it if you could help me.'

'I'll see what I can do,' said Morgan with a smile and then returned to his desk.

Foster felt bad taking money from the company. Even if it was being done legitimately, what would his father have thought? He'd worked so hard over many years to establish the business and now his son might be putting the company at risk. If it went bankrupt, then that would make his own position even worse. He put his head in his hands. His situation was dire even without the trauma of these murders, and the worsening relationship with his sister.

～

Emily Foster and Janice Anderson were having lunch in a cafe on the square. They usually did this on two working days a week in order to get out of the brewery building and have a proper break. It was difficult to stop work when you were at your desk, with people bringing problems to you. You often ended up wolfing a sandwich down while working at your computer and getting indigestion.

'I'm glad that graffiti business is over,' said Emily as she ate a tuna salad. 'We were right to tell the police. I've had enough of the way some people think they can treat us. I have to admit I was relieved this morning when there was nothing else written on the gates.'

Janice was eating a cheese and ham panini. She gave Emily a knowing smile. 'Oh, don't worry about that. We won't have any more trouble from him.'

Emily looked up. 'From who? Do you know who did it?'

'Yep. It was that gruesome character, Tony Handley. He works in the warehouse up at your brother's. He's got plenty of form for parading his racism and sexism.'

'How do you know?'

Janice took a bite of her panini before replying. 'I suspected it was him and I got the truth out of Paula Adamson. She's a local, lived here all her life, and knows everybody and everything. She confirmed it was him. Her sister was out late with a group of her friends and they saw him.'

'Isn't that just rumour?'

'I don't think so; news travels quickly in a small community like this.'

'I don't know him, but he sounds a nasty piece of work. Do you think he could have had anything to do with the murders?'

'I doubt it. People like him are all bluster and mouth.'

Emily looked at her partner suspiciously. 'Anyway, what did you mean when you said we won't have any more trouble from him?'

Janice finished her sandwich and wiped her hands and mouth. 'I got Paula and her mates to go round and repay the compliment.'

'What? You mean they graffitied his house?'

'Yeah, all over the walls and windows. Why not? I paid them to do it. We have to show that we're not intimidated by people like that, and we can fight back if necessary. It sent a message to him and to anyone else who thinks we might be a pushover.'

Emily shook her head. 'Bloody hell, don't you think that's a bit reckless? We don't want the whole thing to escalate. And what if the police find out it was you?'

'They won't. Paula won't blab, she's got too much to lose. I think Handley will be shocked and cowed by it. He didn't expect any retaliation and he won't go to the police. They already suspect that it was him who graffitied our gates, and this would just confirm it.'

'Even so, it seems a bit extreme.'

Janice smiled. 'That's why I didn't tell you. I knew you would think it was going too far. But with bullying types like that, you've got to stand up to them. They prey on the weak.'

'Well, I hope you're right.'

'The police won't know, trust me.'

Emily looked curiously at her partner. She was seeing a tough, even ruthless, side to Janice that she'd not encountered before. In one sense it was admirable, but it was also a bit disturbing.

~

Oldroyd drove his old Saab up the winding drive to Swinfield Hall with Andy in the passenger seat. They passed an ornamental lake surrounded by huge banks of rhododendrons, some of which were coming into flower, and a large stable block with a traditional domed clock tower. There were a number of horses and riders in the yard and a woman watched them go past.

'Wow, this is some posh place, sir,' observed Andy, grinning as they got out of the car and mounted the steps up to the door.

'Yes,' replied Oldroyd, looking around. 'Magnificent! I just hope our visit is worth it.' Oldroyd was not keen to waste valuable time reassuring local bigwigs that order and peace would soon return to their patch once the trivial matter of a few murders had been sorted out. It was at times like this that he shared Walker's contempt for their chief constable, who seemed to place his status and social connections before everything else.

Oldroyd had half expected the door to be opened by some functionary in a uniform who intoned, 'This way, sir, his lordship is expecting you.'

However, it was Langford himself who greeted them and ushered them into his study. The detectives sat down opposite him, Oldroyd looking rather stony-faced. Langford offered them a drink which they declined. He poured himself a large whisky.

'I wanted to have a word with you about a somewhat delicate matter,' began Langford. 'I'll come to the point, Chief Inspector. I told Watkins I was concerned about the impact of a prolonged murder inquiry on the area, but I was not being entirely frank with him.'

Oldroyd raised an eyebrow. 'I see,' he said.

'Yes, it's actually a much more personal consideration that concerns me: my daughter. I thought it better to speak to you directly but in private. I'm sure you understand.' He laughed rather nervously, seeming a little embarrassed.

'How is your daughter affected by this?'

Langford took a drink of his whisky and paused before continuing. 'She had a relationship with Brendan Scholes which lasted for quite a time. Obviously I disapproved of this when I found out and put pressure on her to end it. Eventually she did, but I think it was more to do with his infidelity than anything I said.'

Oldroyd was frowning. 'You say it was obvious that you disapproved of the relationship. Why was that?'

Langford laughed. 'Come now, Chief Inspector. Sophie has a future ahead of her. She can't ruin that by fraternising with the locals, especially men quite a bit older than her with a reputation for womanising. I've invested a substantial amount of money in Sophie's education in order to equip her to enter society.'

Oldroyd was liking him less and less. 'Where exactly do we fit into this? We're very busy at the moment, as I'm sure you understand.'

'Oh, yes, well, the point is, this case is now attracting a great deal of attention from the media. It would be a disaster if Sophie's name was mentioned in connection with the victim and then the reporters started to dig around and find things. It could destroy her reputation, as I've told her. She's under strict instructions from me not to mention anything to anybody.'

Oldroyd glanced at Andy, who raised his eyebrows, then he turned to Langford.

'I'm not sure what you're asking us to do. Now that you've declared this connection between the victim and your daughter, we will obviously have to speak to her.'

Langford's face fell. He had clearly not expected this. 'Is that necessary?'

'Of course. If she was a rejected lover, then she could be said to have a motive.'

'But surely . . . I mean . . .' Langford was struggling for words.

'I'm afraid we will have to interview her. But as far as the media are concerned, we don't reveal who we've spoken to until someone is charged, unless there are special reasons. We won't be feeding the reporters information about your daughter's past.'

Langford nodded.

'If you were expecting,' continued Oldroyd, 'that, somehow, we could prevent the media speaking to people and investigating things, then that is impossible. I don't like the sensationalising approach they often take, and I handle them very carefully. But it is an essential part of a free society that the police, as an arm of government, do not control them.'

Andy smiled at this powerful little speech – and its effect on Langford, who took a while to reply.

'Quite,' Langford said at last. 'I accept that. I just wanted to urge you to finish the investigation as soon as possible so that the media will move on and not . . . you know.'

'Discover anything unpleasant,' said Oldroyd, completing the sentence.

'Exactly.'

'Well, I can assure you that we are doing everything possible to solve these crimes. We have a significant number of officers working on this case from Harrogate and Ripon.' He got up. 'I think at this point the best thing is for us to get on with it.'

'Of course,' replied Langford, who was much less jaunty and confident than when they had arrived at Swinfield.

'While we're here I think we'll take the opportunity to speak to your daughter. Could you call her in if she's around?'

'Yes, she's out in the stables.' He also got up. 'Please stay here and I'll get her to come over.'

'Bloody cheek, sir!' exclaimed Andy when Langford had left. 'As if we've nothing better to do than to make sure his precious daughter doesn't get into the news. And as if we could control the press.'

Oldroyd shook his head. 'I know, he's the kind of entitled person who thinks the world revolves around them.'

'Do you think he will complain to the chief constable?'

'I hope not. If Matthew Watkins harasses Superintendent Walker any more, I think he'll blow his top. But seriously, Langford's completely out of order calling us in like this for what effectively would be a favour: leave his daughter out of the investigation, which we can't do because she had a relationship with the suspect. I think he knew he was on dodgy ground; that's why he didn't tell Watkins the truth.'

There was a knock on the door and Sophie came in. She sat down as the detectives introduced themselves.

'I want to apologise for my father,' she said immediately. 'He's a ridiculous snob and an arrogant man who thinks everyone's there at his beck and call.'

Oldroyd had to laugh. 'Well, I must say that's very frank. I take it you and he don't see eye to eye on certain things.'

'That's an understatement. I take it you want to talk to me about Brendan?'

Oldroyd nodded.

'OK. I met him at a gig in Ripon about two years ago. We were together for over a year. I kept it secret from my father because

I knew he'd disapprove. Brendan was local, he didn't have much money and he was a lot older than me.'

'But none of those things concerned you?'

'No. I'm not like my father. He sent me to boarding school, and then to this dreadful finishing school in Switzerland. It was there that I realised what the whole thing was about: separating us from other people who were not in our class. I think it's awful. Brendan was great fun; it was like a breath of fresh air after the stuffy life I'd led.'

'How did he treat you?'

'Very well to begin with. I was a bit naïve, though I knew all about his reputation. Things went pretty well until I got pregnant.'

Oldroyd raised his eyebrows. 'Your father didn't tell us that.'

'No, he wouldn't. In his opinion, it was too scandalous, and would make me damaged goods for potential suitors. That's the way he thinks, Chief Inspector, and the language he uses. He's stuck in the nineteen-fifties – or maybe the eighteen-fifties. Brendan couldn't deal with it either. He was the kind of person who couldn't handle any responsibility. He started seeing other women.'

'And what did you do?'

'I wanted a termination, but, unfortunately, I needed my father's help, so I told him. He paid for it.' She took a deep breath. 'It was a big mistake, looking back; it just gave him more power over me.'

Oldroyd thought for a moment. 'From what you've told me, your father must have had a very hostile view of Scholes.'

'Yes.'

'Hostile enough to want to kill him or have him killed?'

Sophie's demeanour changed. She looked worried. 'No, he wouldn't.'

'You don't sound very sure.'

She was struggling with something. 'He wouldn't go that far. It's just that I'd been seeing Brendan again recently and I wonder if he'd found out. He would have been very angry.' She looked at Oldroyd with a pleading expression. 'You don't think . . .'

'I'm afraid I can't say. We'll need to talk to him again now that we have some new information. And what about you? Scholes didn't exactly treat you well, did he? Was he cheating on you again and was that the last straw?'

'No, Chief Inspector, I'd never hurt Brendan. I knew him for what he was, but I . . . I cared about him.' She suddenly began to weep.

'OK,' said Oldroyd gently. 'When was the last time you saw him?'

'A few weeks ago. His father died and I didn't hear from him. I expect he was too upset or busy arranging things.'

'I just have to ask you where you were on Monday evening.'

She dried her eyes on a tissue. 'I was here. I spent the day giving riding lessons and I watched a film in the evening in my bedroom.'

'Can anyone support that?'

'Daddy and I saw each other around the house during the evening. You're going to want to know where he was. He was here with a couple of friends. They were having drinks. So I suppose we can support each other's alibis.'

∽

'It's a bit too convenient that they can vouch for each other's where-abouts on the night of the Scholes murder, sir,' said Andy later, when the detectives were driving away from the hall. They'd had another brief word with Langford who'd said he didn't know that Sophie had been seeing Scholes again and of course denied any involvement in the murder, confirming his daughter's story that they both spent the evening at the hall.

'There's clearly a motive there, especially if he's lying about finding out that she was seeing Scholes again. He would have most likely employed someone to do it. It is unbecoming for a gentleman to be involved with violence, at least to some people. They don't mind blasting their guns away at birdlife.'

'What do you think about her?'

Oldroyd frowned. 'Well, it seems unlikely. She seems to have genuinely cared about him. It's difficult to see that she could have carried out that brutal murder, and it would have been much harder for her to get help with it.'

'But they remain on the suspect list?'

'They do.'

~

Back at Harrogate HQ, Steph was finishing off her work and getting ready to leave when her phone went. She didn't immediately recognise the number.

'Hello.'

'Steph, it's me.' It was a London accent. Her father.

'Dad? Hi . . . I, er, didn't expect this.'

'No, I . . . I'm going up to Edinburgh tomorrow to see a friend and stopping off in Leeds for the night. It's too far in one day on the coach – the economy ones stop all over the place. I'm staying in a bed and breakfast, and I thought maybe we could just meet up for a quick drink, catch up a bit, you know.'

'You never mentioned this before. I thought you were coming up in a couple of months.'

'Well, yes, I am. This was a bit of a spur of the moment thing, going up to see Alan. I wasn't going to ring you – I don't like, you know, to impose . . . but then I thought why not?'

Steph paused to think for a moment. 'OK, we could meet in a cafe in town, say about eight o'clock? It'll just be me. It's too short notice for Lisa.'

'Oh, that's OK. She won't mind on this occasion, will she?'

'No, probably not. So, Cafe Nico, near to the station?'

'Yes, I know it. See you there at eight tomorrow. Bye, then.'

'Bye.'

Steph sat down and breathed deeply. She always felt unsettled when she spoke to her father, although from his hesitant manner he clearly found it even more difficult to speak to her. She'd been able to prepare for the meetings she and Lisa had had with him, but this seemed very abrupt. The previous meetings had been OK, without any animosity, but rather awkward. It had been difficult to talk about the past, which lay heavy and unspoken in the atmosphere. She wasn't certain that there was a future in them meeting regularly. Nevertheless, his conduct throughout the time he'd reconnected with them had been good and she felt that she wanted to carry on the contact, or that she ought to – she wasn't entirely sure which. But she could not honestly say that she was looking forward to it.

~

Richard Foster felt exhausted in the afternoon so decided to go home early. When he arrived he knew straight away that something was wrong. He came in through the side door into the kitchen and there were dirty cups and plates on an unwiped table. This was completely out of character for house-proud Christine. There was no sign of any meal being prepared, no smell of anything cooking; instead there was an unusual odour . . . of spirits?

He called out, 'Christine?' and went into the lounge. She was lying on the couch in her dressing gown, asleep. Her hair was draped untidily over a cushion. There was an empty gin bottle on the floor.

'Christine? What's going on? Have you drunk all this bottle?' He tried to rouse her gently.

She woke and turned a bleary face towards him. 'Oh God! Go away,' she said and put her head to the back of the sofa.

'Christine? What's wrong? I don't understand.'

Her shoulders started to shake. She was crying.

'Christine?'

After a while she turned to him again. Her face was tear-stained. 'I drink, Richard. I'm probably an alcoholic. I've kept it a secret, but after yesterday . . . I couldn't stop drinking this afternoon.' She put her hands to her face and spoke through her fingers. 'I didn't think you'd be back yet, but I don't care any more. I know what a great irony it is. You work at a brewery and have an alcoholic wife. Oh, it's so humiliating!' She sobbed.

'Where are the kids?' asked Richard.

'They've gone to their friends' for tea. I managed to stay off drinking until Julie had gone, but then I couldn't resist it any longer.'

Foster was near to tears himself. The shock of finding out and seeing her like this was terrible. He felt as if he was in an awful nightmare and that this wasn't really happening.

'But . . . why? Is it my fault?'

She sat up, leaned back against a cushion and spoke slowly, as if it was a great effort. 'It's got steadily worse since this gambling business started. I couldn't deal with the worry of not knowing if you were losing all our money.'

Foster hung his head. He didn't know what to say. All the time he'd been struggling with his addiction, she'd been developing hers. And he hadn't known. He'd been too bound up with his own problems to notice hers.

'Then yesterday, you admitted you'd gone back to gambling, and that was it!' She turned her face away for a moment and then suddenly got up. 'Oh, God, I'm going to be sick!'

She ran into the downstairs toilet and reached the bowl just before she retched.

Foster sat with his head in his hands. It was a huge shock, but also a potential turning point. For both of them. There was only one thing to do: make a clean breast of everything and help Christine to recover. The crisis was deeper than he thought.

Eventually she staggered back into the room and Foster had a glass of water for her. 'Thanks,' she said and collapsed on to the sofa again, white-faced and completely drained. He waited for her to come round.

'Look,' he began. 'I absolutely promise you there's going to be no more lying and secrecy. I don't blame you for this and I'm going to help you recover.' He gritted his teeth. 'I still haven't been completely honest with you about my losses.' She gave him a bleak look but didn't have the energy to say anything. 'The truth is, we didn't only play on the usual sites, we went on this poker site, where the stakes are higher.'

'Richard!' Her voice was a wail.

'But don't worry, we're only talking about another couple of thousand in losses and I've spoken to Peter Morgan. I think the brewery will be able to loan me something to tide us over.'

She didn't respond. The fight had gone out of her.

He put his arms around her shoulders. 'This has really made me realise what damage I've caused. I'll work hard to make up those losses and I'll never gamble again, I swear. If necessary, I'll get some help. I won't let you down this time.'

He thought she might push him away contemptuously; he had said that to her and promised the same a number of times before. It was a pivotal moment in their relationship. She turned to look at him, saw the agony on his face and then held on to him. Maybe she sensed that this time he really was determined that things would be different.

At least it was a start.

~

Oldroyd enjoyed the drive from Markham to Ripon. It was late in the afternoon. They had decided to call it a day in Markham and stop at Ripon on the way back to Harrogate to conduct another search of the house.

It was breezy and white clouds were moving quickly across the sky, interspersed with intervals of strong sunshine. Spring flowers of various colours were blooming in the pretty village of West Tanfield as they drove through and turned right over the bridge across the River Ure. As he did so, Oldroyd glanced at the famous scene that appeared on so many calendars: the cottages with their gardens leading down to the river, the fifteenth-century Marmion Tower, and the church surrounded by trees. Just across the bridge he pulled over and Andy stopped behind him. Oldroyd went over to speak to his puzzled sergeant.

'Sir?'

'Just get out, and come look at this.'

Andy obliged and followed his boss on to the bridge where they stood and gazed at the beautiful view. Some ducks flew overhead and settled on the river further down.

'That's beautiful, sir.'

'Yes. You know this reminds me of your first day here. We stood on the bridge over the Wharfe at Burnthwaite and then skimmed stones across the water – or at least you tried to.' He laughed at the memory.

'I remember, sir,' said Andy. 'It seems a while ago, but I've never regretted coming up here for a moment. I think I fell in love with Yorkshire that very first day.'

'Well, I'm glad to hear it,' replied Oldroyd. 'Who wouldn't when you can see views like that?' He continued to gaze at the scene for a while. 'Come on, then, we can't look at views all afternoon. We'd better move on and get to that house. We've got work to do. We're not on top of this case yet.'

'We will be soon, sir, or should I say, *you* will be, judging by how I've seen you solve mysteries like this since I came up here to join you.'

'Well, you have a touching faith in my abilities,' replied Oldroyd as they walked back to their cars.

'It's based on experience, sir,' replied Andy, who decided this would be a good time to mention his interest in a possible move. He explained about the inspector jobs coming up.

'I'm going to talk to Steph about it, sir, and then see what I think.' He laughed. 'One thing's for sure: you've got someone desperate to come and work for you.'

'Young Jeffries, yes. Well, don't let him push you out if you're not ready, but I think you should consider it seriously, as I said before. You're definitely capable of it.'

'Thanks, sir.'

Oldroyd was very thoughtful as he drove on to Ripon. To be honest, he wasn't keen on the idea of losing Andy; they had developed such a good relationship. But he would never stand in the way of someone who deserved promotion.

However, there was nothing like the beauty of the Yorkshire countryside to make you feel better. And also, contemplating the often painted and photographed scene from the bridge at West Tanfield had given him another idea.

When they arrived at the terraced house it was locked up, with incident tape hanging around the door. Andy opened the door with a key that had been provided by the ever-efficient Jeffries. The electricity was turned off but there was still plenty of light in the house. Downstairs the gruesome evidence of Barry Green's murder was visible in the form of a large bloodstain on the carpet and the items he was about to steal were still strewn around where his body had been.

'So,' began Oldroyd. 'Jeffries and his team subjected this house to a search before Green was killed, but found nothing of significance. I don't think there's any point in going through drawers and cupboards again. I think if that recipe does exist, Wilfred Scholes would have hidden it carefully. After that view we looked at, I'm thinking about pictures and what Duffield said. I wonder if . . .' He tailed off as he started to look around the walls and on the top of the old sideboard. He saw the pictures and photographs that Jeffries had examined a couple of days before. He picked up the one showing David Foster, Wilfred Scholes, and others at the awards ceremony in 1995. He looked closely at the triumphant group in the photograph.

'Now this one is interesting,' Oldroyd said. 'Look, there's Wilf Scholes and Bert Duffield.' He turned it over. 'I wonder. Where better to hide it than here? Get a thin, sharp knife from the kitchen, will you?' Andy disappeared and rummaged around for a while, then he returned with a suitable knife and handed it to Oldroyd who looked at the photograph again.

'You see this is a photograph, maybe the only copy, of one of their proudest moments when Wensley Glory Bitter had won the Beer of the Year award. So, let's have a look.' He turned it over again and started to carefully cut the tape that fastened the back of the photograph to the mounting. After this he was able to remove the photograph and, tucked in the corner, concealed behind the mounting, was a folded piece of paper.

Oldroyd removed it carefully. 'Well, would you believe it?' he said with a smile. He slowly opened the folds and dust fell out. He laid the paper on a table to reveal a handwritten recipe.

The title at the top said 'Wensley Glory Bitter' followed by detailed accounts of barleys, hops, process times and other technical details. It was signed by David Foster and afterwards there was a little note: 'Wensley Glory Bitter was made by myself and my father Brian Foster. It took many years to get right. This recipe must be followed exactly if the beer is to have its proper flavour.'

'Good God, sir, you've done it!' declared Andy. 'What did I say earlier on?'

'Yes, we've found it! So, it does exist . . . and I suspect this is what our killer was looking for. Wilf Scholes was telling the truth that time when he was drinking with Bert Duffield: he did have a copy and, look, it was hidden behind the photograph that he's in. No wonder he was laughing when he told Duffield – it was his cryptic little joke.'

'Do you think Brendan Scholes knew it was concealed there?'

Oldroyd looked again at the fragile document. It was fraying along the lines of the folds. 'If he knew it was there, he'd left it alone. The tape fastening it to the mount looks as if it hasn't been disturbed for some time. It looks like his killer thought it was in the house somewhere. I can't be more specific than that.'

Andy had a close look at the paper. It was written in uneven, spidery writing, as if the writer didn't regularly put pen to paper, which David Foster probably hadn't. 'And what now, sir?'

Oldroyd thought for a moment. 'I'm not sure, but I think we'll keep this discovery to ourselves for the time being. I think it will prove useful.' He placed the recipe in a small plastic bag and fastened it up. Then they locked up the house and continued on their way to Harrogate.

~

When Norman Smith was released from Ripon police station that morning, he immediately made his way back to Markham. He'd lost a day's work through being in custody and he could ill afford it. He was also concerned about his reputation. Would people want to employ a joiner who'd been in trouble with the police if that became public knowledge? It was all that blasted Scholes' fault. The man was still harassing him, even though he was dead. It was a shame about Barry Green, but that was what happened when you broke into people's houses.

When he got home, he rang the person for whom he was scheduled to do a job, apologised profusely, made an excuse for not turning up and promised to be there within a couple of hours. The task was fitting an external door and he had all the materials ready but there was no food in his house. He would have to make a trip to the little supermarket down the road before he went to work.

The shop was near and as he walked round with his basket collecting milk, a loaf of bread, some vegetables and frozen meat, he tried to keep a low profile. He wasn't ready to talk to people yet. He wondered if anyone had seen him being taken away by the police. Very little escaped notice in this small community.

'Hello, Norman. I thought it was you.' Smith turned round to see an elderly man for whom he'd recently repaired a garden shed. He was a gossipy old character and the last person Smith wished to see. 'I didn't expect to see you here at this time. Aren't you working today?'

'Yes, I am,' replied Smith. 'Just on a dinner break as it happens and got to get back . . . Nice to see you, but I'm sorry, I must be off.'

With that he turned and went straight to the checkout and escaped further conversation. As he hurried home, he reflected again upon his situation. Did the police believe his story about discovering Scholes' body at the brewery? He knew they were sceptical and if that was the case, it was likely that he would remain a suspect and they would come for him again soon. There really did seem to be no escape from the curse of Brendan Scholes.

~

Late in the day, when the work was about to finish, an unexpected person appeared at the Ewe's Ales Brewery. Tony Handley walked slowly through the gates that he had recently defaced and stood sheepishly by the big door of the works entrance. He tried to summon up the courage to knock, but before he could do it, he was spotted by some of the female workers in the yard.

'What the hell are you doing here?' said one. 'Have you got your paint with you to splatter some more disgusting slogans on the walls?' This was Paula, whom Janice had called into the office.

'No . . . I . . . I've come to say sorry.'

The women regarded him curiously. 'Are you serious?' said one.

'Yes, I am. I'm sorry I put all that . . . that stuff on the gates. And I'm particularly sorry that it said nasty stuff about your bosses.'

'Right, OK, then. Are you scared of us, now that we've shown you we're capable of fighting back?'

'No. It's my wife. She's made me realise that . . . that kind of attitude is wrong.'

The women had gathered around him and some of them jeered at this. He felt very uncomfortable.

'I'm glad there's a woman who's made you change your mind. You should carry on doing what she says. She sounds like a sensible person.'

He looked around the group but was too embarrassed to maintain eye contact with any of them.

'So have you managed to clean your walls and your door yet?'

'I've had a go,' he said.

'I bet you have. She's made you, hasn't she?'

It was intensely humiliating. He had to control himself. If he got angry it would only make matters worse. 'Yeah . . . well, I'll be off then.' He started to walk away in the direction of the gate.

'That's it, there he goes with his tail between his legs,' called a mocking voice. 'Back to report to his wife; tell her you've been a good boy and done as she said.'

Raucous laughter broke out at this, and Handley's cheeks reddened as he exited the gate with some relief. It turned out that women were not the soft target he'd thought they were.

'If you do anything like that again, we'll rip your balls off,' one woman called out to more laughter from her workmates.

Janice Anderson had been watching this encounter from her office window, which looked on to the yard. She decided not to intervene and to let the others deal with it. It appeared that Handley had come to make peace. He wasn't being aggressive; on the contrary, his body language was cowed and defensive. She smiled as she heard the women laughing and saw him beat a hasty retreat. As she'd said to Emily, it was important that the message went out that they were strong and not intimidated by any acts of hostility towards them.

⁓

That evening, Andy and Steph sat out on their terrace overlooking the River Aire. It was the first time in the year they had been able to do this, but a warm April evening had enticed them out. They were enjoying a glass of wine together.

Steph told Andy about her father's call. 'It still unsettles me when I speak to him.'

Andy sipped his wine. 'I suppose it always will, to some extent. There's too much unpleasant history there and so many years when he was completely out of your lives for you ever to be entirely comfortable with him.'

'I suppose you're right, but I think if he continues to behave as he has since we met up again, things could settle down into a reasonable pattern.'

'I don't see why not. By the way, what does your mum think about it?'

'I haven't told her about tomorrow. She's left it to Lisa and me to decide what to do about seeing Dad. I don't think she wants to make contact with him, and he's never said that he wants to see her again.'

'That's understandable. Their relationship is – what do the lawyers say? – "irretrievably broken". I doubt if they could face each other ever again after the things you've told me happened.'

'You're right.' Steph took a sip of her wine and looked over to the other side of the river where people were sitting outside at bars and restaurants. It was turning into a lovely evening that brought a foretaste of summer. 'That's why I think it's so generous of her to allow us to contact him. It can't be something she ever wanted. She must cringe at the prospect of her daughters seeing the man who made her life a misery for so long.'

'Maybe she does, but she probably thinks it's better for you to repair your relationship with your father. She must worry that what happened left its mark on you and Lisa.'

Steph cocked her head to one side and looked at him. 'What a sensitive soul you've become,' she said.

'What do you mean "become"? I've always been like this.'

'Maybe, but you were more of a "lad" when I first met you and still under Jason's influence.'

Andy smiled at her. 'Well, you've brought out the best in me. And I'm getting old now. Wisdom comes with age.'

'Aw, what a flatterer!' She laughed, finished her wine and got up. 'Let's go in and eat, I'm starving.'

'Me too.'

'By the way, what are you going to do tomorrow when I'm seeing Dad?'

'I thought I might go out and get roaring drunk. Who says I'm not still under Jason's influence?'

'You wouldn't dare!' she said, and Andy laughed.

'Anyway,' he said, 'there's something I wanted to ask you about.' He explained about the possibility of moving for promotion. 'I didn't mention it before, because I've never been looking seriously, but when the boss said how we were both capable of going up to the next level, it made me think. You know, if he thinks we're good enough, then, well . . . The thing is I just enjoy working with him so much.'

Steph nodded. 'I know, but if it's what you want, you should go for it. You'd definitely be in with a chance. Think of the reference you'd get from the boss and how seriously that would be taken.'

'I know.' He looked at her. 'Have you considered promotion yourself?'

She shook her head. 'Not really. Maybe I ought to, but I'm even more settled in Harrogate than you. I've been there since I left school. I suppose the boss is right – we shouldn't get too stuck in our ways, but it's difficult. I think you have to do it for yourself and not because he's encouraging you.'

'You're right, good advice. I'm going to leave it for a while and see how I feel.'

They quietly enjoyed the clear evening as the stars came out.

～

Back in Harrogate, Oldroyd's sister Alison had been invited round for a meal. Deborah had made a meat-free lasagne as both she and Alison were vegetarian. Oldroyd, who wasn't, was nevertheless happy to eat the same food at these family meals (his daughter, Louise, was also vegetarian), because he enjoyed the social occasions so much. He'd spent too much time alone when he'd separated from his wife, and his son and daughter were away at university.

'Well, how's the parish?' asked Oldroyd as they ate their lasagne, which was accompanied by a mixed leaf salad, crusty bread, and a nice red wine.

He always like to hear what was happening in her traditional rural parish. He felt quite nostalgic about it. He and his sister had attended church on and off when they were young near where they lived on the other side of Harrogate. After her rebellious teenage years, Alison had studied theology and had been one of the first women to be ordained when the Anglican Church started to accept women as priests.

'It's very much as normal, Jim,' replied Alison. 'By the way, this is very good, Deborah, you've got such a variety of flavours in here.'

'Very kind of you to say so,' replied Deborah with a smile.

'Yes,' continued Alison. 'Well, not much changes in Kirby Underside. But of course that's what a lot of people like about it.'

'But not you?' asked Deborah.

'No. I've always believed that the Church might have at its core an eternal message, but many things in society – attitudes, norms, cultural values and so on – change and the Church has to change too or it becomes strange and moribund.' Alison paused and picked up her glass. 'But I think I'm coming round to the idea that it's time for me to retire.'

'I'm glad to hear that,' said Oldroyd. 'I've been encouraging you to do it for some time.'

'I know. I'm getting tired of the place and it's all a bit too easy. I could just carry on there for I don't know how many more years. I don't think anyone in authority would try to get rid of me.'

They certainly wouldn't, thought Oldroyd. His sister was a formidable presence in the diocese, and he believed the hierarchy of bishops and archdeacons was scared of her. If she'd been born some years later, she could have been a bishop herself, but she was a little too old for that now.

'I need a new challenge, though I don't know exactly what that might be yet. I'm working on a few ideas.'

'I'm sure they'll miss you in Kirby,' said Deborah.

'Maybe, but it will be good for them, too, to have a new person. They could do with someone young who would stir them up a bit.'

'You've done plenty of that, I'm sure, especially on social justice issues,' said Oldroyd with a laugh. 'I think one or two won't be too sorry to see you go.'

'You may well be right, Jim.' She turned to Deborah. 'Anyway, how's the house hunt going?'

Deborah rolled her eyes. 'Not too bad . . . when I can get him to show some interest.' She pointed at Oldroyd, who covered his face with his hands. 'We've been to see one and we've got a viewing tomorrow. They're outside Harrogate; we fancy a move to a village. And I'm really keen to get back to gardening. I had a good plot in our family house before I split up with Roger. It's getting the balance between a property that needs too much doing to it and one which has had everything done but not to your taste.'

Alison nodded. 'Yes, I can see the problems, all of them,' she said as she turned to her brother. 'You've got to pull your weight, you lazy oaf. Don't leave it all to Deborah.'

Oldroyd laughed. 'I know, but it's really not my thing and I'm occupied with this brewery case.'

Alison turned back to Deborah. 'There's always been an annoying part of him, you know. He could be a bit of a brat when we were small.'

'Who, me?' said Oldroyd with mock surprise.

'Yes, you used to make a nuisance of yourself when my friends came round; hiding and jumping out to scare them. You once got the hose pipe out and sprayed Carol with water as she was leaving. She was soaked.'

'I don't remember that,' said Oldroyd, the impish look on his face suggesting that he recalled it very well.

'In the end, Mum banned you from the house when my friends were there.'

'She did,' admitted Oldroyd and he reflected that sibling relations can ebb and flow, and are not always easy. He was so happy that he and Alison had become close as adults. It didn't always happen, as with Richard and Emily Foster and, seemingly, the Scholes brothers as well.

'Anyway, how's the case going?' asked Alison.

'We're a bit stuck. The theory at the moment is that the first victim was killed by his brother. We found the missing recipe and that could have been the motive. But there are a number of things that don't stack up.'

'I see. One brother killing the other; that's a terrible thing. And you say it could have been over this recipe for beer?'

'Yes.'

'I wonder if they'd been close at one time. Was there a big difference in age?'

'No, not much more than a year between them and they . . .'

'I ask because sometimes there's a history of bullying between siblings which can have bad repercussions in later life and . . . Jim? Are you listening?'

'Whoops!' said Deborah. 'The cogs are moving in the old brain, I think. He's oblivious of everything when this happens.'

'I know.'

Oldroyd shook his head. 'Sorry, it's just that something made me think, then. It's a bit of a wild idea, but I'll have to look into it when I get back to work.'

'That's not tomorrow or Sunday, remember, unless there's an emergency. You promised to take time off so we can visit this house tomorrow after the parkrun and then do some walking on Sunday.'

'Yes, that's fine. I'm looking forward to it.'

'Good.'

'The walk, I mean.'

'Jim!' exclaimed Deborah, and Alison laughed.

Five

The York Brewery is a relative newcomer to the brewing scene, but its beers are widely distributed around Yorkshire and Lancashire and the brewery owns pubs in York. One of its most popular beers is Minster Ale, a fruity and hoppy bitter. The name suggests a link between brewing and the church in the ancient city. The coopers, who made the wooden beer barrels, took part in the city's medieval mystery plays alongside other craft guilds. Traditionally they played a scene called the Fall of Man, something which was probably regularly acted out in a non-religious context in the city's taverns!

'I hear we had a visitor at work yesterday afternoon,' said Emily Foster. She and Janice had finished breakfast and were doing some housework – part of their Saturday morning routine. Emily would have liked to employ a cleaner, but her partner said it was a waste of money when there were two of them.

Janice was kneeling on the kitchen floor, wiping it over with a floorcloth, while Emily was cleaning the sink. 'Oh yes,' she said. 'I forgot to tell you. Can you believe it? That neanderthal Handley came to apologise for graffitiing the gates and insulting us.'

'I wonder why?'

'The women who met him near the gate said he mentioned his wife. It seems she made him come to apologise and he's afraid of her.'

Emily laughed. 'Would you believe it? So, you were right; it was him.'

'It was. He admitted it. Some of these men have a complicated and weird view of women, don't they? They think most women can be targeted for a bit of misogyny but there's often one – wife, mother – who they're afraid of or idealise.' She wrung the floorcloth into a bucket. 'I don't pretend to understand it, but I think we were right to show that we can stand up for ourselves.'

'Yes,' replied Emily, who was still a bit uneasy about it all. 'Anyway, what's the plan for today?'

'I've got to pop down to Ripon to collect my new sunglasses. After that why don't we go and watch the cricket? It's their first match of the season against North Tanfield. They've lost Barry Green and that must have been a terrible shock. I think they need all the support they can get. Also, it doesn't do our profile any harm as a local business supporting community activities.'

'That's a good idea.' Emily swilled the sink and then polished the taps. 'Well, I'm going to go round to see my brother when we've finished here.'

'Really?'

'Yes. Now that I think we've put this banners and graffiti business behind us, it's time to make peace and see if the two businesses can get on together amicably.'

'Are you sure he'll be receptive to your overtures?' There was an edge of sarcasm to Janice's voice.

'I think so. He wasn't supportive of me having a role at the Yoredale, but I think he accepts us now as a business concern, except it's more competition for them, I suppose.'

'But does he approve of us, of our relationship?'

Emily was surprised; Janice hadn't raised this question before. 'Richard? I haven't talked to him about it, but I've never felt any hostility from him about us. Have you?'

Janice shrugged. 'I don't suppose so. We've not spent a great deal of time with him, have we? Him and that wet wife of his.'

'Christine? She's OK.'

'She's so suburban, in her tasteless, perfectly ordered house with her two children and business-owning husband.'

'Hey!' laughed Emily. 'Who's being intolerant now? Just because she's more conventional than us.'

Janice held up her hands. 'OK, I plead guilty. Anyway, I'll probably grab something to eat in Ripon, so I'll meet you at the cricket ground about two thirty. I think it starts then.'

'Sure, I'll see you there.'

～

Oldroyd and Deborah were travelling out to view their latest property of interest in another village near to Harrogate. They were a little behind time, as it had been a busy morning after a relatively late night with Alison. They had completed the Harrogate parkrun, eaten a hasty brunch, gone back home to shower and change and made it out to the viewing just in time. Oldroyd had complained about the tight schedule, but this was the only slot available for the day and Deborah was determined to press on with their plans to move.

Oldroyd drove the old Saab nippily through the country lanes outside Harrogate past more clumps of daffodils in many of the roadside verges. Rounding a corner, they saw the sign that they were entering the village.

'Well, it hasn't been a long drive from Harrogate, has it, Jim? You wouldn't have a long commute from here.' She looked at the map on her phone.

'No,' replied Oldroyd. 'Is that it there? There's a man who looks like an estate agent standing outside.'

'Yes, it must be. You can just park on the roadside here.' She pointed to a parking space.

The agent, looking nearly identical to the one at the last property in his smart suit, greeted them and almost immediately launched into his sales description of the property.

'As you can see, the house occupies a particularly generous level plot with no steep steps up to the door and with the advantage of a double garage and electric doors. My parents have doors like these. They find them very convenient, especially since my dad started getting arthritis in his shoulders.' He gave them a big smile and pointed a remote at the doors.

Deborah and Jim exchanged a meaningful glance and Deborah suppressed a giggle.

As the noisy demonstration of the electric doors progressed, Jim whispered in Deborah's ear, 'Bloody hell, how old does he think we are? He'll be suggesting we look at a bungalow next or order a stair lift.'

'OK, let's move into the house now,' continued the agent. 'The hall is very spacious and on your left is a stunning open-plan kitchen . . .'

He carried on with his patter and didn't seem to notice that Jim and Deborah were sniggering like schoolchildren behind him.

'Well,' said Deborah, once she'd regained her composure, 'the kitchen is very large, and I love the bifold doors.'

'The what?' asked Jim.

'They're doors that concertina when you open them and bring the outside in; the garden and the kitchen become one room – great for entertaining and the kitchen is flooded with light.' She winked at Oldroyd and the estate agent looked impressed.

'The kitchen units are German,' said the estate agent, 'and flat-panelled, as you can see. Very minimalist, with integrated smart appliances. All Miele. No cheap brands. The sink has a boiling water tap and waste disposal unit.'

'Very sleek,' said Deborah. 'And no handles to interrupt the streamlined flow. What do you think, Jim?'

Oldroyd didn't seem to notice the irony in her tone.

'I think it's a bit clinical with white cupboards and white work-tops. There's nothing left out on top, not even a kettle.'

'No need for a kettle,' said the estate agent. 'As I say, the sink has a top of the range boiling tap.'

Oldroyd wasn't impressed.

Deborah, who was trying out one of the island stools, pointed to the large induction hob on the other side.

'Look at this, Jim – very green, and so easy to clean.'

'Where's the extractor fan?' asked Oldroyd.

'Built into the hob, sir; everything is sucked down through the grille in the centre.'

'Is it indeed?' said Oldroyd, his tone sceptical.

They moved on to view the office/snug, utility room and downstairs toilet, and then into a very large living room with white walls, more floor to ceiling bifold doors, grey shelving with cleverly arranged objets d'art. For a moment Oldroyd thought he saw a real fire in some kind of stove. The agent saw him looking.

'That's a biofuel fire, sir. No flue needed – it's smoke free.'

'Good Lord.' Oldroyd felt dazzled by the new technology but he didn't really like the room.

'No chimney breast,' he remarked. 'I do like a chimney breast. It makes a living room more cosy.'

'It's the modern style, sir,' responded the agent.

'Mmm,' said Deborah. She was not liking the house either but decided to reserve her judgement so as not to influence him. 'Let's have a look upstairs, shall we?'

185

On the tour of the en-suite bedrooms and highly technical monochrome bathroom, the agent continued to wax lyrical about the hi-tech specifications.

At the end of the viewing, they thanked the estate agent for his time and made their way across the grey block-paved drive to the car.

'The garden's very low maintenance, Jim, virtually all lawn. We could get one of those sit-on mowers.'

'What? I'm surprised by how much you like this place,' said Oldroyd. 'You've always admired older properties with quirky features and character.'

'Of course I don't like it, Jim. I'm being sarcastic.'

'Phew, that's a relief because I prefer the last one.'

'Really? The doer-upper?'

'Well, more ideal would be a house like this one, in that it's already been done up, is close to a good pub and within our price range,' laughed Oldroyd. 'That shouldn't be too difficult to find. By the way, you're in a very ironic mood today.'

'I know,' she said, smiling. 'These agents amuse me. Anyway, that wasn't too difficult, was it? You were trying much harder to concentrate there. Come on, let's try out the quaint village pub.'

'Oh, good,' replied Oldroyd, looking forward to his drink.

∽

It was a subdued start to Saturday at the Foster household. Richard had persuaded Christine to go to bed early on the Friday evening and told the children when they returned that she was not well. She was now having a lie-in, as were Phoebe and Tim, it being Saturday and not a school day.

Foster sat by himself in the kitchen eating toast and drinking tea mechanically without really tasting anything. He was looking out of the window at the pleasant weather, but it hardly registered. He was reflecting on the traumatic revelations of the evening before. The consequences of his gambling had had such a damaging effect on Christine, and she'd kept it secret for months. It made him feel guilty and added to the wave of terrible things that had recently happened. He was worn out and didn't know how much more he could take. He was leaning over the table with his head in his hands when Phoebe, who was fifteen, came into the kitchen in her dressing gown.

'Dad? Are you OK?'

Foster sat up. 'Yes, a bit tired; didn't sleep well last night.'

She got a bowl from the cupboard and poured some cereal into it. 'How's Mum?'

'Still asleep. I'm going to take her some tea in a minute. She'll be OK. Just a bit of a cold, I think.'

Phoebe poured milk on to her cereal. 'Jo and Phil are coming round later. We're going to do some gaming.'

Jo and Phil were a brother and sister around the same age as Phoebe and Tim. Normally Foster might have tut-tutted a bit about them staying in the house on a nice day, but today it was very convenient that they were occupied.

'That's good. If Tim gets up in time.'

'He will. I'm going to drag him out of bed when I've eaten this. They're coming at half ten.'

'OK. I'm going out and Mum will be resting. You can make sandwiches for your lunch, can't you?'

'Yeah, no problem.'

Foster made a cup of tea and took it upstairs. Christine was still under the covers, but she was awake. He put the tea on her bedside table. She sat up, looking bleary-eyed.

'Thanks. Was that Phoebe you were talking to?'

'Yes.' He explained about the children's plans. 'Look, it's a nice day and the first cricket match of the season down at the ground. Why don't we go over this afternoon and watch it? It'll get us out of the house and the kids'll be all right here.' They both enjoyed watching cricket and were regular spectators at the Markham club.

'Oh, that's a good idea. I'd forgotten about it. I haven't been able to think about anything except . . . you know.'

'Right. Well, this will take your mind off things.'

Christine seemed to be somewhat energised by this prospect and she got out of bed. 'I said I'd go round to see Mary this morning. She's a gambling widow, too.'

It was her first attempt at humour and Foster smiled with relief. 'Good. Only coffee to drink, though,' he said good-humouredly.

'I know, and no betting on the cricket match.'

'Touché!' He took her in his arms. 'Don't worry, I'll help you through this and we'll both get the support we need. I'm going to pop down to the works to see if everything is OK. We've got a firm in doing some repairs to the boiler while we're not brewing. Why don't you call into that deli in the marketplace, pick up some food, and we'll have a little picnic down at the ground?'

She smiled at him. 'OK. I will.'

∾

Philip Welbeck arrived at the Markham Cricket Club at ten o'clock. It was a fine day and reasonably warm; the ideal weather for the first match of the season. It was his job as captain to unlock the clubhouse, make sure all the kit was ready and check that the pitch was in a good condition for the game. He looked out over the green expanse of the turf to the river on the left and to the old houses on the right above the water. The prospect of the game in such a lovely setting excited him. He'd been missing it all winter.

An elderly man in a flat cap, corduroy trousers and wellington boots appeared; this was Alf, who acted as an unofficial grounds-man for the club.

'Mornin', Philip. It's a good day for it.'

'Aye, it is, Alf. Can you get the roller on the wicket? I'm going to go round the boundary with the whitener and then I'll leave you to do the crease when you've finished rolling.'

'Right you are,' said Alf, and went to start up the small sit-on roller that the club owned. Welbeck opened a tin of whitener, took a paint brush and spent a pleasant hour etching in the boundary where the white marks had faded. After this he returned to the clubhouse and went through the equipment: bats, pads, wickets, balls. Players were expected to bring their own shirts and shoes. Everything was very clean and fresh for the new season.

At half past twelve, he and Alf sat down in the small stand, and ate the sandwiches they had brought with them. Shortly after this John and Miriam Evans arrived and unloaded boxes from their car. John and Miriam were a couple who volunteered to work in the kitchen on match days, preparing the sandwiches, pork pies, cakes, teas and coffees which were eaten by both teams in the interval between innings. Welbeck welcomed them with a smile. Everything was going well. His last job was to check that everything was working with the scoreboard and that the scorer was in position.

At half past one, players from both teams started to arrive and there was much good-humoured banter between the sides. Spectators began to fill up the benches around the boundary. When the umpires got to the ground, Welbeck went with the North Tanfield captain to the coin toss, which he won. He then went into the home changing room to rally the team.

'Right, lads, we've won the toss, so we're batting. Terry and Pete, get padded up. Ian, you're in at number three so get your pads on, too.'

189

'OK, skipper.' The team were all smiles and jokes. It was clear that they were looking forward to the new season too. Morale was very high and if they could beat North Tanfield today, they would be off to a great start. Welbeck was glad to see that recent events didn't seem to be affecting the players' mood, while, outside, the spectators seemed animated and excited at the prospect of the first match of the season.

~

Christine Foster had gone to visit her friend and Richard was just about to leave for the brewery when, much to his surprise, his sister Emily arrived.

'Is this a good time to have a little chat, Richard?' A glance at his face told her that it probably wasn't.

'Well, come in,' he replied. 'Let's go in here.' He led her inside a small sitting room behind the kitchen. She could hear the electronic sounds of gaming coming from upstairs. They both sat down.

'Kids having a good time, then?' She smiled.

'Yes, they've got their friends over.' He looked tired and stressed.

'What's the matter, Richard? I wanted to talk about all this graffiti business, you know, and clear the air a bit, but you don't seem very well.'

He sighed and closed his eyes for a moment. 'No, there's a lot going on at the moment, and I don't just mean these terrible murders.'

'Oh?'

'Yes. Look, I appreciate you coming round, but I can't go into details at the moment. As far as the things that have been said about Ewe's Ales Brewery and about you and Janice go, I'm very sorry. It was nothing to do with me. I think the person who graffitied the gates has been outed so hopefully we'll have no more of that.'

'Thanks, Richard. But can I help at all?'

Foster shook his head. 'Chris and I have to work it out.'

'Oh! You're not splitting up, are you?'

'No, we need one another more than ever.' He looked at her. 'Don't say anything to anybody and the kids don't know what's going on, but, basically, I've got a gambling problem and, mainly because of the anxiety that caused her, Chris has turned to drink and it's serious.'

Emily put her hand to her mouth. 'Richard, I had no idea!'

'Of course you didn't. Addicts keep their habit secret.' He paused. 'It's all my fault. I drove her to it.' Suddenly there were tears in his eyes. 'I feel so guilty.'

Emily reached over and put her hand on his shoulder. 'Don't despair; you two can work through it, Richard. And I'm here if you need help.'

He took her hand. 'Thanks. I can't tell you any more just now, I haven't got the energy and there isn't time. I've got to make a quick trip to the brewery.'

'No, that's fine. I'm glad you've told me what you have. It puts everything else into perspective, doesn't it?'

'Yes.'

'I won't stay long, but let me get you a drink.'

As she went into the kitchen to make coffee, Phoebe was there, getting some cans out of the fridge.

'Hi, Auntie Emily! Haven't seen you for ages. How come you're here?'

'Just popped round to visit your dad. How are you and Tim?'

'Great, thanks! See you!' And off she went back to the gaming session, leaving her aunt smiling. Emily returned with the coffee.

'Janice and I are going to watch the cricket this afternoon. You could come with us.'

'Thanks. Actually, Chris and I have already decided to go, so we'll see you down there,' said Richard, sipping his coffee.

'Good – and don't worry, I won't say a thing to anybody, not even Janice.'

He gave her a wan smile. 'Thanks for coming round.'

At two thirty, prompt, the umpires in their long white jackets and black trousers walked out slowly on to the pitch, followed by the North Tanfield team, who were fielding. Shortly after this, the Markham opening batsmen left the clubhouse and headed for the crease, to the applause of the home supporters. The rest of the Markham side looked on from the benches outside the clubhouse.

The weather had remained fine and now the benches were nearly full with a really good crowd to watch the opening match. Some people had brought picnic chairs, which they placed just outside the boundary, while others lounged on rugs and opened plastic boxes of food and Thermos flasks of tea for refreshment. Welbeck was doing a final walk around the ground to check that everything was OK before the match started. Bert Duffield, who played for Markham when he was younger and was now a regular supporter, came over to him.

'Well, you lads give 'em some stick, then. Philip, we're right behind thi. If there's one team we always like to beat it's North Tanfield; always been our bitter rivals. Ah suppose it's because they're so close. Anyway, best o' luck.'

'Thanks, Bert,' said Welbeck, smiling, and he continued his circuit of the ground.

Emily Foster had finished off the housework when she got back from her brother's house, eaten a sandwich for lunch and then set straight off to the cricket ground. She arrived just as play began and managed to find one of the few remaining bench seats. She looked around but couldn't see Janice or her brother and his wife.

The first few overs passed with little drama. The openers were playing themselves in and opting for mostly defensive shots, although one of them struck a handsome cover drive for four.

~

Richard Foster had been detained longer than he'd expected at the brewery. One of the plumbers had explained in great detail about a problem they were having, and what they intended to do about it. The technical details were unintelligible to Foster, and he found himself saying 'yes' repeatedly as the man droned on. All Foster wanted was for the problem to be fixed.

He then had to walk quickly down to see the match, hoping he hadn't missed the start. By the market square, there was a narrow ginnel with steps down to the river and the cricket ground. He could hear the famous sound of the smack of willow on leather and realised that the game had begun. He quickened his pace and reached the bottom of the steps.

He was very near the ground, but couldn't yet see it beyond the trees and bushes, when a figure came up behind him and swiftly placed a ligature round his neck. As he was dragged down, he managed to produce a strangulated cry, loud enough to be heard by the nearest spectators.

At this point, the attacker pulled off the ligature and ran up the steps back towards Markham before anyone appeared to help. Two people quickly arrived to find Foster gasping for breath. Putting his arms around their shoulders, they helped him to the clubhouse, where they were met by Philip Welbeck.

'Richard? What's happened?'

'Someone just attacked me! They tried to strangle me!' Foster sat down in the kitchen and was given a glass of water. He coughed, then felt at his neck and shivered with the shock. Welbeck sat to the side of him.

'Are you OK? Where was this?'

'Just coming down from the square. I managed to cry out and then I think they went back up the steps. I heard their footsteps on the stone. They must have been worried that someone had heard me.'

'Bloody hell!' exclaimed Welbeck. 'I'm going to call the police. Do you want us to stop the game? What about an ambulance?'

'No. I'm alright. They hardly got the thing round my neck before they ran off. And don't stop the game. I don't want to spoil things. I'm OK.'

Welbeck saw that he was still shaking. 'OK, we'll carry on playing, but I'm calling an ambulance as a precaution. You've had a terrible shock and you need to be checked out.'

'OK,' said Foster. 'Look, my wife, my sister and her partner will be here in the ground somewhere. We were going to meet up. I'll text Christine.'

'Can you manage that?'

'Yes,' replied Foster, whose hand nevertheless trembled as he tried to use his phone.

'Right,' continued Welbeck, 'I'll go and see if they're here after I've made the calls.'

A number of the players were coming to the kitchen door, puzzled at what was going on. Welbeck assured them that it was nothing serious and encouraged them to go back to watching the cricket. He didn't want the news to spread. If it did, everyone would be distracted from the game, and they might as well abandon it.

He called the police and ambulance, then went back outside. He scanned the ground but at first could see no one from Foster's family present. Then he saw Emily walk behind some seated spectators and sit down on a bench. Had she just arrived?

At that moment one of Markham's openers was clean bowled after a good innings and walked back to the clubhouse to be greeted with applause. Welbeck hardly noticed as he made his way around the ground to Emily and explained to her what had happened. They both hurried back to find Foster still sitting in the kitchen looking dazed and waiting for the ambulance.

'Richard!' exclaimed Emily. 'What on earth's happened?' She sat down by him.

'Someone tried to strangle me.'

'Strangle you! Where?'

'At the bottom of the steps from the square.'

Emily glanced at the silent and shocked faces of people watching. 'But . . . why?'

Foster shrugged. 'I don't know and I'm sick of it all. I don't know what else can happen around here. It's a nightmare.' He put his head on Emily's shoulder and started to cry.

At that moment, Christine rushed into the room. 'Richard? What's going on? I've only just got your message. I was driving.'

'He's been attacked,' said Welbeck. 'He's OK, but I've called an ambulance as a precaution.'

'Oh my God!' She sat at the other side of him.

As Foster had his wife and sister to look after him, Welbeck decided he could return to the game. He found that Markham had undergone a mini batting collapse and that he was due to bat next, so he hastily put on his pads.

DC Jeffries and a colleague arrived in a police car from Ripon and came into the clubhouse. Welbeck, who was now padded up, asked permission for the game to continue and Jeffries agreed.

There was no point in disappointing and alarming people as the crime was nothing to do with the match. Jeffries then spoke to Foster, who described what had happened.

'Did you get a view of the assailant? Would you recognise them again?' asked Jeffries.

'No, they came from behind me. It was all over too quick. I didn't even see them run off. I was too busy gasping for breath.'

'They didn't say anything?'

'No.'

'Did they try to rob you?'

'No, they just put some kind of band round my neck and tightened it. It was terrifying.'

From outside came the incongruously pleasant sounds of bats striking balls and spatters of applause. Jeffries paused. Was this anything to do with the other two murders or just an attempted mugging? It seemed unlikely to be the latter unless the sleepy country town of Markham had suddenly become full of violent people.

'Do you have any idea who might want to attack you?' he asked.

Foster shook his head. 'No, but it seems everything in this town is going mad, so I'm not surprised.' He looked completely exhausted.

At this point the ambulance arrived, provoking some curious glances from both players and spectators. It drew up at the rear of the clubhouse, and Foster got in with Christine.

Emily saw them off before texting Janice to see where she was. She left a message to meet by the clubhouse, and then sat down on the grass, lost in her thoughts and barely watching the game.

After a brief examination of the crime scene, which yielded nothing, Jeffries arranged for a local PC to come to the ground and stay until the match was over in case the attacker reappeared. There would be an announcement at the end of the game explaining what had happened and asking people to take care if they were walking home and not to go alone. Jeffries wondered whether he should immediately inform DCI Oldroyd about the day's events. In the end he decided that, as no one had been seriously injured, he would investigate the attack himself and not disturb the DCI when he was off duty at the weekend. He could do another search of the crime scene and ask around in the town to see if anyone had seen anything suspicious. He could also organise some statement taking. He smiled to himself; DCI Oldroyd would be pleased with that.

Back at the cricket ground, Emily was still waiting for Janice to arrive from Ripon. The Markham innings were nearly over when she finally saw her partner's car turn into the car park.

Janice came running to the clubhouse. 'I've only just seen your message,' she said. 'I was driving. What's happened?'

'Richard's been attacked. Someone tried to strangle him, over there in the bushes at the bottom of the steps.' She pointed to the spot.

'What? You're not serious?'

'I am, he's gone with Christine in the ambulance to the hospital.' Emily looked at Janice questioningly. 'What took you so long?'

Janice shook her head. 'Oh, I got delayed in traffic. But that's awful! Poor Richard.'

'Yes, well, I'm sure he'll be OK. Let's get a seat. It's nearly the interval between innings.'

'Are you sure you want to stay after what's happened? I don't mind if you want to go home.'

'No, I'd like to see the rest. I think we'll get a good score and hopefully we can bowl them out for less. I can tell Richard about it later. I feel so sorry for him. He must wonder what's going to happen next.'

'Don't we all?' added Janice.

They watched the rest of the match, which Markham narrowly won by eight runs. It was a thrilling finish culminating in cheers and applause for the Markham side as they walked off the pitch smiling and laughing, followed by the disappointed batsmen.

But though she enjoyed the cricket, Emily felt strangely anxious for the rest of the afternoon about her brother and other things.

~

Saturday was also Pam Handley's day for cleaning. She worked full-time as a carer, and usually ended up doing all the housework as well. She frowned as she vacuumed the living room. As usual she got very little help from that stupid husband of hers. Their two daughters had helped when they were around, but they were now living with their partners in Leeds and Harrogate.

Where was he now? After lunch she'd asked him to clean the filters in the dishwasher. He said he would, but he just had to pop out for a minute. That was about three hours ago. She shook her head. He always had time to tinker with his car. He'd be in the pub now drinking with his mates, unless they were ostracising him over this graffiti business. She hoped they were. At least he had gone round to the Ewe's brewery to apologise.

It was nearly four o'clock before she heard him come in. She was sitting in the living room with a magazine and a cup of tea. He put his head round the door and grinned sheepishly.

'Hi, love. Sorry I've been so long. I just went for a quick drink and some of the lads were going down to watch the cricket, so I went with them.'

She carried on reading and didn't look up at him. 'Very nice. Didn't you have your phone with you? You know, send me a message, tell me where you are?'

He put his hand to his head, rather too dramatically. 'Oh no, I forgot it!'

Now she looked at him sharply. 'More likely you daren't send me a message, you big, useless oaf. I don't know how I put up with you.'

Handley chuckled nervously. 'I'll just get those filters out, then, love.'

'Yes, and not before time! After that you can clean the toilet and bathroom. And make sure you do it properly!' She rustled her magazine and returned to reading it.

～

Foster's visit to the hospital was brief. He had no serious injuries and was told to rest at home to recover from the shock. A friend came to collect him and Christine and dropped them back in Markham. Christine had arranged for Phoebe and Tim to go to their friends' house for a while.

Foster collapsed on to the sofa while his wife made cups of tea.

'Have you any idea who it could have been?' she asked when she returned and sat next to him.

Foster sipped his tea. At least his hand had stopped shaking. 'The police asked me the same question, but I couldn't think of anyone at the time. Now, however, I just wonder about that idiot Tony Handley.'

'Why?'

'Over this graffiti business. I told the police I thought it was Handley and they interviewed him. Maybe he found out somehow that I'd told them, and he was out to get revenge on me.'

'But how? And would he have tried to kill you?'

Foster shrugged. 'I don't know. I doubt it, really, but we've had two shocking murders and it makes you wonder what's going to happen next. I wouldn't be surprised by anything now.'

'I know and that's without our own problems.' She put her hand on his leg. 'Look, you'll have to stay off work for a couple of days to recover from this. You were under a lot of stress even before it happened. Call the police and talk it through with them.'

'OK.'

'I'll be here and, as you said, we can begin to support each other with our problems. I feel much more positive about things now.'

He nodded. 'It sounds good.' He looked at her and decided he should tell her about his sister's visit. 'By the way, Emily called round this morning. She really wants us to get on together. I told her a bit about our difficulties. I think it's good if someone else knows and can help us. She won't tell anyone, not even Janice.'

Christine nodded. 'That's OK. I've always liked Emily. It would be nice if we were all able to be together as a family again. I've felt for a while that you didn't want to have much to do with it because of this brewery thing.'

'You're right. But I'm determined to change that, too. I want some good to come out of all this.'

~

At eight o'clock that evening, Steph walked into the Cafe Nico in the centre of Leeds. It was a large, spacious cafe with lots of alcoves and side rooms. She looked around to see if her father had arrived. She always felt rather nervous when she was meeting him. She soon found him sitting alone at a table near to the door. His clothes were shabby, and he looked tired.

'Hi,' she said, and he smiled as he got up to greet her. There was no physical contact; things still seemed too awkward for that.

'Lovely to see you,' he said. 'Sit down. What can I get you to drink?'

'I'll have an americano with warm milk, please.'

He went to the counter, leaving Steph wondering what they might talk about. In the two meetings she and Lisa had had with him, the distant past when they were young girls had not been mentioned. He was chiefly interested in how they were doing now in their jobs and relationships. She was not sure she could talk about those days before he left. He returned with her drink and sat down. He was drinking a black espresso.

'I . . .' he began and then stopped. His hands were shaking, and he couldn't look at her. 'I thought maybe we could talk a bit about what happened when you were little – you know, clear the air a bit. It seems like it's become the elephant in the room.'

Steph took a deep breath and felt herself go hot. 'OK, but it won't be easy.'

He took a sip of his coffee. 'No, that's why I've come now and just to see you alone. It's easier to talk to only one of you and Lisa's younger; she won't remember those days as well as you.'

'OK,' repeated Steph. She couldn't think of anything else to say.

He paused, and nervously took another drink. 'What I want to say is how sorry I am for how I behaved, especially towards your mum. And I want to explain what was going on – not to excuse myself but so you can understand a bit more about why it happened.'

Steph sipped her coffee without registering the flavour and felt knotted up inside. It was hard to concentrate and part of her wanted to say 'No!' and rush out of the cafe.

'I was an alcoholic.' He shook his head. 'No, I am an alcoholic; it's always possible to slip back. It started when I went out with the blokes after work. It was sort of competitive; you had to prove you could take your beer. I went out once or twice a week, then it became every evening and then for longer. In the end, most evenings I was coming home drunk late after you and Lisa had gone to bed.'

'I remember. We were glad we were in bed, so we couldn't see you staggering around. You were frightening. A different person. Not like our dad at all. But we always heard you shouting at Mum.'

He winced and looked away. His face was genuinely anguished. At that moment, Steph realised that he was indeed truly sorry for what he'd done.

He held his cup and fiddled with it, still finding it difficult to look at her. 'Some people, they get lively and good fun when they're drunk, but with me, I felt aggressive, I don't know why, and . . . and I hit your mum lots of times.' Suddenly he burst into tears. Steph was shocked and at first didn't know what to do. Then she leaned over and put her hand on his arm. 'I'm sorry . . . I'm so, so sorry,' he kept repeating.

'I know you are,' she replied in a quiet voice and waited for him to continue. He took a handkerchief from his pocket, wiped his eyes and blew his nose.

'I've paid for it, big time,' he went on. 'When I left you all and went back to London, I carried on drinking, and I could scarcely hold a job down. It ruins you, Steph. Alcohol ruins you. It destroys your mind and body.' He looked at her and she saw the misery in his yellowy eyes. His face, which had once been handsome, was pinched and blotchy; his blond, wavy hair had practically gone. He was thin and frail before his time.

'I lost everything: my family, my home, and my marriage. Eventually I got help from the AA and I'm sober now, except once you've been an alcoholic as bad as I was, you can only live a day at a time and there's always the chance you'll drop back. I now live by myself in a tiny rented flat and I'm poor.' At last, he was able to look at her. 'I've missed you all really badly for all those years and I still do. I didn't see you grow up and now look at you and Lisa: a detective sergeant and a nurse. I'm so proud of you both and I . . .' He stopped and tears came into his eyes again.

Steph got up and went round to sit beside him. She thought of the long, dismal years of loneliness and struggle that he'd endured.

'Dad,' she said for the first time in many years, and she found that she was crying, too. She felt for his hand and held it.

~

Andy was watching a film when she got back to the flat rather later than she had expected.

'How did it go?' he called out as she came in. She didn't say anything but came into the room, sat beside him and watched the film for a few moments. She felt exhausted after such an emotional encounter. It had stirred memories and feelings long forgotten.

'Well?' asked Andy, glancing at her.

'Andy, I think for the first time I really understand what forgiveness means.'

'Whoa! That's deep!' He paused the film. 'What happened?'

She told him how her father had broken down. 'He was in tears, and I believe it was genuine. When I looked at him, I saw how the drinking had destroyed his body. He used to be strong and healthy, now he looks old. He was really upset when he recalled how he'd hit Mum and he was genuinely sorry for everything.' She looked at her partner. 'I believe him, Andy. I never thought I'd say this, but I understand how the drinking got to him and made him behave like he did and that now he regrets it. He didn't try to blame anyone else for anything.'

'Right.'

'He's lost so much. I always thought he must have created a new life for himself down in London, but he didn't. It was just a constant struggle against the drinking and he was poor and now he's by himself. He had no family and no job most of the time. It must have been awful.'

'So, you think he paid for what he did to you all?'

She thought for a moment. 'Yes, I think I do. Nothing completely excuses what he did. He could have killed Mum on more than one occasion, but we've had much better lives than he has despite the trauma he caused.' She looked down. 'The thing that really got to me was when he said how he'd missed seeing Lisa and me grow up, and that he was so proud of us now.' She started to cry again. 'How could I not feel something when he said that?'

Andy put his arms around her. 'Of course you felt something. But it's good. It sounds to me as if he really feels sorry and wants to start again. It couldn't have been easy for him to say those things.'

She dried her eyes. 'I don't think it was.'

'I think he'll feel a lot better after tonight and you've started to feel differently about him. You'll just have to see how it goes. Is he coming up again in a few weeks?' She nodded. 'Well, who knows? You may be on the way to having a dad again.'

'I'd be pleased about that, but I don't know how Mum would feel about it. I have these guilty feelings that I'm betraying her.'

'Well, you're not. Knowing your mum, I'm sure she will be pleased if you could establish some relationship with him. Didn't she encourage you to meet him in the first place?'

'Yes, but . . . I don't know. I need to talk to Lisa about what happened tonight. And then we'll see.'

~

Back in Markham, the Wensley Arms was packed with the celebrating cricket team, and as the evening progressed, things were becoming noisy as the younger players started to laugh raucously and sing songs.

Philip Welbeck smiled at them as he sat at the bar drinking beer, and talking to Bill Lawrence.

'Good start to the season, then, Phil?' said the barman, drying some glasses as he talked.

'Yes, it was close in the end, but we got there. They had a good seam bowler, but Ian, our number three batsman, was in good form. I didn't make many runs, though, I was too distracted.'

'You mean by the attack on Richard Foster? That's a funny do, isn't it? I suppose we're going to get the police all over the town again.'

'Probably. At least he got away with minor injuries.'

'Aye. Who the hell do you think it was?'

'I've no idea.'

Lawrence shook his head. 'It makes you wonder what the world's coming to – muggings in a place like this.'

'At least we managed to finish the game. The police were very good about it. I think it was important for the town. After what's been going on recently, we needed a morale boost.'

On the other side of the bar things were getting a bit out of hand and somebody ended up with beer poured over their head, followed by howls of laughter. It was all good-humoured, but Bill Lawrence went over to calm it down.

'OK, lads, let's go steady now. I'm giving you some cloths and you can mop that up off the floor,' Welbeck heard him say as he took a drink from his beer. It was good to see people enjoying themselves, but he felt that there was still a threat hanging over the town. Was this attack linked to the murders? It would be up to the police to find out.

On Monday morning the detectives, in their incident room at the brewery, were discussing the very issue that Welbeck had been considering. Oldroyd and Andy had received a full report from Jeffries, who had been very busy over the weekend.

'You searched the crime scene but didn't find anything?'

'That's right, sir. And I've called for more witnesses, but no one has come forward.'

'Is this the same person at work, then, sir?' asked Andy. 'It seems a bit of a botched job after the other two attacks. Could it have been a random mugging?'

Oldroyd shook his head. 'Well, I doubt it. Muggers don't usually try to garotte people. It makes it difficult for them to hand over their wallets.' He turned to Jeffries. 'You say nothing was taken from Foster?'

'No, sir, but then the assailant ran off quickly when Foster cried out. We've spoken to the two people who came to Foster's rescue and they confirmed his story as much as they could. Neither of them saw the attacker.'

'Right. If it was our murderer, then what intrigues me is that this attack was carried out in much more pressurised and risky circumstances than the previous ones: outdoors, with people nearby. It was always possible that it could go wrong. It suggests an urgency . . . a need to get rid of Richard Foster quickly. But why?'

'When I took Mr Foster's statement, sir, and asked him if he knew of anyone who might want to attack him, he said the only person he suspected was Tony Handley,' said Jeffries, consulting his notes.

'Handley the Graffiti Man. I assume that's because he wondered if Handley had found out that Foster had suggested his name to us about that incident?'

'That's right, sir.'

'It seems a bit drastic,' said Andy. 'He didn't seem like a murderer to me, just a bloke with weird ideas. He doesn't have any history of violence against people. I suppose if he lost his temper or something, it might explain why it was badly planned – just lying in wait and taking his chance. Unless he never meant to go through with it, and only give Foster a fright.'

'That's possible. It just seems very unlikely that we've got more than one person behaving so violently in a small town like this.' Oldroyd drank some of his coffee, which Jeffries had brewed for them earlier. He started to look around for a biscuit and then stopped himself.

'OK,' he continued with a sigh. 'We'll have another talk with Mr Graffiti but if it turns out that he has a cast iron alibi, we're back to thinking about what the motive might be for this attempted murder. So I'm giving that job to you, Jeffries. Handley should be here at the brewery; if not, you've got his home address, haven't you?'

'Yes, sir.' Jeffries left, glad as ever to be useful to the chief inspector.

'We don't really know for sure yet what the motives are for any of these attacks, do we, sir?'

'Don't remind me!' replied Oldroyd, shaking his head and again feeling very dispirited at the lack of progress. 'Let's go and find Welbeck. He probably saw more than anyone else down at the cricket ground. He might have noticed something significant.'

~

Oldroyd and Andy found Welbeck down in the works by the fermentation tanks. He took the detectives into a small, cluttered office where they all sat down.

'I've already made a statement to DC Jeffries,' said Welbeck, looking rather tired after what had been a mixed weekend of triumph and trauma.

'Yes, but I just wanted to go through it with you; see if you noticed anything that might prove important. It could be just a small detail.'

'OK. The match had got underway. It was about three o'clock and a number of people, including me, heard a cry. We were looking in the direction that it came from, which was behind some bushes where the steps down from the square reach the bottom. I saw two men, who were the closest, run behind those bushes and they soon returned helping Richard Foster slowly over to the clubhouse.'

'What kind of a state was he in?'

'Very shaken; mark round his neck. We gave him a drink and then I called the police and the ambulance. He told me his wife, his sister and her partner had all arranged to be at the ground. I went out to look and I saw Emily Foster taking a seat; maybe she'd just arrived. I don't know.'

Oldroyd, who had been listening, as he often did, with his eyes closed, opened them at this point. 'And what about the other two?' he asked.

'Christine arrived soon after and went to the hospital with her husband. The police had got here, and we decided, with their permission, to continue with the match. Soon after that I went out to bat.'

'So you didn't see Janice Anderson?'

'Yes. I saw a car arrive in the car park a bit later and she walked over to meet with Emily.'

'What time was that?'

'Probably about half past four. Our innings was not far off the end.'

Oldroyd paused and seemed to be thinking. 'Was there anything that struck you as odd about the whole business?' he asked.

Welbeck shrugged. 'I think everything about it was weird. Richard Foster, owner of a famous local business in a small town, attacked by the cricket field? It's not the sort of thing you expect round here. I suppose you have to wonder . . . why there? And why do it at all?'

'Indeed,' said Oldroyd, who would have loved to have been able to answer those questions. He had his own suspicions, but he needed proof.

∽

'What did you make of that, then, sir?' asked Andy when the detectives returned to the office.

'What's intriguing me is the question of who knew Foster was going to be at the cricket ground.'

'Yes, and the arrival of all those women at the ground after the attack. They all knew he was going to be there. But did they all know he was going to the brewery first and was likely to walk to the ground via those steps?'

'Let's go steady,' replied Oldroyd. 'The person who was most likely to know that was his wife. But we've no idea of any strong motive on her part. His sister, not on good terms with him, hardly had time to attack her brother and get to the ground before Welbeck saw her, which leaves Janice Anderson who arrived much later – which did give her ample time to get away and then return in her car.'

'What might her motive be, sir? And how did she know that Foster was going to be coming down those steps?'

'I don't know, but I think we need to talk to those two couples. If we're lucky, we might uncover the answer to this whole affair.'

∽

Markham was quiet on this Monday morning. It felt as if the recent shocking incidents had cast an invisible pall over the little town. Residents were venturing out of their homes with some trepidation, shaking their heads at each other as they passed in the street and gathering in small groups to talk about what had happened in hushed voices.

At lunchtime the Wensley Arms was almost deserted. Norman Smith didn't usually drink in the middle of the day, but these were such stressful times that he took a break from his job erecting a greenhouse in the garden of a house on the outskirts of the village and walked over to the pub. He had a look at the sandwich menu and ordered a ham and cheese toastie. Bill Lawrence pulled him a pint of bitter.

'What the hell was going on at the cricket ground on Saturday, then?' Smith asked. 'I hear someone was attacked.'

Lawrence frowned and shook his head. 'Aye, it was Richard Foster. Apparently, someone tried to strangle him.'

'What?'

'Aye, can you believe it?'

Smith was speechless for a few moments. 'This town will never be the same again after all this,' he said eventually. 'People won't trust each other. It's a shame.'

'Oh, I don't know,' replied Lawrence, trying to strike an optimistic note. 'We've got enough resilience in this community to come back from it all. Why not?'

'Well, I hope you're right. I'm going to miss old Barry. He was a character, what with his bikes and everything, wasn't he?'

'He was.'

'I went on some biking trips with him.'

'I didn't know you were a biker.'

'Oh, I used to be. Years ago. I remember we once went across Pateley Bridge over to Grassington, then up Wharfedale and off the road down the old track to Semer Water. It was rocky going down that fellside but great fun. It was a hot day and we stripped off and swam in the lake.' He took a drink of his beer as he enjoyed the memories. 'Good times.'

Then his face darkened. 'It's all about that damn Scholes, somehow. He caused so much trouble in this town. Why the hell did he come back? He got what he deserved, in my opinion.'

'He was certainly a nuisance, but who finished him off and killed poor Barry? That's what's on everybody's mind. It means there's some killer here in the town and that makes people very uneasy. The same person probably attacked Foster.'

Smith shook his head but didn't reply, not wanting to get on to the subject of suspects. His sandwich arrived and he took it over to an empty table as Lawrence went to serve another customer. He ate the sandwich, finished his beer and went back to work. It was better if he kept a low profile for the time being.

~

'So I left the brewery, walked across the square and down the steps quite quickly as I could hear the match had started. When I got to the bottom, someone came up behind me and put some kind of cord round my neck and pulled it tight. Luckily, I managed to cry out quite loudly. Then suddenly the cord was released, and I heard the person run off up the steps. It all happened in a flash.'

Oldroyd and Andy were at the Fosters' house. Richard Foster, who was still resting after his ordeal, was describing what had happened. He sat on the sofa next to Christine, looking tired, with a bruise visible on his neck. Oldroyd and Andy sat opposite.

'Did you catch sight of the attacker?' asked Andy.

'No, none, as I said in my statement. They came up behind me and ran off before I had a chance to see them. I couldn't even say if it was a man or a woman.'

'They didn't say anything?'

'No.'

'And you have no idea who it could have been, apart from Tony Handley?'

'No. Who on earth would want to kill me?'

'One of our officers has established that Handley has an alibi,' said Oldroyd. 'He was in the Wensley Arms at the time you were attacked.' He paused and looked at Foster. 'I understand that it was arranged that you and your wife would meet with your sister and her partner at the cricket ground?'

'Yes. We didn't arrange it before Saturday, but Emily came round here in the morning that day. We were all going to see the match so we said we would meet up.'

'How would you describe your relationship with your sister at the moment? We know that there have been hostilities between you concerning your rival businesses.'

Foster looked pained. 'Yes, that's true. But we're working through it. When she came on Saturday, we discussed a private matter, and I felt she was very supportive. The idea that my sister would attack me is ridiculous, Chief Inspector.'

Oldroyd had heard such declarations which later turned out to be false too many times to be deterred from pursuing the point. 'What did you talk about? I'm afraid it's relevant to this murder inquiry, however personal it is.'

Foster looked at his wife, who nodded. He explained about the problems they'd had with alcohol and gambling.

Oldroyd looked from one to the other. 'So, your husband's gambling has caused you a great deal of distress?'

'It did,' replied Christine.

'And you must have resented him a lot, putting your family's financial security in danger.'

'That's why I turned to drink. But I never wished Richard any harm, if that's what you're getting at. I think we're just beginning to deal with the issues and it will be good to have Emily's help if we need it.'

Oldroyd looked at them again. 'OK. How about your sister's partner, Janice?'

'What about her?' replied Foster.

'Do you get on with her? And how do feel about your sister's sexuality?'

Andy smiled. He was still sometimes faintly shocked at how direct his boss could be. He had many techniques of questioning that disarmed the person he was interviewing. He always seemed to get what he wanted.

Foster stumbled a little. 'I . . . It doesn't worry me, Chief Inspector. It's entirely her business. Janice is . . . well . . .' He turned to Christine.

'We've never spent much time with her,' said Christine. 'She's not been over-friendly with us. I think she believes that Richard and I don't accept her and their relationship, but it's not true.'

'Has she ever expressed any direct hostility towards either of you?' asked Andy.

'No,' said Foster. 'And I really think it's very far-fetched to think she would try to strangle me by the cricket ground.'

'Maybe,' said Oldroyd. In fact, he had seen far more unlikely hypotheses turn out to be true. 'As far as your gambling goes,' he continued, 'I take it this unfortunate habit has placed you in financial difficulties?'

'Yes, but I'm dealing with it.'

'But a quick fix would be very helpful, wouldn't it?'

Foster looked exasperated. 'If you're referring to that recipe again, I've told you before: there's no evidence that it even exists, never mind that I could get hold of it to pay my gambling debts.'

He slumped further into the sofa. 'Is that all, Chief Inspector? I'm not feeling well, as you can imagine.'

Oldroyd got up. He wasn't going to reveal that the recipe had been found. He wanted the killer to think there was still a chance of finding it, if this did turn out to be the motive. 'OK. I'm sorry we've had to press you hard on these matters in the circumstances but I'm sure you realise that we really need to get on and solve this case before there is any more violence. We have to follow every possibility.'

The Fosters nodded without saying anything. They both looked exhausted.

~

'It was interesting to hear about their family reconciliation, sir. Something like that is happening with Steph,' said Andy as he and Oldroyd walked across the empty market square towards the Ewe's Ales Brewery. He explained about her meeting with her father, from whom she'd been long estranged. Oldroyd listened with interest. He was very fond of his young detective sergeant; he'd mentored her since she joined the force from school.

'I'm pleased about that. I know she hasn't had much contact with him since she was very small. And wasn't he a drinker?'

'That's right, sir.'

'Well, there's another parallel. It's always nice to hear about people conquering their addictions.'

'Do you really think Foster could have bumped off Scholes to get that recipe, sir? That was your original theory, wasn't it, when we interviewed him on the first day?'

'Yes, and now it seems more likely because of his debts and the fact that we know the recipe does exist. Foster may have believed that Scholes had it, but he couldn't afford to pay him anything due to his gambling debts.'

'The problem is: who attacked him if he's the murderer?'

'There could have been more than one of them involved and they fell out. And also, how do we know that it really happened? No one saw the assailant. It's very easy to mark your own neck with a cord.'

'True, sir. I never thought of that.'

'It's always important not to easily accept what you're told, or sometimes what appears to be before your eyes. Magicians misdirect you into thinking something is real when it isn't. Anyway, do you fancy a bite to eat? We haven't had any lunch. This looks like a nice place.'

'OK, sir.' Andy smiled to himself. His boss never went very long without eating something or drinking a pint of beer.

They sat down at a table outside a cafe. It was a warm April day and Oldroyd looked around the pretty square. 'This is the first time I've sat out this year. It really makes me look forward to summer.'

'I know, sir. It's always a good feeling, isn't it, the end of winter?'

They ordered sandwiches and coffee, and Andy told Oldroyd a little more about Steph's meeting with her father.

'I've been lucky with my family,' said Oldroyd. 'My sister and I were always close, and we got on well with our parents. We know from our work that family breakdowns can be terrible and even . . .' He stopped.

Andy looked up. 'Sir?'

Oldroyd thought for a moment before replying. 'Oh, nothing really. An idea just struck me. But I've no evidence. I'm interested in talking to Emily Foster and Janice Anderson. I wonder what Anderson really thought about her partner's brother and his wife.'

～

After lunch they continued their walk down the pleasant lane to Ewe's Ales Brewery. Oldroyd listened to the birdsong and noticed a blackbird with nesting materials in its mouth. Suddenly he stopped. 'Listen, Andy.'

They both went quiet and after a few moments there was the sound of a cuckoo in the distance.

'Wow! I don't think I've ever heard that before, sir!'

'It's a lovely sound. They're very shy birds; they always seem to be a distance away and you don't often see them. Anyway, here we are.' They had reached the brewery.

'Come in, Chief Inspector. Sergeant.' Emily Foster welcomed the two detectives into her office.

'Thank you. We'd like to speak to your partner, too, after we've spoken to you. I presume she's at work today.'

Emily looked a little flustered. 'Yes, she is. I'll call her and tell her to wait in the room next door. What's this about?'

'I know you've already made a statement, but can you tell me about Saturday, and the attack on Richard Foster.'

Emily sat down. 'Janice and I had arranged to meet at the ground when she got back from Ripon. I got there just as the game began and, not long afterwards, I saw there was something going on at the clubhouse, but I couldn't see who was involved.'

'What do you mean by "something going on"?'

'Somebody was being helped by two other people into the clubhouse. I was too far off to see that it was Richard. Then Philip Welbeck came over to tell me that Richard had been attacked. I ran over and found him sitting in the kitchen looking dazed. I spoke to him for a few minutes, then Christine came in. We were all going to meet at the ground, you see.'

'Yes. Carry on.'

'The ambulance arrived, and Christine and Richard went off together.'

'What did he say to you about the attack?'

'Not much. He said he had no idea who could have done it and he was very upset. He cried on my shoulder. He said he was fed up of all the awful things that had happened: the murders and that business with the graffiti. And now he'd been attacked himself. It was just too much.'

'There were other things, weren't there? Did you know about their personal problems?'

'Yes,' she said reluctantly. She clearly felt very uncomfortable talking about it. 'Earlier that morning I'd called in to talk to him because I was tired of all this animosity between our breweries. He looked very stressed, and he told me briefly about what they were going through.'

'You didn't know previously that he had any money worries?'

'No.'

'Or that Christine had a drink problem?'

'No.'

'OK. How do you feel about your brother and his wife now?'

'I feel much more positive about our relationship. The fact that he confided in me about their problems shows that, deep down, there's still a bond between us. I've always got on well with Christine, although I've not seen that much of her since Richard and I started to become estranged over the business.'

'Do you think your brother accepts your relationship with your partner?'

Emily was a little taken aback by Oldroyd's directness. 'I've never felt any hostility from him or Christine about that. Richard's not homophobic, even if some of his workers are. His problem, as I told you when you first spoke to me, was that he couldn't accept women in the world of brewing. But, actually, I sense he's changing his mind.'

'Thank you,' said Oldroyd. 'Can you call Janice in, please?'

Janice was wearing overalls and she brought in with her an odour of yeast and hops. She sat down looking rather sullen and resentful.

Oldroyd began as abruptly as ever. 'Do you have any problems with Emily's brother, Richard? By that I mean, do you think that he accepts you as a lesbian couple?'

Janice's eyes narrowed as she looked at Oldroyd. 'You don't mess around, do you, Chief Inspector? Frankly I did find him and his wife difficult. I don't mind admitting it; I've got nothing to hide. I've spoken to Emily about it. I don't think she notices, but I always feel that they're cold towards me. I think they're very conventional people – this little town is full of them – who find our relationship difficult.'

'And how do you feel about the rift between the breweries?'

'It's misogynistic. Richard, and others like him, can't accept that women are capable of running a brewery.' Her expression changed and her eyes glinted. 'You have to fight those attitudes, just as we fought against the graffiti.'

'It seems that you may have replied in kind to the graffiti on your brewery gates.'

She shrugged her shoulders but said nothing.

'Are you prepared to do things that are against the law, and even violent, when fighting those "attitudes", as you put it?'

Again, she said nothing.

'I understand that Emily and yourself had arranged to meet at the cricket ground when you returned from Ripon?'

'That's right.'

'What was the purpose of your visit to Ripon?'

'I went to collect my new sunglasses.'

'But it seems you were delayed on this visit. You didn't arrive back in Markham until nearly four o'clock.'

'Yes. I made the mistake of going to get a bite to eat first as I thought I wouldn't be long at the opticians'. It turned out there was quite a queue of people in front of me, then they couldn't find my sunglasses for a while, and then I had to have them fitted. It was after three o'clock before I got out. And on the way back, I was held up by an accident which had blocked the road.'

Oldroyd considered all this information before continuing. 'I'm wondering about your late arrival. I think you knew that Richard was going to the cricket ground and that he would walk over from the brewery. Maybe you had seen him go to the brewery earlier on. Did you lie in wait for him at the bottom of those steps and then try to strangle him? You had ample time to drive off from wherever you had concealed your car and then return later. You could even have gone into Ripon for a brief visit as an alibi.'

He looked directly at her, but she remained steady and controlled. 'And why would I do that?'

'Because you disliked him and his attitude to you and your partner and because his brewery was a threat to your business, and it would be easier with him out of the way.'

She laughed scornfully. 'You'll have to do better than that, Chief Inspector. Of course I didn't hurt Richard. You can check at the cafe I went to and the opticians'. I'm sure your colleagues in traffic will tell you about the road accident.'

'We will check it all, so please leave us the details. And stay in town for now.'

'So, I *am* a suspect! Is that for the murders, too?'

'Not necessarily, but it's possible,' said Oldroyd. 'Did you know Brendan Scholes?'

'Yes. When I was a teenager, I used to belong to a group of friends that he was part of. I hadn't seen him for years until he turned up in the beer tent on the day of the festival. He looked the same although his voice was a bit deeper – age, I suppose. I don't think he remembered me. He didn't want to talk to me.'

'Did you have any reason to feel hostile towards him?'

219

'No, why should I? We had some good times together in that group, going to gigs and stuff.'

Oldroyd thought for a moment. 'OK. That's all for now, thank you.'

She got up and left the room looking rather angry.

Andy was intrigued. 'It sounds a bit far-fetched, sir, if you'll forgive me.'

Oldroyd laughed. 'Sometimes if you put a half-baked theory in front of someone, they can react in a way that tells you if you're on the right lines even if the details aren't quite correct.'

'Did you feel that with her?'

'To be honest, no. I think we'll find that the alibi stands up. She's a tough cookie, though I wouldn't eliminate her completely. Funny how she's the only person who has said anything positive about Scholes.' He thought again for a moment, slapped his legs, got up and sighed. 'Anyway, I think we've finished here. The problem with this damn case is that there are suspects but you can't pin anything on them. I think we're missing something, or at least something has yet to come to light.'

He didn't know that the case was about to take a strange turn.

Six

Saltaire Brewery is sited in the World Heritage village of Saltaire near Bradford. The village was built for the brewery workers by the mill owner Sir Titus Salt, who ironically forbade 'beershops' in his new village, probably so that workers would not be absent due to being inebriated! The brewery operates in an old generating station that once powered Bradford's trams, and now sells beers in sixty-eight countries around the world. Two of the most famous are Saltaire Blonde – a malty and hoppy beer – and Titus, a traditional bitter named after the famous philanthropist.

It was on Tuesday morning that DC Jeffries was finally presented with the dramatic information about the case he'd so longed for to impress the chief inspector.

He was at Ripon HQ when he took a call.

'DC Jeffries. Yes, hello.' He listened for a while with growing astonishment as the caller spoke. 'What? That's impossible. I mean, are you absolutely sure? . . . Right. OK, thanks.' He ended the call and immediately rang DCI Oldroyd.

'Sir, it's Jeffries. I've got some very strange news. Do you remember there was a badly decomposed body found in a drainage tunnel before these murders in Markham and Ripon? Mr Groves and I attended the scene . . . Yes, well, I've just had a call from a dentist in Ripon who finally tracked down the dental records of the victim. It was Brendan Scholes . . . Yes, sir, they said there was no doubt, and they remembered him coming to their surgery. I remember you wondered whether there was a connection between that murder and the case we're investigating, and you were right, sir, there was . . . I know, sir, we'll have to re-evaluate everything. Brendan Scholes was not the brewery victim. That body in the fermentation tank wasn't him. He'd already been dead at least two weeks.'

~

Christine Foster was feeling much better and was already benefiting from Richard's support in resisting alcohol. She was sitting on the sofa in the lounge, holding hands with Richard. He was still some-what shaken by his ordeal, but every bit as determined that crucial things in his life and in that of the Foster family as a whole were going to change. He had already spoken to his gambling friends to say he was not going to attend any more meetings and they were not to contact him about it.

'I've decided that some radical action is necessary to repair my relationship with Emily,' he said. 'What do you think of the idea of merging the breweries?'

'Gosh, that is radical. Do you think she would agree?'

'Yes. Because I would stand back and let her take charge.'

Christine looked at him. 'Richard? Are you sure? I thought it meant a lot to you to have succeeded your father in running the brewery.'

Richard sighed. 'Well, it did, but I've realised now that other things are much more important: the family for one thing. We'll all be much stronger together. One family brewery again in Markham;

it would be awesome. I'm not bothered about prestige and status any more. We were facing disaster but we're coming through.' He turned her face towards him and kissed her.

∼

At the incident room in the Yoredale brewery, Oldroyd, Andy and Jeffries were discussing the implications of this dramatic turn in the investigation as they drank coffee.

'Of course, this changes a great deal, but it confirms some of the doubts and questions I had about the facts and narrative we were presented with,' began Oldroyd, who seemed excited by the news.

'In what way, sir?' asked Andy.

'The first thing I found odd about this case was that Norman Smith said Scholes didn't seem to recognise him that day when he ran into him at the festival . . . and yet Scholes had been messing around with his wife. He must have known what the husband looked like, even if only to keep away from him. And, anyway, everyone knows each other in a small place like this. Smith thought Scholes was pretending not to recognise him, but it seemed strange. And yesterday Janice Anderson said something similar: that Scholes didn't want to talk to her in the Ewe's brewery beer tent. But surely he would have had some kind of conversation with her, as they'd been friends in the past. Also, she said his voice was different. Now that could be due to him being older and having a deeper voice, but I thought there was something not quite right about it.'

'I see where you're going, sir,' said Andy. 'You're saying that these things suggested all along that that person wasn't Brendan Scholes. And now we know for sure that it wasn't.'

'Correct. Another thing that bothered me was why he agreed to meet the person who turned out to be his killer at the deserted brewery after dark? That person must have had a reason to kill

Brendan Scholes, so why would Scholes meet them in such a place, which was a gift to a killer?'

'Because it wasn't Brendan Scholes, and he didn't know that the person he'd arranged to meet had a reason to kill Brendan?' suggested Jeffries.

'Exactly!' said Oldroyd, and Jeffries beamed.

'But if the first victim wasn't Brendan Scholes, sir, who was it?'

'I think there's only one person it could have been . . . and that's his brother, Frederick. We know they were close in age and in appearance. So, after he'd killed his brother, Frederick grew a big beard and dressed in his brother's clothes. That was one of the reasons why there was a gap between Brendan's death and Frederick appearing in public pretending to be his brother; he had to grow the beard. Other than that it wasn't too difficult for him to impersonate Brendan. I began to wonder vaguely about something like this when my sister asked me if there was a big age gap between the brothers. We didn't know that Frederick was around then, but it came to me that if someone had been impersonating Brendan, that would explain certain things.'

'So, what was going on, sir?'

Oldroyd drank some of his coffee before continuing. He was so animated at this breakthrough that he didn't even think about a biscuit.

'We'll never know for sure. We were talking about family break-down in the office and that started to ring bells for me. I thought for a time that the problems in the Foster family could be behind all this, but it turns out it was the Scholes family. However, both brothers and their father are dead so we can only try to reconstruct what happened between them, just as Gandalf does in *Lord of the Rings* with the story of Gollum's early life.

'Remember that word "precious" was at the back of my mind? I think what I said to you at the time was right. Frederick did come back after his father's death. The brothers did fall out about the recipe. And Frederick did kill his brother. We had the sequence right, but not the timing. In fact, Frederick didn't kill Brendan that night in the brewery. He killed him much earlier. Probably in anger because Brendan wouldn't tell him where the recipe was.'

'Do you think Brendan knew himself, sir?'

Oldroyd shrugged. 'I don't know. The fact that when we found it, the recipe didn't seem to have been disturbed for a while suggests that maybe he didn't. But he most likely knew it was in the house somewhere. I think his father must have told him that it did exist, but not where it was. Sadly, he didn't trust his sons. And with good reason.

'So, after his brother was dead and he'd concealed the body, Frederick had an idea. He could impersonate his brother and try to sell the recipe to likely buyers like the Fosters. He looked like him and Brendan didn't have a regular job at that time. He must have been sure that no one had seen him arrive at the house in Ripon. He was relying on the fact that he would find the recipe. I thought the interloper who killed Barry Green in the house in Ripon was Frederick searching for it, but clearly it wasn't. Frederick was dead by then, so it must have been the person who murdered him.

'Anyway, this scheme prevented people from wondering where Brendan was. And once he'd sold the recipe, you can be sure Frederick would have disappeared back to wherever he'd come from. As we couldn't trace him, we can assume that wherever that was is a long way away and under an assumed name. If the body of his brother hadn't been found, Brendan's disappearance would have remained a mystery, but not out of character for that family. And if the body was found at some point, what was there to link the killing with Frederick?'

'But the flaw, sir,' continued Andy, 'was that he had been away for a long time, and he didn't know about Brendan's activities and his enemies, so without realising it he gave his killer the opportunity to murder the person he thought was Brendan Scholes.'

'Correct. We'll need to get forensics to verify that the body in the tank was Frederick, but I'm certain they will.'

'I'll get on to that, sir,' said Jeffries.

'What he failed to take into account was his brother's colourful history in Markham,' continued Oldroyd. 'He didn't know about the baggage from his brother's affairs and debts, and he didn't know who had been his brother's friends in the past, so he failed to respond in the right way. That's why Smith said Scholes didn't seem to recognise him when he encountered him at the beer festival and the same was true with Janice Anderson.'

'But, sir,' said Andy, 'I think you're right about the Scholes brothers, but where does that leave us in the investigation?'

'I'm afraid it means that we're back to the drawing board, as they say. Some things have been clarified, but we still don't know who killed Frederick Scholes and Barry Green, and who tried to kill Richard Foster or why. The good news is, I have a plan that might reveal who it is.'

'There's something timely coming through from Harrogate HQ, sir,' said Andy, who was on his laptop. 'Apparently, Sharon Warner has managed to track down Frederick Scholes. I don't know how she did it. The trail went cold, but knowing he'd trained in engineering, she pursued that line. She followed up some of the people who were at the army college with him to see if he might have joined them. Sure enough, she found an Antony Scholes working at a firm in Liverpool, owned by the father of someone who'd been in the army with him. He probably passed this off as his name instead of Frederick. There were some pictures on their website, and she recognised him from the photo Jeffries got at the house in Ripon. He clearly didn't want to be found, even before all this madness.'

'There may be some other things he was involved in that will come to light later. I think if he'd succeeded in selling the recipe, he would have left that job, gone even further away and changed both of his names,' said Oldroyd. 'Well, good on DC Warner. She's shaping up very well. I'll mention that in my report to DCS Walker. The information has come too late to make much difference, but she's showing a real flair for research.

'Anyway, let me tell you what I have in mind to catch the killer . . .'

~

'I'm leaving tomorrow, Daddy. I've had enough.' Sophie confronted her father in the massive entrance hall at Swinfield.

Langford looked around anxiously but there was no one else nearby. 'What're you talking about?' he said dismissively.

'I've had an offer from a large riding school down in the Midlands. I've been thinking about it for some time, and I've decided to accept it.'

Langford looked contemptuous. 'So, you want to spend the rest of your life messing around with horses and teaching spoiled young girls how to ride?'

Her face flashed with anger. 'At least it will be my own life, and not simply doing what you've decided for me. I'm sick of you controlling me.'

'Everything I do is for your benefit.'

She looked at him with her head to one side. 'Is it? Or is it to keep up the family name and its prestige? "Lord Markham's daughter has become engaged to the son of Earl Whatever." You'd love that to appear in the society section of some posh newspaper, wouldn't you?'

'What's wrong with that? Look, you're an attractive young woman, but these chances will pass. You could still establish yourself in society.'

'Can't you get it into your head that I don't want to? I might not be very clever at doing exams and things, but I'm worth more than being a pretty little thing accompanying some boring man with a title. I like working with horses and teaching riding, and I'm good at it.'

Langford waved his hand dismissively. 'You'll never have the lifestyle and the place in society you could have if you don't follow my advice.'

Sophie looked at him almost with pity. 'You just don't get it, do you? Anyway, I'm leaving in the morning. I'll text you my address when I've found somewhere to stay.'

Langford had thought that he could easily change her mind, but now he saw that she was serious. It seemed only yesterday that she had been an obedient little girl; now a determined young woman stood before him. He didn't know how to respond.

She turned and walked out of the hall. There was no hug or other physical contact. After a few moments he went into his study and walked to the window. As he looked out on to his extensive estate, which was beautiful on the bright spring day, it occurred to him that he was now alone in this huge house – maybe for the rest of his life. His wife was dead; his son was living a busy life in London, and he rarely saw him. And now Sophie was gone, unlikely to return.

He was a wealthy man, but his future looked bleak.

∽

'I know it's not easy to believe, but I think he's genuinely sorry for what he did, and he's suffered a lot because of his alcoholism.'

Steph was in the lounge of her mother's house in Harrogate with her mother and sister Lisa. It was the evening of the same day. Lisa had driven up from Sheffield for tea and to stay for a while in the evening. Steph was describing what had happened when she met her father in Leeds.

Lisa rolled her eyes. 'That may be true, but he's caused other people to suffer – mainly Mum.'

'I know,' replied Steph, 'but you should have heard what he was saying. He's very proud of you becoming a nurse and I really think he's devastated by the fact that he didn't see us grow up. I'm sorry you weren't there, but it was all arranged at the last minute. I don't think he would have opened up as he did if we'd both been there. He found it very difficult as it was.'

'Did he say anything about Mum?'

'Not much, except he admitted that he'd been violent and that caused him to burst into tears. I don't think he's easy talking about how he treated Mum.'

'I'll bet.'

'But that doesn't mean he isn't sorry.'

Lisa turned to her mother. 'Mum, you're not saying much. How do you feel about it?'

Her mother frowned. 'Look, my main concern is you two. I'm glad Steph feels that your dad is sorry, and that he has some feelings, as a father, for you both. I think my relationship with him was damaged beyond repair, but it could be different for you. As I've said before, he is your father. And if he's genuinely reaching out to you, I don't think it would be right for me to stop that.'

'Oh, Mum, that's such a generous view. You're so good,' said Lisa, shaking her head.

Her mother laughed. 'Thank you. I've always believed it was wrong to cling on to bad feelings. I don't hate your father for what he did to us. Not any more. If I'd stayed with how I felt at the time it would have made me very bitter. Also, I knew then that it was because of the alcohol; he was never violent unless he'd been drinking. It didn't make it any easier for me and I was glad when he left, but it sounds as if he has changed and finally dealt with his problem. Maybe he should be rewarded for that.'

Steph nodded. 'I wouldn't dream of asking you to meet him, Mum, but I think he does have a real regard for me and Lisa.'

'What are you suggesting?' said Lisa, still sounding sceptical.

'Nothing dramatic, just that we carry on seeing him – and with an open mind, not with our attitude fixed against him. I felt like that the first time we met. I didn't think there was anything he could say that would change my view of him. But now I think I was wrong.'

'What you're saying is that we should give him a chance,' said Lisa.

'Something like that, yes. I think we can both tell whether someone is being genuine or not. If it works out then . . .' She paused and struggled for the words. 'I suppose we become his daughters again. I think that would mean a great deal to him, but I know it would be difficult for all of us.'

Lisa took a deep breath. 'I'm just not sure I can do it. Could I ever trust him? Could I ever get near to him after what he did?'

'I know, love,' said their mum, 'but I think you were right in what you said: he deserves a chance. It sounds as if he's paid the penalty – his life has been pretty bleak since he left us. And now . . . I don't know. It's up to you two.' She smiled at them both.

'He's coming up to Leeds in a couple of months. Let's just meet him and see how it goes,' said Steph. 'I think we should try to be as open and as welcoming as we can – resist the temptation to freeze him out, and listen to what he has to say.'

Lisa pulled a face and shook her head but eventually said, 'OK.'

It was quite late when Steph arrived back at the apartment in Leeds. Andy was still up watching a film. She took off her jacket and, with a tired-sounding sigh, sat next to him on the sofa. Andy paused the film and turned to her.

'How did it go?'

'Pretty well. It's exhausting going through this stuff, but it was OK. I managed to convince Lisa that it was worth persisting with Dad.'

'It's understandable that she would be reluctant.'

'Yes, it was interesting that she was the one who raised the idea of giving him a chance, so I think it must have been in her mind at some level, even though she was fairly hostile to the idea on the surface.'

'Deep down people don't want to disown members of their family if there's any chance that there can be some kind of reconciliation. I'm seeing it with my current case: the brother and sister who own the rival breweries. You can sense it pains them to be at loggerheads with each other.'

'I think you're right. We'll see how it goes when Dad comes up next month.' She smiled at him. 'Thanks for being so thoughtful and understanding about this. You've really encouraged me.'

'That's fine. In a way, I envy you.'

'How's that?'

'Well, difficult as it is, it's possible for you to sort of regain your dad, but mine's dead and he's never coming back.' There was suddenly a very sad look on his face.

'Oh, gosh, I never thought of it like that. Come here.' She leaned over and gave him a big hug. 'Do you still miss him?'

Andy took a deep breath. 'Yes. Not like I used to. It doesn't upset me any more to think about him, but let's say if I was in your position, I would leap at the chance of getting a father again.'

Steph nodded. 'I can see that. So,' she said, changing the subject, 'how's the investigation going?'

Andy gave her a summary of the day's dramatic developments. 'Thanks to you, and also thanks to Sharon's efforts, I think we've turned a corner. The boss was very impressed and he's putting in a commendation for Sharon. She's a whizz with the old research, isn't she?'

'Yes. Do you know, I think technology develops so rapidly that even people of our age are getting superseded. She's only about twenty and everything in IT comes so naturally to her and she does it all at an incredible speed.'

Andy laughed. 'My God, on the scrap heap in your early thirties! What a fate!'

'Well, imagine Superintendent Walker – he wouldn't know where to start.'

'I'm not sure the boss would be much better, but they've still got fine minds, haven't they? And a wealth of experience. The boss has a plan to catch the killer and, knowing him, I'll bet it works. He always has a few tricks up his sleeve.'

'What's that, then?'

Andy explained. 'He's going to speak to the media tomorrow. He loves the idea of them doing some work for us without realising it. Then it could involve quite a bit of tedious vigilance over the next few days, but we'll see if his gamble pays off. And by the way, I've decided that Jeffries can wait. I don't want to move from Harrogate at the moment. I think I've got a lot more to learn, particularly about being in authority. As an inspector, I would be in charge of investigations. I'm not sure I'm ready for that yet.'

'Well, you've thought it through very carefully so that's fine.' She smiled. 'I'm pleased, actually. It wouldn't be the same if you weren't in the team and I couldn't get one over on you by working the case out first!'

'Get lost!'

'I've called this press conference to bring you up to date on the investigation into the brewery murders.'

It was the next day and Oldroyd was speaking to the assembled reporters and television crews outside the Yoredale Ram Brewery. Andy was at his side. Interest in the case was now intense and nationwide.

Before he could continue a reporter jumped in. 'Is it true there was another attempted murder at the weekend, Chief Inspector?'

You had to give them credit, thought Oldroyd, they had amazing sources of information, and weren't afraid to be upfront with their questions.

'There was an attack on someone, yes, but I can't confirm that this was linked to the murders. We continue to advise people to take care and also to ask anyone with any information to come forward. This latest attack took place near the cricket ground on Saturday afternoon and the attacker made off up the steps towards the square. They may have been seen.'

'Are you near to making an arrest?' asked an eager reporter who then thrust a microphone towards Oldroyd.

'Without going into details, I believe that we are not far from that. Our main suspect is Frederick Scholes, the brother of the first victim. We believe that he killed his brother in a dispute about their late father's legacy. It is important that anyone who has any information about Frederick should speak to us. He is a dangerous man and shouldn't be approached. We will be issuing a description of him.'

'Did he kill the second victim, Barry Green?'

'We believe so, yes.'

'Didn't know Brendan had a brother, Chief Inspector . . . Where's he sprung from?'

'Frederick Scholes has not been around in this area for some time. As a boy he got into quite a bit of trouble at school and so on, and, as soon as he was old enough, he left the area. That's about fifteen years ago now.'

'Chief Inspector, we've heard that this might all be about a lost recipe for a type of beer – Wensley Glory Bitter. Is that true?' This was from a young reporter at the back of the crowd who was wearing some kind of hoodie.

'We think that's unlikely. I'm sure that many of you are aware of what I might call the legend of Wensley Glory Bitter, which was brewed some time ago by the late David Foster. It won many prizes, but the recipe has long been missing.'

'Maybe it turned up.'

'Very unlikely. There has been an extensive search of the house in Ripon that was the home of Wilfred Scholes, the father of the Scholes brothers, until he died recently. This has not uncovered any relevant documents and we have concluded that the recipe does not exist. We have completed our investigation at the house, which is now locked up.'

The reporter in the hoodie spoke again. 'If the recipe was found, it would be worth a lot of money, wouldn't it, Chief Inspector?'

'Yes, I'm sure a brewery would pay a handsome price for it. It would be extremely good for business if they were able to sell Wensley Glory Bitter.'

Oldroyd took a few more routine questions and then ended the meeting. He smiled as the reporters left and there was a twinkle in his eye. He seemed very satisfied with how things had gone.

'Well done, sir,' said Andy. 'I think that worked well.'

'Yes, now let's see if our prey takes the bait.'

∼

'This sounds amazing. "This delightful four-bedroom Edwardian end-terrace is the perfect combination of stunning original features and quality contemporary styling . . ."' Deborah was reading the estate agent's description as Oldroyd drove them to their third house viewing. It was late in the afternoon and theirs was the last viewing of the day. It was possible that, if they liked it, it would be too late to put in a bid.

'My mother always used to say, if it sounds too good to be true then it probably is,' said Oldroyd.

Deborah laughed. She'd heard many stories about Oldroyd's mum, who was known for her directness and no-nonsense, down-to-earth manner. 'Well, let's try to keep an open mind, shall we?'

The car turned off the main road, over the railway and into New Bridge, a village just two miles from Harrogate. Deborah pulled a sheet of A4 paper and a pen out of her handbag.

'Tick,' she said, glancing sideways towards Oldroyd and smiling.

'What's this?' he asked.

'A spreadsheet.' She held it up. 'It's got all our requirements listed.'

Oldroyd looked perplexed.

'First two boxes ticked,' said Deborah. 'Public transport and pub.'

'Such efficiency,' replied Oldroyd.

He was very familiar with the train station, and he'd enjoyed many a good pint of Ewe's Ales at the Bridge Inn, after which he'd been whisked back to Harrogate town centre on the 36 bus, which had been taking passengers between Leeds, Harrogate and Ripon for as long as anyone could remember.

As they pulled up, Oldroyd was genuinely impressed by the look of the house. 'Now that *has* been very well maintained, at least on the outside.'

The estate agent, who looked almost identical to the previous ones, was waiting for them on the front path and wasted no time in pointing out the many advantages of the house.

'. . . benefits from an end-of-terrace position with a garage, so no need to worry about finding a parking place on the street . . . etched windows, characteristic of the Edwardian era . . .'

Whilst Deborah ticked more boxes, Oldroyd took a closer look at the window frames.

'That's good,' he said. 'UPVC replacements, but high spec so you can't really tell until you get close up.'

'Well, they had me fooled,' said Deborah.

'The front door is the original,' said Oldroyd as they followed the agent inside. 'Great quality hardwood, it'll last forever. You don't get doors like this any more.' He was making a big effort to be engaged in the viewing.

'I didn't realise you were such an expert on timber,' quipped Deborah and Oldroyd stuck out his tongue.

The estate agent ushered them around the different rooms and Oldroyd could not find any major faults with this house. The owners had obviously put a lot of money into it; the solid wooden floors alone must have cost a fortune.

Deborah was keen to see the kitchen, which was large, bright and big enough for a table and a small sofa. French doors opened out on to the garden.

Oldroyd was impressed.

'I like this – plenty of space and not clinical like the kitchen in the last house we looked at. I'd be up for giving these pine cupboards a lick of Farrow and Ball Drizzle.'

'Mizzle! Not drizzle,' said Deborah, smiling.

'Or maybe Dead Trout.'

'Dead . . .' Deborah was laughing so hard she couldn't get her words out. 'It's Dead Salmon.'

'Who on earth thinks of these names?'

'I don't know but . . .' Deborah broke off. Her eye had been caught by the cat flap in one of the doors. She pointed it out to Oldroyd.

'Don't worry, love,' he said. 'I could easily block that up.'

'There'll be no need for that,' said Deborah as she held up her spreadsheet. 'Cat flap . . . tick. It's on my desirable list.'

She smiled at Oldroyd as they were led into the living room and invited to admire the original tiled fireplace, picture rail and cornice. It was all very tasteful. They would not be paying for any horrible modern fixtures and fittings that neither of them liked, and they could easily live in this property without doing anything.

The final part was the garden. They went through the French doors and walked around. It was the perfect size and in good condition, with some nice herbaceous borders. There was also scope for Deborah to make some changes and improvements, notably by installing a pond and a rockery.

They went back inside to have a word in private.

'Cat flap?' said Oldroyd, teasingly. 'So, you'd like a cat, would you?'

'You know I like cats, Jim. This house would be ideal. Lovely garden for it to roam around in.'

'I see. Well, the good news is, I really like this one. I think we've found what we're looking for.'

Deborah was delighted as she felt the same way. They decided to put an offer in straight away. They both hoped that they were not too late.

~

At the Wensley Arms it was a quiet evening. Bill Lawrence wondered whether people were still reluctant to leave their homes at night given the terrible recent events. Some of the regulars were gathered at the bar – Philip Welbeck, Bert Duffield and Norman Smith – but nobody was playing darts and most of the tables were empty.

'Not many people in tonight, Bill,' said Welbeck, echoing Lawrence's thoughts.

'Aye,' replied Lawrence. 'It won't get back to normal until the police solve these murders and clear off. People are unsettled by it; they don't want to be attacked. They're staying at home.'

'What's wrong wi' folk?' said Bert. 'Ah'd like to see anybody havin' a go at me in t'street. They'd know abaht it, ah can tell thi.'

'As long as you weren't so drunk that your savage blows missed their target,' joked Welbeck with a laugh.

'Get away wi' ye,' replied Duffield, and squared up to Welbeck, who cowered down in mock fear.

'I don't know what's taking the police so long,' said Smith. 'Surely there are only so many people it could be?'

'Does that mean you're off the suspect list, then?' asked Lawrence cheekily.

Smith was sanguine about it. 'Well, they haven't been back to me again. I've nothing to hide, anyway.' He finished his beer.

'So who do you think did it, then?' asked Welbeck.

Smith frowned. 'Who knows? Scholes had so many enemies, but I still wonder about that beer, you know.'

'Wensley Glory? I wish we had it on tap here. It was in a class of its own, apparently.'

'Aye, it wa',' said Bert. 'T'best beer ah've ever tasted.'

'And Scholes was going round telling people he had a copy of the recipe. It would have been worth a lot of money to bump him off for,' continued Smith. 'And then you've got these breweries at each other's throats. I think it was someone connected with one of them.'

'Well, I think it was Bert,' said Welbeck mischievously. 'He wanted to get the recipe so that he could brew that beer for himself. Didn't you know he has a little brewery in his shed at the bottom of his garden?'

'Get away wi' thi,' said Bert, laughing with the others. 'But ah'll tell thi this . . .' He raised his finger. 'Ah could still brew ale as well as any man living.'

'Or woman,' said Welbeck.

'Aye, well, ah don't know abaht all that . . .'

'No,' continued Welbeck, grinning, 'but I know another thing: you can also drink ale as well as any man or woman.'

They collapsed into laughter again.

~

It was after midnight a few days later, and the town of Ripon was quiet. There were very few people around on the streets.

In the lane behind the terraced house, a hooded figure climbed over the wall into the small yard of the former Scholes residence. They moved silently but quickly, as if they were familiar with the place. Breaking in was not necessary as they brought out a key, opened the back door – which they then shut softly behind them – and switched on a small torch. They headed stealthily through the kitchen towards the stairs where they stopped and began to look at the pictures on the wall. Suddenly there was a click. They turned round and were blinded by a bright light, which shone straight into their face.

'So,' said Oldroyd, who had emerged from where he was hiding in the living room. 'I think our plan has finally worked. Who have we got here?'

An officer came up behind the figure and tore off the hood. A shocked face blinked in the strong torchlight.

'Well, if I'm not mistaken it's Peter Morgan, the finance director at the Yoredale brewery,' continued Oldroyd. 'Good evening. I think we once met in Richard Foster's office. I wasn't expecting to see you here.'

Morgan could not respond to Oldroyd's wit; his face looked like that of a bewildered animal startled by a car's headlights. He turned and it seemed as if he was going to try to run for it, but he was quickly surrounded by officers. Andy moved in and put on the handcuffs.

'Peter Morgan,' intoned Oldroyd, 'I am arresting you for the murders of Frederick Scholes and Barry Green and for the attempted murder of Richard Foster. You do not have to say anything, but it may harm your defence if you do not mention when questioned something which you later rely on in court. Take him out.'

Without saying a word, Morgan was marched briskly outside to where a police car had drawn up. Oldroyd and Andy came to the door as the car sped off into the night.

'Congratulations, sir,' said Andy with a smile. 'It's taken a little while, but your scheme has flushed the killer out.'

'Yes,' replied Oldroyd. 'I banked on the lure of finding the recipe being too much to resist, though I have to admit, I didn't expect it to be Morgan. It will be interesting to find out what on earth brought him to this. The press can be very useful,' he continued with a laugh. 'Even if they don't realise they are being used. They accepted my insistence that there was no recipe, while still describing how valuable it would be if it were to be found. Given that we know the killer had already been to search the house once, it was likely that they would return, especially if they saw me on television saying that the police would no longer be around the house.'

'Jeffries did well, didn't he, sir?'

'He did – played his part as a young reporter feeding me questions about the recipe very nicely. Tell him what I've said if you see him.'

'I will, sir. I think it will make his day.'

Oldroyd yawned. He and Andy had been part of the team that had kept watch in the house for a number of nights and days.

'We'd better get home and get some sleep. We'll question Morgan at Harrogate tomorrow. I'm eager to see what tale he has to tell. Find out his address and get forensics round. It shouldn't be too hard to find something to link him with the crimes. He hasn't had time to hide anything. But it can all wait until tomorrow.'

'OK, sir. Goodnight.'

~

Next morning, a tired and defeated-looking Peter Morgan sat facing Oldroyd and Andy in an interview room at Harrogate Police HQ. Oldroyd sensed no arrogance or hostility in him and decided to take a gentle approach.

'So, what's behind all this?' he asked. 'You don't seem like a man who would get involved in violence.'

Morgan sighed and closed his eyes as if contemplating the awfulness of his position. 'Gambling,' he said, summing up his terrible fate in one word. 'I've lost large amounts of money over the years. I've managed to keep it from my family and my employer until now. But it's all over. At least I won't be able to gamble any more.' He slumped back in the chair and brushed away a tear.

'How did Scholes fit into this?'

'He was blackmailing me, so I was losing even more money. I've been siphoning off money from the Yoredale brewery for quite a while. That's one of the reasons the business has been struggling. When he worked there in the office, Scholes must have suspected what was happening – he examined the records and found me out. He wasn't stupid, just a bastard!' For a moment his eyes blazed. 'He asked for money, or he would tell Richard. I couldn't deal with it. I was still losing money and having to pay him as well.'

'How did you feel about taking money from your employer?'

'Bad, but I was desperate. I justified it by telling myself that Richard was partly responsible for the state I was in. I started gambling with him and his friends playing poker games. I dropped out of that, and Richard thought I had given up the gambling . . . but I hadn't. I was playing at home online for higher stakes and for longer periods.'

'Why didn't you get help?'

Morgan shook his head. 'I was too ashamed, especially as an accountant – a person who knows about figures and how to handle money. People don't expect you to throw money away. I didn't feel I could tell anyone.' He looked down. 'Now I wish I had.'

'What did you decide to do about Scholes?'

'To get rid of him. He was a nasty piece of work. Somehow, I had to break out of the trap he'd caught me in. I thought if I could get him somewhere secluded, then I could finish him off. I knew he had lots of enemies, and the suspicion would fall on them. Not that I wanted anyone else to go to prison for what I'd done. I just thought there would be nothing to link him with me.'

'So, on the night of the murder, you called him, I presume?'

'Yes, I'd heard he'd been going round during the beer festival claiming to have a copy of the recipe for Wensley Glory Bitter. I didn't know if he was lying – his father had died recently so there was a chance that he could have inherited it if David Foster had given Wilf Scholes a copy. Anyway, I knew I didn't have enough money to pay him for it, but I thought it was a chance to lure him to the brewery, which would be deserted late at night. I thought he might be reluctant to meet me there and I was ready to spin him a story saying I was interested in the recipe but didn't want to be seen with him in public or it might get back to my wife. It was a bit flimsy, but the strange thing was he agreed straight away. It was almost as if he'd forgotten me or that there was this blackmailing between us. I thought he would be more suspicious. Anyway, I took the chance. I have a set of keys for the brewery, and I was able to set the trap up. I lay in wait for him to come in.'

'I'm afraid your instinct was right. You see, it wasn't Brendan Scholes who met you there and who you murdered.'

Morgan looked up. 'What?'

'His brother, Frederick, had already killed Brendan. He was then impersonating him and trying to get money for the recipe.'

'Bloody hell, that explains a few things. Of course, he wouldn't know that Brendan was blackmailing me. When I encountered him briefly before I smashed him over the head, I thought he looked the same, but his voice had been a bit different on the phone.' Morgan laughed sardonically. 'Well, he got his just deserts, then. He was no better than his brother by all accounts.'

Oldroyd leaned down and pulled something out of a bag by his chair. 'You used one of these to hit him over the head, didn't you?' He held up a hammer that had a broad, flat head on one side and a wedge-shaped pein on the other. At the tip of the wedge was a narrow groove.

Morgan looked at it. 'Yes. How did you know?'

'The forensic pathologist saw a peculiar pattern on the head wound. It confused us. The wounds looked like they were caused by a hammer, but we couldn't explain that pattern. It was caused by this groove. This is a cooper's hammer, the kind someone would use to hammer the hoops on to the barrels. You used the same hammer to kill Barry Green and I think you got it from the museum room at the Yoredale brewery. I saw there was one missing from a collection. Am I right?'

Morgan shrugged. 'You seem to know everything. I stole that hammer before Scholes arrived at the brewery that night and then I hung on to it and took it with me to Ripon.'

'Were you looking for the recipe when Barry Green broke into the house in Ripon?'

'That and any documents Scholes had relating to my fiddling of the books at the brewery. I had the set of keys I took from Scholes – Frederick, you're telling me – before I heaved his body into the tank.'

'So, you believed that the recipe existed?'

'I thought there was a chance, and it would be in the house somewhere.' He looked at Oldroyd. 'When you're desperate for cash to pay for an addiction, you'll grasp at anything and fall into traps, like I did – twice.'

'And Barry Green recognised you?'

Morgan put his hands to his face and broke down weeping. He seemed genuinely remorseful about the murder of Green. After a few moments he managed to continue. 'I didn't want to kill him – or anybody else. I crept downstairs with the hammer thinking I could frighten off whoever it was, but I wasn't wearing my hoodie. He must have heard something; he turned round quickly and recognised me. I panicked and hit him over the head. I should have just hidden until he left the house.'

'Weren't you worried that he would find the recipe?'

Morgan shook his head. 'Maybe, but Scholes owed Green money, didn't he? I imagine the poor bloke was just looking for cash or valuable things to pinch because he thought he'd never get his money back. If only he hadn't seen me. I'm really sorry about it.'

'Why did you attack Richard Foster?'

Morgan gave another grim laugh. 'That was so ironic. Richard's got a problem with his gambling, too, and he asked me to look at ways he could take some money out of the firm in a legitimate way. He didn't know I'd been stealing it for a while. He wanted really detailed accounts and I was afraid that he would notice all the minor irregularities I'd managed to cover up. On the day of the cricket match, he came into the brewery to check on the work that was being done and I was there. I'd come in to see if there were any other ways I could conceal the fact I was skimming off the top. He didn't see me, but I overheard him say to one of the workmen that he was going to the cricket later, and so I took the opportunity . . .' Morgan stopped and his face looked anguished.

'I didn't want to harm him either, but I was desperate. I waited at the bottom of those steps and came up behind him. I got the cord round his neck, but he managed to cry out. I panicked again and ran off.' He paused and seemed to be struggling to carry on. 'I'm glad he did cry out. I haven't got his murder on my conscience, at least.'

'And then, presumably, you saw my press conference and decided it was worth another look for the recipe?'

Morgan laughed. 'Yes. I was following your investigation all along. When you said you'd stopped searching the house in Ripon, I thought this was a chance for me to have another look. The odds were against it, but odds don't matter when you're a gambler and you don't think straight. I walked into your trap.' His face was drained of colour, and he slumped forward on to the table, apparently exhausted.

~

'It's a sad story really, isn't it, sir?' said Andy when the interview was over. Morgan had been taken back to the cells and they were making their way to their office.

'It is. His family are going to be devastated when they get the news. It's not a pleasant thing to contemplate.' Oldroyd grimaced at the very idea of it. 'It's another tale of addiction; we seem to be encountering a lot of them at the moment, what with the Fosters . . . and even Steph's dad. How is she, by the way?'

'Fine thanks, sir. It's been very positive for her to re-establish contact with her dad and to start to see what made him behave like he did.'

They reached the office. Oldroyd put on the coffee, and they sat down. 'That's a very mature attitude. The few times she mentioned him in the past she used to say that she hated him and never wanted to see him again.'

'Well, I think she's changed her mind, sir. That's how she felt as a girl after how he treated her and her sister and their mum, but she saw how broken he was by his alcoholism, and he told her how sorry he was, and how proud he was of Steph and her sister. I suppose she saw that he wasn't all bad.'

'I see.'

'I'm sure it's partly because of you, sir.'

'Me? What on earth did I have to do with it?'

'You know we were talking the other day, sir, about when I first came here to work?'

'Yes.'

'Well, in those days, and I think Steph was probably the same – I used to believe that criminals were evil people. "Catch and lock 'em up" was my attitude. But you've taught us to think differently: that people who do bad things are mostly damaged themselves and maybe they were trapped in circumstances where another person might have behaved in the same way. Something pushed them over the edge. You know what I mean, sir?'

'I do.'

'And you've taught us to put ourselves in the shoes of the criminal: they're human, like the rest of us, and mostly think the same way. I don't think I'm explaining this very well.'

'Yes, you are,' said Oldroyd, 'and I'm very touched by what you've just said. I suppose the word is empathy. I don't want to sound sanctimonious, but whenever we get to this point in a murder inquiry and the killer is going to prison, I never feel any sense of triumph. Maybe satisfaction and relief that we've solved the case and put away a dangerous person, but the dominant feeling for me is what a tragic waste it is – for the victims and their families, but also for the perpetrator and their families whose lives are ruined. Then I always reflect. It could have been different; why wasn't it? What evil combination of factors came together and caused this to happen?'

'I suppose in the end that's one of the mysteries of life, isn't it, sir?'

'I think you're right.'

They were brought back down to mundane reality from their deep reflections by Oldroyd's phone ringing. It was Tom Walker.

'Well done again, Jim,' Walker said when Oldroyd answered. 'I'm glad you got to the bottom of it. You-know-who should be satisfied. He can go back to sleep in his office now. One brother killed the other over a secret beer recipe, I hear?'

'That was part of it, Tom, then there was the firm's accountant who was a gambler and was being blackmailed. He killed two people and attacked a third.'

'Well, it all happens in the little towns up in the Dales, doesn't it? It's bloody amazing. By the way, how did you get on up at Moneybags Hall or wherever it was?'

Oldroyd laughed. 'There was more to it than Watkins realised. The bloke wasn't really concerned about the local impact of the investigation, he was trying to protect his daughter who'd had a relationship with one of the victims. He didn't want her name to crop up in any of the media coverage.'

'Right. I'll bet he didn't. It might ruin her chances in the high-class marriage market.'

'You've got it, Tom.'

'I know how these people think. It's all about them, never mind three people were killed. Anyway, are you on for a drink this week some time? It's been a while since we had a chat.'

Oldroyd met Walker occasionally in a local pub for a drink and they agreed a date. Fundamentally he liked the old boy, who was a good boss to have; they shared the same views about policing and Walker always allowed Oldroyd a great deal of freedom in investigations. The evening was usually reasonably pleasant if the 'chat' didn't consist of Walker going off on his rants about Watkins, modern policing or any other of his pet hates.

~

The next day everyone was hard at work at the Ewe's Ales Brewery when the news came through about the dramatic events of Wednesday night. Janice came running up to Emily's office in a state of high excitement.

'We've just had the local radio on. Peter Morgan's been arrested. You know – Richard's accountant? There was a statement from the police saying the arrest was in connection with the two murders and the recent attack in Markham.'

Emily sat back in her chair. 'What?!'

'Yes, he must be the killer. They also said that the first victim, the one at the Yoredale, had been wrongly identified. It was Frederick Scholes, not Brendan.'

'Frederick!? But . . .'

'Yes, apparently Brendan's been dead for several weeks and they think Frederick killed him. His body was found a while ago in a drainage tunnel.' She sat down after blurting out this news. 'I knew there was something odd about him, and his voice was definitely different. Well, it wasn't him after all!'

'Wow!' Emily was stunned and finding it difficult to take in. Privately she was very relieved. She could never tell Janice, but her partner's hostility to her brother and her late arrival at the cricket ground had prompted some very dark thoughts. 'So, it's all over?'

'Yes, I think so, thank God. It's been a terrible pall over the town. Hopefully we can all think positive and move forward together.'

'Yes,' said Emily, smiling, and, as if on cue, there was a knock and her brother came in.

'Richard!' she said. 'Come in and have a seat.'

'Thank you,' he said, nodding to them both. 'Nice to see you, Janice. It's been a while.'

'Yes, it has,' replied Janice rather coolly.

'Well, I intend to change that. Christine and I want you both to come round for a meal this Friday evening.'

Janice and Emily exchanged a glance.

'Thank you, Richard,' said Emily. 'We'd love to.'

Janice did not feel quite as positive, but she wanted to make the effort. 'Looking forward to it,' she said. 'I'd better get back to work, I'm holding things up. I'll leave you together. Bye for now.'

Richard sat down. 'Have you heard the news?' he said.

'Yes, that must have been a shock for you, Richard.'

'Yes. The police have been in touch. It was his gambling that was behind it all. He was badly in debt and had been stealing from the company. No wonder we weren't doing particularly well. Mind you, I was planning to take money out myself, although it would have been above board. He thought I might get on to him when we looked in detail at the accounts, which is why he tried to get rid of me.'

'That's awful!'

He looked at her with a puzzled expression. 'I know, but I actually feel more sorrow and pity than anger. I understand how gambling addiction can make you desperate enough to do all sorts of shocking things: lying, stealing, being violent. He never told anyone or got help. It was all bottled up inside him and none of us knew.' He paused and shook his head. 'He was part of our poker group at one time, but he dropped out and I never thought things were a problem for him. I suppose you think an accountant can always handle money sensibly. But, actually, why should that be the case? Everybody's human. I should have joined the dots and maybe I could have done something but I never suspected him at all. It was the same as with Christine; I was too bound up by my own problems to notice someone else's.'

'Don't be hard on yourself, Richard; it wasn't your fault. I'm sure he was very clever about concealing everything.'

'Yes.' He shook his head as if to dismiss the thoughts. 'Anyway . . .' He paused as if about to make an announcement. 'I've come here with a special proposal.'

'What's that?'

'I want our breweries to merge. Actually, I want Ewe's to take us over.'

'Richard?' For the second time that morning, Emily was astonished.

'Look, after the money I've lost, and through Peter Morgan taking it out of the company, we're in a weak position and it just doesn't make sense to have two breweries, effectively run by the same family, competing in this small town. If we merge, you will be chief executive and I will take a secondary role. I'm sure Philip and Janice can work together.' He put his hand to his head and looked weary. 'I'm completely exhausted after all that's happened. I need to spend time tackling this gambling thing and help Christine. It's not compatible with running a business. I'll be happy if I can earn enough to enable us to survive, even if the kids have to change schools. The local secondary school is fine. I sometimes wonder why we bother sending them to that private school in Ripon, anyway.' He stopped and looked at her. 'What do you think?'

'Richard, I don't know what to say.'

'I was completely wrong to believe you shouldn't be involved in the brewery. Dad was right. I was being selfish, silly and old-fashioned. You're a very talented businessperson and your partner is an excellent brewer.'

'Oh, Richard, thank you – and never mind about what's happened in the past. It's worked out well in the end.'

'Does that mean that you agree to my proposal?'

'Well, I can hardly get my head round it, but yes, yes, of course. It will be great to work together again. What shall we call the new business?'

'That's for you to decide, but what about Wensley Brewery? But maybe not just yet. I think it may be a good idea to keep the identities of the breweries separate for a while so as not to confuse our loyal customers.'

'That's a great idea.' She shook her head and beamed. 'I'm so delighted, Richard. It was stupid to compete with each other instead of pooling our expertise.'

He gave her a sly smile. 'That's good, because I've kept the best thing until last.'

'Oh?'

'The police found the recipe for Wensley Glory Bitter in the Scholes house in Ripon. It did exist after all. Dad must have given a copy to Wilfred, the only person he trusted.'

Emily gasped. 'Oh my God! I can't believe it!'

'It's true and now we can brew it again. It will be a fantastic boost for our new business.'

'I wonder why neither Dad nor Wilfred passed it on to us?'

'I don't know, but I wonder if it was something to do with the fact that we were estranged from each other and running separate breweries. He didn't want to give it to one of us and leave the other out. He never thought that we would end up competing with each other and he didn't like it.'

'And I suppose Wilfred didn't want to favour one of us either. I wonder if Dad told him not to? I can just imagine him saying, "If I die afore thi don't give t'recipe to either of 'em, Wilf, unless they start working together age'an. All this carryin' on, they don't deserve it."'

Richard laughed at his sister's impression of their 'broad' Yorkshire father. 'You know, I think you're right, and wherever he is, he must be pleased that we are coming together at last and that his famous beer will be brewed again. Let's shake on it.'

Laughing, they leaned over the table and shook hands.

∾

Another clear and warm spring evening a few days later found Oldroyd, Deborah and Alison eating pizza in an Italian restaurant in Harrogate. There was a bottle of Chianti on the table.

'So, you're going to be moving at last?' remarked Alison.

'Yes,' replied Deborah after swallowing a piece of her Margherita pizza. 'We've had an offer accepted on that house in New Bridge. It's really exciting. I'm particularly looking forward to the garden. I hope we can move in before too long so I can get working at it this spring to prepare it for the summer. It's years since I had a garden.'

'How about you, Jim?'

Oldroyd was tucking into a ham and mushroom pizza. He'd mentioned the Meat Feast, but a look from Deborah had ruled that out. 'Yes, I'm really looking forward to it: nice house, lovely village, good pub.' He took a drink of his wine and his eyes glinted mischievously.

'Yes,' said Deborah, with a note of warning in her voice. 'That's the only thing that concerns me – the local pub is very close . . . I can see you propping up the bar on a regular basis. Especially after you retire . . . whenever that is.'

Oldroyd smiled and didn't comment, except to say he had no plans to retire yet.

'But, Jim,' said Alison half seriously, 'think about the dangers of too much alcohol. It was a feature of the case you've just been investigating, wasn't it?'

'Yes, and for my detective sergeant.' He told them about Steph and her alcoholic father. 'The whole case really turned on addiction more generally. The killer turned out to be the accountant at the brewery. His gambling and debts drove him to commit murder and nearly bankrupted the business. And all this in a small town. It's certainly a myth that these problems only exist in cities.'

'Yes, well, there you are, Jim. We're all frail, you know.'

'Yes. But a good thing about this case was that it wasn't all bleak in the end as they sometimes can be. There were some positive outcomes. Not for the tragic Scholes family, who are all dead now, but I think Richard Foster and his wife will both be able to conquer their addictions. They're supporting each other.'

'That's good news,' said Deborah. 'A well-established addiction is not easy to overcome without professional help, but a supportive partner and family can be a great help.'

'The other really good thing is that there was reconciliation between those two Markham breweries where the brother and sister had been at loggerheads for quite a while.'

'What was it all about?' asked Deborah.

'To put it bluntly, it was Richard who couldn't accept his sister working in the brewery and this drove her away to form her own very successful venture. To his credit, he seems to have admitted he was wrong and allowed his talented sister to run the new company.'

'Well, good for him,' said Alison.

Oldroyd turned to Alison. 'I remember when I came over to see you at the beginning of the case. I told you about the Fosters and you commented on how it was sad when close relatives fell out.

That remained with me somehow and it turned out that it applied with even greater force to the Scholes family. It made me start to consider if the conflicts in the family had a bearing on the case.'

'It's always nice to be helpful,' laughed Alison. Oldroyd's family were used to things they said stimulating ideas in his mind about a case he was working on.

Oldroyd continued. 'And I think the community in Markham is even more accepting of the gay relationship between Emily and Janice. Most of them certainly seem to celebrate the new brewery and I think the bigots have been silenced.'

Oldroyd finished his little exposition about the case. He looked at the table and then slyly at the two women. 'You know, I think we need another bottle of this. We haven't toasted our moving house yet, nor the success of the new Markham brewery, nor the—'

'Jim!' interrupted Deborah. 'What have we just been saying about alcohol?'

Oldroyd looked a little sheepish but didn't back down. 'Well, I know, but it's a special occasion, isn't it?' He picked up the bottle and looked at the label. 'And you must admit it's a very fine wine.'

Alison laughed and Deborah rolled her eyes.

'Oh, go on, then,' she said.

Epilogue

Black Sheep Brewery is the second brewery in the town of Masham. It was founded by a member of the Theakston family after Theakston Brewery was taken over by a large company. It occupies premises that were previously used by the former Lightfoot Brewery. Its most famous beers are Black Sheep Bitter – a classic Yorkshire bitter – and the strong, fruity Riggwelter. This is named after the Yorkshire dialect word for a sheep on its back.

Some years later, the Facebook page of the Yorkshire Ale Society contained a photograph of Emily and Richard Foster smiling as they received the Beer of the Year award for Wensley Glory Bitter. The accompanying text ran as follows:

'Wensley Glory has made a triumphant return after many years during which the recipe was thought lost, seemingly for good. It is more than thirty years since the beer, brewed in conditions of some secrecy by David Foster, the father of the current winners of the award, first won the title of Beer of the Year. How proud David Foster would have been of his son and daughter, who merged their breweries in Markham several years ago and began to brew the famous beer again. Wensley Ales has a roughly equal male and female workforce and is regarded as a model business in terms of equal opportunities and in the creation of a harmonious working atmosphere. The revived beer was first served at local pubs in Markham, including the Wensley Arms, but sales picked up rapidly and are now worldwide.

'Chief Executive Emily Foster was asked what was special about Wensley Glory but was unwilling to give any details except to say that it was a beer with a unique flavour. She said that the recipe had been developed a long time ago by her father and grandfather. It was now being skilfully brewed by the head brewers at Wensley Ales, Janice Anderson and Philip Welbeck, who had been entrusted with the recipe. There is a long tradition in the family that the details of how Wensley Glory Bitter is made are kept secret within the company, and the intention is for it to remain that way.

'She added that a copy of the photograph of her and her brother receiving the award would be framed and placed in the new brewery museum, next to one of her father and his head brewer, Wilfred Scholes, receiving the same award many years before.'

Acknowledgements

As ever, I would like to thank my family, friends and members of the Otley Writers' Group for their help and support, and the many people around the world who buy my books.

Many readers will quickly realise that Markham is a thinly disguised Masham in Lower Wensleydale, though the history of the rival fictional breweries in the story is very different from the actual one. I would like to thank all the brewers in Yorkshire for making it such a great place to drink beer. Many breweries also offer fascinating tours of their premises, which usually end with a welcome sample of the produce!

The West Riding Police is a fictional force based on the old West Riding boundary. Harrogate was part of the old West Riding, although it is in today's North Yorkshire.

About the Author

John R. Ellis has lived in Yorkshire for most of his life and has spent many years exploring Yorkshire's diverse landscapes, history, language and communities. He recently retired after a career in teaching, mostly in further education in the Leeds area. In addition to the Yorkshire Murder Mystery series, he writes poetry, ghost stories and biography. He has completed a screenplay about the last years of the poet Edward Thomas and a work of faction about the extraordinary life of his Irish mother-in-law. He is currently working (slowly!) on his memoirs of growing up in a working-class area of Huddersfield in the 1950s and 1960s.

Follow the Author on Amazon

If you enjoyed this book, follow J. R. Ellis on Amazon to be notified when the author releases a new book!
To do this, please follow these instructions:

Desktop:

1) Search for the author's name on Amazon or in the Amazon App.
2) Click on the author's name to arrive on their Amazon page.
3) Click the 'Follow' button.

Mobile and Tablet:

1) Search for the author's name on Amazon or in the Amazon App.
2) Click on one of the author's books.
3) Click on the author's name to arrive on their Amazon page.
4) Click the 'Follow' button.

Kindle eReader and Kindle App:

If you enjoyed this book on a Kindle eReader or in the Kindle App, you will find the author 'Follow' button after the last page.